THE

23RD MIDNIGHT

JAMES PATTERSON

& MAXINE PAETRO

GRAND
CENTRAL

New York Boston

Grand Central Publishing
Hachette Book Group
1290 Avenue of the Americas, New York, NY 10104
grandcentralpublishing.com
twitter.com/grandcentralpub

Originally published in hardcover and ebook by Little, Brown & Company in May 2023
First trade paperback edition: February 2024

Grand Central Publishing is a division of Hachette Book Group, Inc. The Grand Central Publishing name and logo is a trademark of Hachette Book Group, Inc.

WOMEN'S MURDER CLUB is a trademark of JBP Business, LLC.

The publisher is not responsible for websites (or their content) that are not owned by the publisher.

The Hachette Speakers Bureau provides a wide range of authors for speaking events. To find out more, go to hachettespeakersbureau.com or email HachetteSpeakers@hbgusa.com.

Grand Central Publishing books may be purchased in bulk for business, educational, or promotional use. For information, please contact your local bookseller or the Hachette Book Group Special Markets Department at special.markets@hbgusa.com.

Library of Congress Control Number: 2023930485

ISBNs: 9781538710623 (trade paperback), 9780316402989 (ebook)

Printed in the United States of America

LSC-H

Printing 1, 2023

Dedicated to our friends and fans of the Women's Murder Club. This book's for you.

THE 23 RD

MIDNIGHT

PROLOGUE

MONDAY

One

AT DAWN THAT morning, a man dressed entirely in black backed his gray Ford sedan up to the curb on Taylor Street. To the east, the morning sun struggled to rise through the clouds over San Francisco Bay. It was still dark but the man, who was now in "Blackout" mode, knew this street as well as he knew his own mind.

He cut his headlights, released the trunk latch, lowered the seat back a few inches and adjusted his video glasses in the rearview mirror. With his unobstructed view of Victorian row houses and the wooden staircase behind him in the rearview, Blackout waited for Catherine. She was always on time, one of the many things he liked about her.

At twenty-five, Catherine Fleet was a beautiful mother of a baby girl named Josephina, and an integral part of the masterwork he was creating. He wished he could talk with her about it, but there wouldn't be time. She was leaving her house on Leavenworth now. She would turn down Macondray Lane, the quarter mile of footpath that ran downhill and at a right angle to Taylor.

The lane parted a smattering of trees and hugged the walls of the large homes until it merged with the wooden staircase that ended only feet from the rear of Blackout's stripped-down cop car.

Catherine would pause there, Josie strapped into her front-facing carrier, and together they would take in the magnificent view of dawn breaking over San Francisco Bay. Moments later, she would head south to Ina Coolbrith Park for their morning walk.

As he rounded off that thought, Blackout saw a flicker of movement in his rearview mirror. Catherine was halfway down the staircase, as regular as a metronome. Her unbuttoned dark coat revealed a garnet-red, snowflake-patterned sweater over dark pants. Her long, dark hair spilled over her shoulders and floated around the redheaded baby's ears.

Perfect. She was perfect.

Blackout secured his video glasses, worked his gloves over his large hands, and got out of his car. In only a few strides he'd reached the foot of the staircase. Catherine looked down briefly, gripping the banister, giving the good-looking young man a brief smile.

Blackout smiled back, took the first two steps upward, snagging the toe of his shoe on the third. As he'd calculated, he tripped and fell facedown spectacularly, sprawling with his arms spread like a large broken bird.

She called out, "Oh, my gosh. Are you all right?"

"I, uh, don't know," he said. "I think I slammed my knee on the edge of the riser…"

Blackout was awkwardly working himself up into a crouch when Catherine reached him.

"Can you stand up?"

The concern in her voice sent a wave of pleasure through him as he looked up into her blue eyes, the irises rimmed with gold halos. The baby was awake, beating her fists against the air.

"I'm good," said Blackout. "Embarrassed, is all. I try to impress with finesse."

Catherine laughed, saying, "Forget it ever happened," never seeing the small vial Blackout had secreted in his clenched hand. Called "Down Dog," it was an inelegant name, but it got the job done. He aimed the sprayer at Catherine Fleet's golden blue eyes and thumbed the lever.

Her reaction was instant, sharp, pained. She cried, "What did you do?" She sat down hard, tearing up from the pepper spray and palming her eyes. The baby girl was gulping air, exhaling wails that could be heard through brick walls.

Blackout had to move fast, before someone else came down the stairs on their way to the park. He scrambled up and got behind Catherine, cradled her lovely neck between his forearm and biceps. She could barely draw breath, gasping, "Don't. Hurt. My baby."

"Don't worry. She's in good hands."

Catherine tried to push off the step, to get away from him, but Blackout held her in place and spoke gently to her as he squeezed.

"Don't fight me, Catherine. It'll be all over soon. Shhh, shhhh. I've got you."

In fifteen seconds, Catherine was unconscious. In forty seconds, a woman who'd been at the peak of life was dead. But the baby was wailing.

Blackout assessed their combined weight at a hundred and twenty pounds. He checked in all directions. They were alone. He gathered up mother and child and carried them to his car's unlatched trunk.

He stowed them without trouble and was reaching inside to kill the baby, when a man's voice called out.

"Pardon me. Do you need some help there?"

Two

BLACKOUT TURNED TO see a jogger in shorts and a tennis shirt materialize in the gloom, coming slowly toward him. He had seen him before, a man in his seventies, stiff, arthritic, now winded from climbing the hill.

"We're fine," Blackout shouted back. "We're all fine."

The jogger's expression showed confusion, then, as the baby's cries filled the air, the old man put it all together. And he held up his phone.

He shot pictures, then, turned and ran surprisingly fast back down the hill, with his phone clapped to his ear. *He was calling 911. Had to be. He had pictures on his phone. Of him. Of his car. Maybe he'd gotten an angle on his plates and the contents of the trunk.*

The baby was shrieking.

There was no time for rage. Blackout covered the baby's mouth and nose with his large gloved hand until the baby had stopped breathing. Then he dragged blankets over the two dead bodies. Slamming the trunk lid closed, he surveyed the field with a chopper gunner's eyes, tipping the street toward him and dividing it into a grid.

The jogger was sixty feet away and gaining downhill speed. Farther down the block, near the Victorian row houses, an impatient woman yanked on the leash of a small, prancy dog before disappearing through a doorway.

And now, the sun was burning off the cloud cover and pinking up the sky. Blackout slid into the driver's seat and pulled the old Ford out of the parking space. Straightening out, he touched his foot to the gas. He trailed behind the old man for a moment before darting around him, braking suddenly, blocking him in. The old man faltered, dodged, then made for the space between two parked cars.

Blackout reached for the weapon lying on the passenger seat. A stun cane. He grasped it, exited his vehicle, and using the stick as a bat, he swung and connected with the back of the old man's head. The jogger fell against a parked van then slumped to the street. He cried out weakly, but the sound didn't carry.

The phone had jumped from the jogger's hand, skidded a few yards downhill. Blackout walked over and crushed it with his heel, then uncapped the stun cane.

The jogger was weeping, helpless. He couldn't stand.

Blackout looked down at him and carefully placed the business end of the stun cane against the jogger's throat.

He spoke in a soothing voice, "What's your name?"

The old man pushed futilely at the stick. His face was red. Tears spilled down his cheeks.

"Don't," he said. "I didn't see anything."

"I said, 'What is your name'?"

He wheezed, "Jay. Cob."

"Jacob. Got it. You took pictures, buddy. Big mistake. Hang on for the thrill of your life."

Blackout pulled the stun-cane's trigger, sending a million volts into the old man's body, enough to light up the entire block. He knew that the human body could only absorb one percent of a charge that strong, but that plus the current knocked the old man out and with luck, stopped his heart.

But no. The old man blinked his eyes. His mouth moved.

The sky was brightening and Blackout had no more time for this. Back in his car, he pulled the classic Ruger Mark IV, complete with suppressor, from his glove box. He walked back to the old man and aimed the gun point-blank at his forehead and fired it. Then put two more in his chest.

With his back to the many-windowed houses on Taylor's west side, Blackout picked the SIM card out of the litter of Jacob's broken phone. He tossed the stun cane back into his car and took the driver's seat, returning the gun to the glove box. The engine was still running and now Blackout allowed elation, that precious, elusive feeling, to fill him up. He heard in his deep and heaving breaths, the soundtrack of his life.

He made a mental note to freeze frame on the bullet hole in Jacob's forehead. Fade to black.

And then he headed the car downhill.

Blackout still had a lot of work to do, of the most important kind.

Three

AS HE DROVE at the residential speed limit of twenty miles an hour, Blackout's immediate plan had been to get off Taylor as fast as he reasonably could. He had taken the first left at Filbert, then turned up onto Leavenworth, passing the house where Catherine and Josie Fleet had lived.

A man he recognized as Catherine's husband, Brad Fleet, had been coming down the front steps. He'd looked both ways and, not seeing his wife and daughter, had no doubt assumed that Catherine and Josie were still in the park. *Poor bastard.*

As police cars, sirens screaming, could be heard on the street below, Blackout proceeded to the location for his most important scene.

Now, hours later, safe at home, he thought how long that drive had seemed with the woman and baby tucked away inside the trunk. And he'd had a few thoughts about the senior citizen who'd seen too much, lying dead on Taylor between two parked vehicles.

He'd charged up his video glasses in the car as he drove and later, filmed the perfect ceremony for his victims — without interference. He'd felt peaceful. Reverent.

That part, the end of their story, was one long four-minute shot that might be even more bittersweet with music. Something classical, he thought. Albinoni's "Adagio in G Minor." Better yet, Ravel's *Pavane for a Dead Princess*. Yes, that was more appropriate, a fitting homage to a killer he'd often thought of as a teacher, almost a friend. He was sure his mentor would like the results of the day's work and pictured him now: a superior executioner confined to a cell at San Quentin. A man named Evan Burke.

TWO DAYS EARLIER

CHAPTER 1

CINDY THOMAS SAT in the back seat of a Lincoln Town Car heading toward Book Passage in Corte Madera. It was Saturday afternoon, the first stop on her book tour, and she had every reason to be excited.

It had been a whirlwind since she'd sold the project. Given the hot subject matter, her publisher had accelerated the production schedule to push out finished copies in record time.

Prepublication reviews had been outstanding. Industry buzz had it that her book could hit number one on the *New York Times* Best Seller list. If that came to pass, it would be an honor and a miracle, but she wasn't feeling the buzz, not even close.

In the course of writing Evan Burke's authorized biography, she'd been repeatedly shocked by Burke's ruthlessness, the pleasure he took in killing. Unable to wall herself off from the sickening details of his crimes, Cindy had come to know Evan Burke too well. And that knowledge had changed her.

Cindy held the book in her lap tightly with both hands. She flipped it over to look again at Burke's photo on the back cover. He looked ordinary: A white man with an unlined face and a full head of hair who could be anywhere from his fifties to his seventies. He'd had work done, too, getting his face sculpted and chemically abraded. That rolled back his age by ten to twenty years. His brown eyes looked kind. But Evan Burke had never felt kindness. He was a psychopath, a serial killer who'd racked up over a hundred murders before he was finally caught in the act.

Injured in a shoot-out with police, he'd been arrested, hospitalized, and charged with murder in the first degree.

That should have been a full stop, the end of the story, but Evan Burke's narcissism couldn't be stopped. While still being treated for his injuries, cuffed and shackled to a hospital bed, he'd asked to see Cindy Thomas, star crime reporter with the *San Francisco Chronicle*.

Cindy hadn't known that Burke was a fan of her work, but he'd told her that he read her column daily and that she would be famous one day. She had gone to the hospital hoping for a quote, and he'd pitched his big idea.

"I want to cement my place in history. What do you say, Cindy? Let's write a book together."

An investigative reporter with an earlier true-crime book to her credit, Cindy remembered being a little dazed in Burke's presence.

It was only later, after she'd seen his vision of a compelling read that would showcase her talent and boost her career, that she'd said, "Okay," to his proposal and even "thank you." Evan Burke would savor his standing in the serial killer Hall of Fame from his cell in solitary confinement.

Early into this agreement with Burke, she'd changed the original title from *Evan Burke's Last Stand* to a new one: *You Never Knew Me: The True Story of Evan Burke, "The Ghost of Catalina."* Bob

Barnett, Cindy's agent and lawyer, had said, "Great title. Very selling. Your name goes first." That's how Cindy Thomas became Evan Burke's confidante, coauthor, and conduit to the world beyond San Quentin State Prison.

Now, holding the finished product, the book looked small when compared with Burke's hellacious crime spree. He confessed to a half dozen murders and helped law enforcement crack multiple unsolved serial killings in exchange for his demands, namely. TV, a no-Wi-Fi laptop, a radio, and private time in the shower. And he wanted an attorney-client room where he could meet with her.

And that's how Evan Burke got monthly access to Cindy's previously wide-open and very fertile mind.

Cindy stuffed the book into her handbag and stared out at the view blowing by without actually seeing anything. She hadn't slept a full night since meeting Burke and her waking thoughts were consumed with bloody murder and the pantheon of Burke's so-called peers; Bundy, Gacy, Dahmer, BTK with a little Son of Sam thrown in. Burke liked the comparisons because by his calculations he stood above them with a gold medal hanging from a ribbon around his neck.

But one unexpected and redeeming feature had come of this total immersion in all things Burke. Cindy had a platform and a bullhorn, and if *You Never Knew Me* became the success her friends and supporters believed it would be, she might actually save lives.

The driver said over his shoulder, "We're here, Miss."

As the car came to a stop, Cindy reapplied her lipstick, ran her fingers through her cloud of blond curls, then got out of the car without waiting for the driver to open her door.

The driver worked for her publisher, had been vetted, validated, and approved. He had expressed no interest in her whatsoever.

But Cindy Thomas no longer trusted men she didn't know.

CHAPTER 2

THE DOOR TO Book Passage swung open before Cindy touched the handle.

She heard Richie call out, "She's here."

Richard Conklin, Cindy's good-looking, good-tempered fiancé, a homicide inspector with the SFPD. He greeted her with a hug and a kiss. Then he held her by the shoulders and looked into her eyes.

"You okay, hon?"

"How do I look?"

"Like a TV personality. Prime time."

"Hunh. So you like me in red?"

He grinned and said, "Wear this more often."

She laughed, "Okay," as Rich released her and Elaine Petrocelli, owner of Book Passage, came toward them. Elaine shook Cindy's hand with both of hers, saying, "Cindy, so good to finally meet you. Tell me what I can get for you."

"I'm just happy to be here," Cindy said and found that, in that moment, she felt it.

Elaine frequently hosted book events and was a friend to authors. Cindy understood that giving a talk at one of Elaine's gatherings was good for her in all ways. *Get out of your shell, Cindy. Now,* she told herself.

Cindy tried to take a panoramic look around, but it was impossible to see the whole store from the doorway. It was designed in a maze of long bookshelves and the aisles were jammed bumper-to-bumper with a crowd of shoppers and browsers. The ceilings were high and the tall plate glass windows on the long side of the store let in the afternoon light.

Elaine escorted Cindy to a rear corner of the store where rows of folding chairs had been set up at the foot of the podium. Behind and to the left of the podium was an easel displaying her book cover, a black-and-white shot of a Burke crime scene in downtown San Francisco, enlarged and printed on foam board. And to the right, a table piled high with fresh new books with her name as lead author.

Across that corner of the room, standing by the wall of windows, were Cindy's best friends: Lindsay Boxer, Yuki Castellano, and Claire Washburn, all members in good standing of the Women's Murder Club. All three crime solving experts in their own realms — Claire as the city's chief medical examiner, Yuki as a top prosecutor, and Lindsay as a homicide detective who partnered with Cindy's boyfriend, Rich — were laughing and talking together and hadn't seen her come into the store.

Cindy turned back to Elaine, who was saying, "I was only going to read a chapter, Cindy, but I couldn't sleep. I finished the whole book by three a.m. My God. What a story."

Tears came into Cindy's eyes brought on by equal parts of humility, gratitude, and a feeling like freedom. That Evan Burke was losing his grip on her just a little. In fact, she never had to talk to or see him again.

Chairs filled and the room hushed as Elaine tapped the podium's microphone, saying, "Everyone, please welcome Cindy Thomas and prepare to be blown away."

Cindy took her place at the mic. Richie sat in the front row with Yuki, while Lindsay and Claire sat behind them. Cindy smiled as Lindsay gave her a thumbs-up and grinned, then kept it going, nodding to strangers who'd come to hear about her book.

Cindy said, "Hello, hello, can you hear me?" into the mic and when the people in the back said she was coming across loud and clear, Cindy, uplifted by the strong sound of her amplified voice, launched into her speech.

CHAPTER 3

GRIPPING THE EDGES of the podium, making eye contact with her audience, Cindy began, "Writing this book has been the most harrowing experience of my life.

"I wasn't expecting Evan Burke's proposal," she said, "but I was prepared. I had already been writing about the Lucas Burke case for the *Chronicle*. When the body of his infant daughter—Evan Burke's granddaughter—washed up on Baker Beach, I was there. I interviewed a schoolgirl who days later was murdered in her car. Many months after that, I was present when the police discovered the murder weapon.

"I didn't know then who was committing these crimes, but I was reporting on them. Later, Evan Burke was shot by police and arrested in Las Vegas. We knew he was the killer. At his invitation, I flew there to meet him, hoping he'd tell me something no one else knew, details that we could publish in the *Chronicle*. I was looking for a quote, but Burke proposed something else. And he gave me this."

Cindy tugged on a red cord she wore around her neck, tucked

inside her blouse, and after pulling it free, she held up a key looped into the end.

"Burke lived in a shack in the desert outside Las Vegas, about four hundred square feet all told. He kept a trunk under his bed and this is the key to that trunk. Two dear friends who are with the SFPD were with me when we unlocked the trunk, but I was not prepared for what we found.

"Burke had been documenting his kills from his first, over thirty years before. He'd filled several scrapbooks with souvenirs and photos. He had drawn maps to where he'd hidden his victims' remains. And along with the scrapbooks, he had a dozen journals detailing his kills. Often he described the women he was about to kill, what they said, how they died, and bits of poetry along with his victims' last words."

Cindy paused, put her hand on the book and looked out at the silent audience. Many in the group looked frightened, as if Evan Burke might just stand up and replace her at the microphone.

She said, "Evan Burke will die in prison. His career as a killer is over. But, along with his trophies and voluminous notes, Evan Burke gave me, gave *all* of us, a priceless gift.

"Ninety-five percent of Burke's victims didn't know him, received no warning, and didn't survive their first encounter. His gift is one our parents gave us as children and is reiterated, no, *proven* in this book.

"It's simply this: Beware of strangers.

"Take that to heart. It comes from one of the most successful serial killers in America.

"Are there any questions?"

CHAPTER 4

APPLAUSE ROLLED FROM the front to the back of the store. Some people stood to reinforce their approval and appreciation and at the same time, a forest of hands shot up. Cindy smiled and, stepping on her own ovation, called out, "The woman in blue on the aisle. What would you like to know?"

"Hi, Cindy. How did the work process go? Were you in the same room with Burke during the interviews or sitting outside his cell?"

"We were in an attorney-client room about as big as a small walk-in closet. It was barred. Burke was shackled and there were guards only feet away. What was I thinking? *Silence of the Lambs*."

As she took questions, Cindy quickly realized that a quarter of the mostly female audience wanted to know about her work process, from what time of day she wrote to whether Burke reviewed the work as she went along.

"When I wasn't physically writing, I was organizing sections of the book in my head. When I slept, I dreamed about the book, the stories, what Burke had done to his victims."

The remainder of those who questioned her wanted to know

more about Evan Burke. Several people asked about the contents of Burke's trunk of souvenirs, what the scrapbooks looked like, and could she compare his first and last entries. Had he become more efficient? How had he evaded the police for so long?

Good questions, all, and Cindy deftly pointed them to find the answers in her new book, even as they began to drive Cindy back into that dark cave where horror lived in her mind.

A well-dressed woman who appeared to be in her fifties spoke up without raising her hand, saying, "I don't think I could be tricked by a man like Burke."

There were some hoots, uneasy laughter, more questions and Cindy fielded them. *Yes, Burke had seen the book. Yes, he liked it. Yes, I feel more vulnerable now that I've spent so much time with him in person and with his things. I am different than I was pre-Burke. I'm more aware of the people around me. That's a good thing."*

A few men, perhaps drawn to her speech, had found standing room behind the chairs. One of them raised his hand. He looked to be in his thirties, wore glasses, and was dressed in khakis and a black leather bomber jacket.

"I come in peace," he joked.

"Hello and what's your question?"

"Cindy. Your presentation sounds like good old-fashioned man-hating to me. How can you say that based on this one killer, women should be wary of men they don't know? Some of the world's best love stories have come from opportune first meetings like that."

Some in the audience shouted the man down, saying that he didn't get it. A few thought that he'd made a good point. The verbal scuffle heated up quickly. There was some loud over-talking and the group camaraderie was broken.

Expressionless, the man stood his ground. He shouted out to Cindy.

"Let me be clear. You say you deplore the killings and the killer. And yet, you were paid for writing this book—"

"I'm sorry, what's your point?"

"Point is, you've hyped this guy and are taking money for doing that and so is Evan Burke. You're rewarding an unrepentant killer."

"You're wrong," Cindy said. "He's not getting paid."

They guy who'd taken her on was not backing down.

"That makes you a man-hater *and* a hypocrite."

Rich, along with his SFPD partner, Lindsay Boxer, and an armed security guard, were moving in, separating the man from the seated audience. Elaine said, "Jesus," and cut a straight path to the door.

The heckler called out as he strode toward the exit, "Good luck with your conscience, Cindy."

Cindy was protected by friends in law enforcement. But she was shaken and knew she'd be asking herself some questions later tonight. *Was that guy dangerous? Or was he just angry and rude? Was commerce a bad thing? How else to get the Evan Burke story to those who needed to read it?*

A woman in the middle of a row of chairs close to the rear of the room called out, "Is that guy one of them, Cindy? A serial killer?"

She said, "We don't know anything about him except that he was inappropriate. To restate my advice, if you're dating, I suggest group outings for a while. And carry a key chain that has a hell of an alarm. By the way, I do believe in love at first sight, but love at third or sixth sight also has merit.

"Anyone else?"

Time passed without even tapping her on the shoulder, and an hour had gone by when Cindy, Rich, and the Women's Murder Club left Book Passage. Yuki drove Lindsay and Claire. Cindy rode beside Rich in his ancient Bronco as they headed south to dinner in Sausalito.

"Did I handle that guy all right?"

"Sure did. Why? Are you worried?"

"Rich, did that guy wander into my talk by accident? Or do you think he planned to challenge me?"

"Don't know," said Richie. "But for sure, Cin, you handled him like a pro. You were polite. Had no apparent nervousness. He challenged you, and you challenged him back. But if you ever see him again, call the cops."

Cindy moved closer to Rich, put her hand on his thigh.

She said, "I think it's time to get a big dog and a small gun."

"You've got me," said Richie. "Big dog. Big gun."

Cindy laughed, snuggled in. Rich took his right hand off the steering wheel and drew her close.

When she woke up, Rich was pulling up the emergency brakes and Lindsay was knocking on the passenger-side window saying, "Wake up, girlfriend. Time to eat."

CHAPTER 5

THE BARNACLE WAS new to me, but the bar was standing room only and the restaurant was filling with Saturday diners. It was a homey, neighborhood tavern with the added attraction of outdoor dining and a front-row seat on the bay.

The sun hadn't yet set, but my stomach was growling. We commandeered a picnic table on the second-floor deck and in the pale light of a dusky-pink sky, we longtime friends settled in and settled down.

I sat between Claire and Yuki and across from my partner, Rich Conklin, and my great friend, Cindy, who'd been grappling with PTSD since spending too much time with Evan Burke. She'd toughed it out, though, and we were all proud of her and her important book.

Our waitress appeared with menus, told us her name was Mandy. We ordered beer and oysters all around, and I said, "Yes, please," to bread and butter. "Two baskets, okay?"

"Beer first," Cindy said to a round of laughter. "I earned it."

Claire picked up where we'd left off at the bookstore.

"About that guy with the big mouth," she said. "His problem with Cindy was that she was paid to write a book?"

Cindy said, "Elaine told me she'd seen him before but he'd never actually purchased a book."

Yuki said, "I might have a picture of him…Hang on."

" 'Good luck with your conscience,' " said Richie. "What a punk."

"Agreed," I said, "but punks have been known to be dangerous—and stupid."

Yuki passed her phone to Cindy," said "No, I don't have a picture of him. But here you go, cutie. Look at you."

"Oh," said Cindy. "Better than I thought."

Yuki said, "I'm calling it. That guy wanted Cindy's attention."

"He liked me?" Cindy asked.

"What else could it be?" said Yuki. "If I'd gotten a shot, we could run his mug through facial rec."

"You gave him nothing," I said to Cindy. "Whatever that jerk was doing."

But the unknown punk stayed with us as the main subject of our conversation. He was wrong about Burke getting paid, but to Cindy's point, was wariness a good enough tool for women who were too trusting?

Yuki sent pictures of Cindy to our phones while telling us that she had a trial starting on Monday.

"I see murder in the defendant's future if he's not locked up."

Cindy said, "I'd like to come watch you, okay?"

"Good. Yeah. I'd like that."

Rich and I were just recovering from a week of gang shootings and had little to show for it. Two dead kids and a dozen living teenage gangsters, who were also not talking. But at that rare moment on the deck overlooking the bay we were together and looking good. It was as though the roughness of the week had been washed away by the pale watery light.

I said, "Here's to Cindy and this freaking gorgeous view."

"To best friends," said Cindy.

Glasses clinked and dinner arrived. The bass was perfectly seasoned and prepared and went down fast. We were summoning our waitress to ask about dessert when my phone vibrated in my pocket.

I ignored it, of course. No phones at Women's Murder Club meetings. My husband, Joe, was home with our little girl, Julie, and this wasn't his ringtone. Still, my phone buzzed again. Then Yuki's phone also went off. Simple math told me that Jackson Brady, Yuki's husband and my CO, was calling. He was probably steamed that I hadn't picked up.

Yuki and I both looked at our phones. She answered hers a split second before I did.

"She's right here, hon," she said into her phone. "Linds. Brady wants to talk to you."

"Brady?" I said. "Who died?"

Rich's phone rang. He stabbed a button and joined Brady's conference call.

"We're all here, lieu. Give that to us again."

Rich raised his hand for the check and Yuki said to Cindy, "I'll drive you home. Don't think twice about it."

Yuki gave her credit card to the waitress, and I said, "Yuki, let me know what I owe you."

I grabbed a hunk of bread, slugged down the last inch of my beer. I kissed cheeks, hugged Cindy again and tousled her hair. "Love you."

"Me, too. I'm glad you were there," she said.

I was sorry to leave my friends and wouldn't do it but for a phone call that could only mean that someone had been murdered.

CHAPTER 6

RICH AND I left the restaurant, both of us feeling bad to leave Cindy on this of all evenings.

Rich said, "I'll make it up to her." He unlocked the Bronco. As we mounted up, he said, "And if this turns out to be an all-nighter, I'm going to challenge Brady to a friendly fight, and then I'm going to break his nose."

I cracked up. Conklin is ten years younger than Brady, but Brady has massive guns. He stretches out his shirtsleeves just bending an elbow.

"I don't want you to die, Richie."

"You gotta believe in me, Lindsay. I've got quick hands. And I can dance."

I cracked up again. I love Richie and after many years of sitting across from him at our facing desks, working innumerable homicides together, having the other's back, always—Rich playing good cop to my badass, my preferred role—we were a good team. More than that, he's the brother I never had. And a friend for life.

Brady is, too. When he and Yuki got married, he became part of the family. Tall, with white-blond hair and pale blue eyes, he and Yuki make a striking pair. She's a size two, daughter of a Japanese mother and Italian-American soldier father, wears slim, smart suits and a navy-blue colored streak in her hair.

After I caught my breath and Rich had stopped punching the air with one fist, I told him that I hadn't heard everything Brady had told us.

"His voice was breaking up," I said. "I only got the gist."

"Man's been found dead in his car…"

"That, I heard."

"…a ten-minute drive from Book Passage."

Sausalito is over the bridge from San Francisco, not our beat. Yet, we'd been drafted because of the victim's proximity to the bookstore? That didn't compute, but between the radio and our siren, no further conversation was possible. Still, I was looking for a reason. All I came up with was that Rich and I had worked the Burke case together when "Quicksilver" or the "Ghost of Catalina" as he'd been called, lived on Mount Tamalpais, about an hour from here. Marin PD had joined us when we were working on their turf. I guessed Brady was returning the favor by sending us.

Rich knew the way. He drove north parallel to Route 101. We took a sharp left at Tamal Vista Boulevard, a mixed-use area that ran past the Corte Madera lagoon waterfront. After a series of quick turns, we took Doherty to our destination. The classic American shopping center was approaching closing time.

Rich slowed to a crawl as we entered a transient scene; people leaving stores, going to their cars, cars leaving, potential witnesses evaporating never to be seen again.

I surveilled the area from the passenger seat, doing a rough count of the shops. About twenty one- and two-story stucco buildings; a bank, a bakery, three fast-food restaurants, a shoe-repair shop, and innumerable boutiques, all forming a ragged semicircle around a parking lot.

As was standard for large suburban parking lots, this one was divided by treed median strips and hundreds of parking spots, nearly all of them filled with cars. At the far end of the lot, flashing police-car lights grabbed my attention.

Six squads were blocking through traffic and forming a wall around the crime scene. As we moved toward the police, I saw that barrier tape had enclosed a third of the lot. Ten uniformed officers were directing traffic, protecting the scene.

I pinned my badge to my breast pocket and Rich and I got out of his car and headed in on foot.

"The Camry," I said pointing to the vehicle three cars in from the main through-road, taped in within the larger perimeter. The Toyota sedan looked six or seven years old, an oxblood red with some rust around the wheel wells.

Checking my watch, I saw that it was seven thirty and shops were closing at eight. Lights went on in the lot. Scattered bells rang and CLOSED signs were hung inside glass doors as they were pulled shut. A CSU van rounded the turn into the shopping center on two wheels followed by another van, this one marked "Coroner" in big black letters.

Pedestrians had quickly gotten a sense of the situation. A crime, probably a murder, had occurred and many of those people whose cars were parked within the taped-off area wouldn't be allowed to leave. I didn't have to hear their voices to know what they were saying to one cop after another. *"I need my car." "I have to pick up my husband." "I have all of these packages." "My mother's alone." "You have to let me leave."*

That wouldn't be happening.

A uniformed cop, about six three, 280, put up a hand to stop us from coming closer. We kept coming but I shouted out my name, rank, and flashed my badge. Conklin added that Marin County's Captain Geoffrey Brevoort was expecting us. The uniform waved us in, holding up the tape so we could duck under it.

"Mancuso," he said. "Tom."

He introduced us to his partner, Chris Fama, and made a general announcement to the team. Then, Fama ran the scene for us.

"We got the call about fifteen, twenty minutes ago. The manager at the Dunkin' was leaving early and his car was next to a Camry. He saw that the rear left door was ajar. The driver's window was open. He looked in, saw what he saw, and phoned it in."

Rich said, "He's being questioned?"

"Yep, probably just got to the station."

I pulled on latex gloves.

"Mind if we take a look?"

"Here. Take my light," said Fama.

CHAPTER 7

RICH AND I stepped over to the red sedan and peered inside. Every murder left a mark on me and questions quickly formed, tumbling one after the other in my mind. *What had happened here? Who had killed this man, how, and why?*

I tried to puzzle it out using only what I could see by flashlight and the glare of the headlights under the darkened sky. I had no blood tests, no fingerprints, no witness statements. Not even the man's name.

But there was evidence in the murder itself.

I made note of the position of the victim's body. His feet had lifted off the floor near the pedals, but his upper body was twisted to the right. He was facedown on the front seat, his head toward the passenger side, right arm under him, the left hanging over the edge of the seat.

I snapped a few pictures, then, said to Rich, "I think he saw the shooter approach from the rear and tried to dive under the dash."

A bad feeling overcame me as I continued to study the body. There was a wad of what looked like a black leather jacket in the passenger-side footwell.

"Rich. Is this that guy from the bookstore?"

"Huh. Could be. Same type of build, anyway."

"On the floor. That could be his bomber jacket."

The victim's face was pressed against the upholstery, distorting his features. Rich focused the flashlight beam on the dead man's face. His skin was covered with blood and flecks of brain matter, which were also evident on the dash and the passenger-side door.

There was so much blood that I couldn't see where he'd been shot. A whack with a tire iron could create the same amount of blood and tissue detritus.

"It's going to be three to six hours before this is sorted out," Rich said.

I agreed. The CSIs would have to document the primary crime scene. Take photos, lots of them, search for bullet holes and casings, anything the killer may have left behind. Until they were finished with their work, the body could not be moved.

Mancuso's partner, Chris Fama, had returned with his notebook in hand. He said, "The tags say that this car belongs to a Ralph Hammer. If this *is* Hammer, he has no priors. He lives outside Mill Valley. I'm going to have to notify his family. 'Scuse me. I'm getting a call."

Richie was training the flashlight beam into the rear compartment, which was some kind of dump filled with plastic shopping bags.

"Look here, Linds."

The only empty space on the back seat was behind the driver seat. We couldn't rummage until CSU processed this mess, but Rich was insistent.

"Right there," he said. "See the Cheesecake Factory bag?"

I followed his beam until I saw a white paper bag reading "Cheesecake Factory." Then, under it, I saw the corner of a book.

Cindy's book.

My partner verbalized his theory.

"He antagonizes people. Someone follows him from the bookstore, here. Waits for him to come out of the Cheesecake Factory with his food and then, when the dude is inside his car, the shooter gets into the back seat and pops him. Uses a suppressor. Then, he disappears into the crowd."

"Pretty good working theory," I said.

We backed out of the Camry, saw clumps of disgruntled shoppers and storekeepers camped out on the sidewalk. A squad car zigzagged through the lot. It was a mobile plate reader, a squad with built-in cameras at knee-level, feeding plate numbers into the car's computer. If an outstanding warrant was triggered, a beep-alarm would sound. At any rate, there would be a record of cars in the lot around the time of the murder.

Rich said, "The killer could be long gone. Or could still be here, you know?"

I had a belated but still valid idea.

"There had to be cameras in the bookstore, right?"

"I'm on it," he said.

Rich punched a number into his phone and moments later had a brief conversation with Elaine. He signed off and said, "Mancuso can have someone pick up Elaine's surveillance tapes. She'll keep the lights on."

"Good. Even with the victim's extensive injuries, facial rec is our friend."

We climbed up into the Bronco, a good spot to watch the moving scene. Going by the book, uniforms canvassed the onlookers, taking statements and photos of driver's licenses. This was the last best chance to find a witness to the crime.

I dialed Brady, filled him in on what we knew, and told him, "Yes, yes, we'll hang in."

I called home. My husband, Joe Molinari, picked up the phone.

I said, "Rich and I got pulled into a case, Joe. We're at a crime scene in Sausalito and I have no idea when I'll be home."

CHAPTER 8

I DRAGGED MYSELF through the doorway to our loft-like flat. Last time I looked, it was after midnight. I hung my weapon in the antique gun safe in the entranceway and locked it.

Joe turned off the TV, stood up and hugged me, rocked me, said, "Give me your phone."

I asked, "How's the Bug?"

"I might as well tell you. She tried on your sunglasses and lipstick. And shoes."

"You took pictures?"

He showed me on his phone.

I had a half a laugh left in me and I gave it to Joe along with my phone. Then, I peeked in on Julie. She was sleeping with an arm thrown over Martha, my sweet old doggy. Neither of them moved or opened an eye, so I closed the door, crossed the living room and sat heavily in the long leather sofa Joe had bought before we were married. That sofa was both a luxury and a pleasure.

Joe said, "Hungry? We have half a chicken and green beans almandine."

"Sounds delish, but, no thanks, Joe. Be right back."

I took a fast, hot shower, and minutes later, I was in fresh PJs, and Joe was in bed waiting for me. I climbed in, snuggled up to him and he stroked my back and my hair. Normally, that would put me out for hours.

But I was utterly awake.

I curled around him and when he said, "Start talking," I told him everything I knew.

"The vic's name is Ralph Hammer. He was surviving on his wits. He did some freelance coding, bartending, and he got a speaking part in a cereal commercial last year. That was still bringing in royalties."

I explained the working theory, how Hammer had come to the bookstore, accused Cindy of glorifying Burke's homicidal career. Just telling Joe about this guy upset me. I said that I hadn't liked the guy, or what he'd done, but he had a right to speak. And now he was dead.

I kept talking.

"I don't know if his verbal attack on Cindy was related to his death or not. But at the time, he was vehement and a little scary, so Rich and I showed him the door. Store owner recognized him. Told Cindy he'd never made a purchase. It's possible he lifted a copy of Cindy's book on the way out because we found one in the back of his car."

"Strange," Joe said.

My husband has worked in all of America's clandestine services and began his career in the Behavioral Science Unit of the FBI. So, if he said "strange," I had to ask why.

Said Joe, "What I meant is that the fact of the book is strange enough to make me ask *why* was it inside the victim's car? Did

Hammer steal it as you suggest? Did he want to know more about Evan Burke? Or about Cindy? Or did he want recompense for being thrown out of the store? Or."

I kicked off the blanket. "No riddles, please, Joe. It's past my bedtime. Or, what?"

Joe laughed. One of my favorite things.

"Or. The *killer* put the book in the car. If so, it makes me ask was he at the bookstore? If so, was he following Hammer or was Hammer a convenient victim?"

"Or," I said. "Other unprovable theories."

"You got the surveillance tapes from the bookstore?"

"Of course," I said, as if that had been my first thought.

"Run facial rec on everyone, including the women."

"I'll pass that along," I said. "It's not our case, really. We just backed up the local PD as a favor for Brady who owed one to Captain Brevoort."

"So why are you still worrying about this?"

"Because, Joe. I saw the guy. I listened to the guy. He was rude to Cindy. And while we were eating oysters overlooking the bay, someone killed him. And they didn't tickle him to death, either."

"Tell me."

"Stun gun to disable him, garrote to kill him. Then, after he was dead, gave him a couple of gunshots to the head. What's the psychology behind that?"

"Jesus. Talk about overkill."

We lay together in silence thinking about that hit. Joe's breathing started to lengthen and deepen. But I kept thinking. The killing felt personal. Hammer's wallet was intact. His car was filled with bags and whatever. He didn't have a record.

I said, "It was a thrill kill, or payback..."

I felt the tears catching in my throat. I coughed them away and worked my way under Joe's arm. He stroked my back and said, "You're overtired, sweetie. Overworked." Then, he fell asleep.

But I couldn't go with him.

The last time I looked at my watch, it was three. I slept poorly and had a dream that Marin County PD was calling me.

I couldn't find my phone.

CHAPTER 9

HERE'S WHAT I remember of Sunday. Julie's flying leap from the floor to my stomach. Staring me in the face, saying, "Get. Up."

"What if I don't?"

"Well. Then you're a lazy head."

"Oh, no."

Julie giggled. She looks so much like Joe with her dark curly hair and dark eyes that I just couldn't be mad at her for more than a minute. "What time is it?" I asked her.

She handed me my watch. It was nine thirty.

"What day is it? Sunday. So, I don't have to get up, right?"

Joe came in with Martha at his heels. She also jumped onto the bed.

"You feeling better, Blondie?"

"I feel…like…a wet sock. Who's on the phone?"

"Here's everyone who called. Rich. Brady. Cindy. Brady, again. Officer Chris Fama. Yuki called and put Brady on the line. Claire just called. She's spoken to the Marin County ME."

"It's *Sunday*," I said with more vehemence than I meant. "Sorry, Joe."

"It's okay. Cindy was crying. Call her when you've had your nap. Your phone will be charging next to the bed. Also, Brady wants a briefing."

"I gave him one last night. I'm sure I did."

"I told him to talk to Richie."

"Oh, boy. Richie's mad at him. What did Claire find out?"

"She confirms the bullets in Hammer's head were for extra credit. He was already dead."

"I'm going back to sleep. Don't try to stop me."

"Officer Fama called to say thanks and if anything breaks he'll be in touch…"

"Okay."

"One other thing. You want it later?"

"Did Marin PD get any tips about the victim?"

"No one mentioned it."

"Martha's had her walk?"

Joe just looked at me.

"See you later," I said, the words slow walking out of my mouth. He leaned down, kissed the top of my head.

I said, "Rich called? What did he say?"

"He said to have you call him."

My lights went out. When I woke up again, afternoon sun was streaming through the bedroom windows. I got up, grabbed my phone from the charger, looked around the apartment. No one was home. In the kitchen, I nuked oatmeal, made coffee, sugared it half to death. I called Cindy first.

She said, "You okay?"

"I think the job is catching up with me."

"Rich, too," she said. "Me, too."

I let Cindy do all the talking while I made food disappear. She had news on the book front. Sales were going through the roof. Thank God something good had come of all this. I asked to speak with Rich.

"He's out cold."

"Okay. I'm calling Brady."

Brady picked up on the first ring. Rich and I both loved him. A former Miami Vice top dog, Jackson Brady had rotated through homicide when he came to SFPD. He'd partnered first with me, then Conklin, and with our former lieutenant, Warren Jacobi.

Years later, Brady had taken the job of homicide lieutenant—commanding officer of our squad—and we were better for it. Brady knew when to be hands-on, when to oversee from his office and he and I had stood shoulder to shoulder during deadly shoot-outs, including one in recent memory.

"I called you about six hours ago," he said.

"Brady. Give me the fricking day off, will you? I'm this close to a nervous breakdown."

"I didn't know. I'll see you tomorrow morning."

"Don't you dare hang up. Did you talk to Marin PD?"

"Yep. ME found nothing on Hammer's body that would lead to his killer. But she found something interesting."

"No. Do. Not. Make me beg, Lieutenant."

"Silicon Valley prototypes. Before you say 'what,' it's what it sounds like. Plans for pricey tech items not yet released to market."

"What do you make of that?" I asked.

"Besides that I want a look at the future? Likely, the documents are stolen. Hammer was a thief. CSU is still going through the bags of merch in his car."

"So, he stole Cindy's book. Case closed."

"Whatever you and Rich did last night, I got a thank-you from Captain Breevoort at dawn."

"Glad we could help," I said.

"And thanks from me. Go back to sleep."

"Copy that, Lieu. See you tomorrow."

CHAPTER 10

EARLY MONDAY MORNING I was still dreaming. A mission was about to go down. We were in a corridor that was lined with SWAT units, ready to take on whatever we found behind a door.

I was wearing tactical gear, a loaded semiautomatic in my hand. Rich was standing beside me, his gun drawn, too. Behind the door was the answer to—everything.

"Get ready," I said to Conklin.

I'd raised my leg and was ready to kick down the door when a body landed on me.

The dream shattered and I saw that Julie had landed on me again and this time there was an old dog involved.

"Hold it," I said. "Julie, you're too big to jump on me."

"I am?"

"Here's what to do. Let me see your arm."

Martha was digging under the blankets and Julie edged toward me, leading with her wrist. I put my hand around her slim forearm and shook it gently.

"See? Shake my arm and say, 'Mom'?"

She shook my arm and said, "Mom."

I said, "Hi, hon. Are you getting ready for school?"

She said, "Me and Daddy are taking Martha out for her walk. And then we're going to hug you goodbye."

"Got it. Dad's putting you on the school bus."

"Come on, Mommmm. You know."

I shook off my troubled sleep with a sharp memory and pang of remorse. Joe and Julie were flying to New York today for spring break, a plan that had been in play for several months and still worried me. But Julie hadn't seen her only grandmother in too long and really wanted to see New York.

Joe called Julie. She and Martha zoomed out of the bedroom.

I yelled out, "Wait a minute. Wait for me!"

I jumped out of bed, found a T-shirt on a chair, dug for clean sweatpants, put on a pair of running shoes, no socks, no makeup, no worries. I caught my family at the elevator. Julie hugged my waist and Martha had a few kind whines for me.

This was a new record; from bed to elevator in under three minutes, but time with Julie and Joe before they flew away was priceless.

Out on the street, I asked Joe, "What time's your flight?"

"Linds," Joe said, "I hired a car to take us to SFO."

"But, why? I can take you."

"You have an appointment, Linds. You're going to be late."

CHAPTER 11

CLEARLY I'D LOST all track of time and after a peppy walk, weepy goodbye hugs, promises to call every single day, I took Martha home and handed her off to our lifesaver of a nanny, Mrs. Gloria Rose who lived across the hall.

I threw on some work clothes and drove to Dr. Sid Greene's office for my final therapy session.

My therapy had been a review-board decision because of my involvement in a fatal incident. I was not held responsible but I was ordered to see a psychiatrist who worked with law enforcement. I felt strongly that my work with Dr. Greene had been worth the time, but I was relieved that in another hour it would be over.

I parked at mid-block across from Dr. Greene's two-story office building. I buzzed the downstairs bell. There was an answering buzz, and I went in, climbed two flights of stairs, and entered Dr. Greene's waiting room. I stared at the door to his inner office and, as in my waking dream this morning, I sensed that the answers to everything were right behind it.

As if cued, the door opened and Dr. Greene greeted me, saying, "Lindsay, come on in."

Dr. Greene was a man in his sixties, round-faced with an easy smile and good reputation inside the Hall of Justice. I liked him but wouldn't miss these weekly high dives into my feelings. I had prepared myself for his summary and mine of what we had accomplished these last months, followed by a goodbye-and-good-luck handshake.

The room was pleasant, about ten by twenty, beige carpet, windows on two white walls, and between the two windows three abstract paintings that I couldn't fathom.

I took my customary seat across from Dr. Greene, who began the session by asking me to tell him about my week. And I did—the good, the bad, and Saturday, all culminating in what felt like the breaking of a dam.

"Whoever killed Ralph Hammer is, by the look of his work, an unusual killer, an overachiever. Hammer was opinionated, vocal, a thief, and perhaps a hoarder and I don't know what else. I'm interested in the case, but it's not mine. And I have no control over what happens with it or on any case on a given day.

"You know, Dr. Greene, I work with great people. We have an ethical and legal code that's honorable and yet we're not writing traffic tickets. Death is always involved. I can't count the numbers of homicides I've tried to solve. I'm feeling overwhelmed right now by Hammer's brutal death and about the individual who killed him. This case has really gotten to me and…and I don't remember one that hasn't."

Dr. Greene leaned toward me, his hands on his knees.

"Let me ask you this, Lindsay. Are you ready to retire and do some other kind of work? Inside police work, administration, for instance."

After a long pause, I said, "I had a job like that once. I had the corner office and the title, and I knew how to do the job. I supervised most of the same cops I work with now. After a few years as lieutenant, I stepped down. I wanted to work the actual cases and at the same time I didn't enjoy giving orders to people who took chances that I didn't take."

"You're conscientious," he said. "This is why you take it all to heart. The cases. The deaths. The lack of control even though you're following orders."

I nodded my agreement and added that my blood pressure was up and I was having trouble sleeping. That I had a medical condition, aplastic anemia, that would take me down if this level of stress continued. I added, "And now, there's more at stake than ever before."

"Julie."

I nodded. "She's getting a half a mother on a good day. If it weren't for Joe and our nanny, I couldn't work."

"Are you ready to quit your job, Lindsay?"

"How do I know if I'm going through a bad patch or hitting the wall?"

He didn't answer, just kept up steady eye contact with me from his seat eight feet away.

Finally, he said, "Think about both sides of that question. Let's talk again next week."

"Dr. Greene. This was supposed to be our last session."

"In my opinion, there's more for us to do," he said. "You can stop, of course, but I think we should keep going for a while longer."

I scoffed, flipped my hands, looked at the clock on the wall, and then at the good doctor's face. I cast my eyes to the paintings between us and said, "If I figure out the art, will that mean that I'm done?"

"We can talk about that once you've done it," he said.

"Another month," I said.

"Good," he said. We shook hands and we both smiled.

Then, I left Dr. Greene's office and drove to the Hall of Justice hoping for a boring day.

CHAPTER 12

YUKI SAT BEHIND the prosecution table and watched Sergeant Philip Birney swear to tell the whole truth so help him, God. An experienced sergeant with fifteen spotless years on the Job, he was the first officer at the crime scene and now he was Yuki's star witness.

But this morning, Birney looked anxious. Stage fright happened, but, please God, not today, not Birney. Yuki had to win this case for the victim and for the People of San Francisco. The public was counting on her and she wouldn't let them down.

Judge Karen Froman asked Yuki if she was ready. Was she? Nick Gaines, her second chair, said under his breath, "Batter up." Sergeant Birney was in uniform. Otherwise, he appeared to be an unremarkable forty-year-old man of average height and weight, brown hair and brown eyes—that were gazing at nothing.

Yuki got to her feet, straightened her suit jacket as she crossed the well of the small unadorned courtroom and stopped just short of the witness stand.

Yuki greeted Birney sharply and got his attention.

"Sergeant Birney. What brought you to Alamo Square on the day in question?"

Birney sighed, and after a long moment, began.

"A 911 caller, Ms. Carol Linnert. She lives next door to the house owned by Lewis and Barbara Sullivan. Ms. Linnert tells the operator that she heard screaming. She's hard of hearing, couldn't be sure but she thinks it's Barbara Sullivan."

Yuki said, "And what happened after you and your partner arrived at the Sullivan house?"

Birney coughed into his fist, cleared his throat, and said, "Okay. First thing I notice is there's no car in the driveway. The front yard is clipped and the actual house is painted and well-kept. Martin Brodsky, he's my partner. He and I go to the front door and knock. No answer. No sounds. I tell him to cover the back of the house."

Birney took another long pause, looked down at his hands.

"Sergeant Birney?"

Birney said, "Sorry. So, I'm alone at the front door. Seems no one is at home. Then I hear a sound. Like an animal, in pain. I try the door and it's unlocked, so I go in. I announce again. 'SFPD. Is anyone here?' Still, no answer. So, I call my partner on the two-way and ask him to find Ms. Linnert while I check out the rest of the house. I see a man's coat hanging from a hook in the foyer. Kids' toys are in the living room. Ahhh, catcher's mitt. A video game still running on the player. The place looks recently vacated and I feel that the homeowners are coming back soon. I hear the sound again. So, I run down to the basement."

Birney seemed wracked by the memory. His face had tightened and he seemed lost. Yuki had an impulse to walk to the stand and grab Birney by the shoulders. Shake him alert. The audience shifted in their seats. Whispers echoed. A ringing phone played a tune.

This annoyed Judge Froman, an attractive blond-haired jurist, mother of five, who'd been addressed as Your Honor for half her life. Now she banged her gavel and demanded quiet. "Phones off. No talking while court is in session. Don't make me say this again."

Birney cleared his throat and looking up at the judge said, "I'm not usually like this. My old dog died last night. Sarge was seventeen."

The Judge said, "Do you need a break?"

"I'd rather just go on," Birney said. "My memory of the events is clear. If Your Honor doesn't mind."

"All right. Go ahead, then."

Birney picked up where he'd left off.

"There's a laundry room downstairs and upon entering I see a Caucasian female, about forty, maybe a hundred fifteen pounds, lying on the floor, her wrists chained to the base of a utility sink."

Birney was focusing now, speaking directly to the jury.

"Her clothes are shredded. Buttons are torn off, pants, ripped open, pulled below her knees, no panties. She's gagged and her ankles are taped to weights. She's bleeding profusely from numerous cuts and gouges. It looks like her left eye is half-popped-out. Blood is pooling around her head.

"I call her name," Birney said. "She doesn't respond, but I hear her wheezy breathing. Soft. Irregular. I radio my partner and tell him we need an ambulance and detectives. I identify myself to the woman. I tell her help is on the way. I ask her who did this, and where is her family and she still doesn't answer. I want to comfort her but I can't risk contaminating the scene. I take pictures from the doorway and zoom in on the implements near her. Pretty soon, I hear sirens."

Yuki asked, "Can you list and describe these implements?"

Birney swiped at his eyes with the back of his hand and flipped to a page in his evidence log.

He read, "Bicycle chain and lock. Bolt cutter. There's a twenty-four-inch tire iron, a long, serrated bread knife, a coil of nylon marine line. Yellow. Uhh, two twenty-pound free weights and a partial roll of Gorilla Tape. This is the tape that was used to keep the gag in her mouth. And to affix her ankles to the weights."

He put down the notebook and added, "One more thing. There's a bloody handprint on the wallpaper near the door and writing that looks like it was made with a bloody finger. It says, 'I love you.' I took some shots of that."

Yuki entered the photos into evidence and passed them to the jury foreman, George Campbell, a retired high-school science teacher. Birney had come through. She'd been moved by how he had managed to overcome his grief and deliver honest, emotional testimony that also affected the jury.

She put one last question to her witness. "Can you confirm the identity of the woman you found in the basement?"

"Barbara Sullivan."

Yuki thanked him and said to Judge Froman, "We have no more questions for Sergeant Birney, Your Honor."

CHAPTER 13

ATTORNEY MAURICE SWITZER, counsel for defendant Lewis Sullivan, stood and said, "The defense has no questions at this time."

Yuki glanced at the counsel table across the aisle. Lewis Sullivan looked straight ahead. He had replaced his bulldog attorney, Cal Talbot, with Mo Switzer just days before trial commenced. Switzer was charming, low-key, and could present a sympathetic face to the jurors before pulling a winning closing statement out of his hat. If the jurors liked Mo as much as she did, his personality alone could tilt the verdict.

Cindy watched from her preferred seat at the back of the courtroom. The charge of attempted murder against the husband and the apparent near-death spousal abuse had the ingredients of a big headline story.

Yuki asked that her next witness be called.

Officer Martin Brodsky, wearing his blues and a smart, stylish haircut came through the courtroom doors. He walked up the aisle to the witness stand and was sworn in.

Brodsky was thirty years old, good-looking, a bit cocky, and Yuki thought he was something of a risk. Birney, however, liked him, saying, "Marty's good police. And he has a sharp eye for detail."

Yuki took a stance in the well that gave her a clear view of both the witness and the jury box.

She said, "Officer Brodsky, did you respond with Sergeant Birney to the Sullivan house?"

"Yes, I sure did."

"When did you see Mrs. Sullivan for the first time?"

"I saw her when the EMTs brought her out on a stretcher. She was totally messed up. Injured and unconscious."

At Yuki's prompting, Brodsky testified that the ambulance drove off with the victim, that he and two investigators interviewed the Sullivans' neighbors, including Carol Linnert, the 911 caller who had identified the victim as Barbara Sullivan.

Brodsky also testified that another neighbor, Peter Hayes, had seen the husband drive off with the couple's two boys, ages seven and eleven, and that Hayes told him where the kids liked to go for lunch.

Yuki asked Brodsky if by "the husband," he was referring to the defendant, Lewis Sullivan. Brodsky said he was and explained what happened next.

"There's an Arby's a half mile from the Sullivan house," said Brodsky. "My partner and I drove there. We found the husband, Mr. Sullivan, having lunch with the boys, Kevin and Stephen.

"Soon as Mr. Sullivan sees us coming in, he gets out of shape, threatens to call his lawyer. I say, 'Be our guest.' Then, as I'm getting him out of his seat, he says, 'Can I talk to you for a minute?' I say, 'For your own good, come quietly. I'll get someone here to bring your sons, da-da-da-da-dah.'"

"And then what happened?"

"He punches out at me and Phil and I throw him to the floor. Food flies everywhere. Kids are screaming and crying. Backup team enters the restaurant. Phil and I take Sullivan and backup takes the kids and we all drive to the Hall. We book Sullivan for assault, attempted murder, and endangering the welfare of minors and wait with them until CPS arrives."

Brodsky's testimony was clear, straightforward, unimpeachable.

Yuki asked, "Were you ever dispatched to the Sullivan house before on a domestic dispute call?"

Before Brodsky could answer, Switzer objected.

Yuki said to Judge Froman, "Your Honor, prior offenses go to a pattern of behavior."

"Sustained. Answer the question, Officer Brodsky."

"No, Your Honor. I've never been to the Sullivan house before."

"I have no other questions. Thank you, Officer Brodsky."

Again, Switzer had no questions for Yuki's witness, but reserved his right to recall Brodsky at a later time.

CHAPTER 14

IT WAS EARLY Tuesday morning.

After my appointment with Dr. Greene, I drifted through Monday, clocked minimal hours at work, missed my call to Joe and Julie.

I was walking Martha when Julie called from New York, where it was half past ten.

"I had a bagel. With a schmear," she hooted.

"That's cream cheese, right?"

"With *everything*."

Joe got on the line saying, "How are you, Linds? We're fine. Grandma showed Julie my old baby pictures. Julie doesn't believe that I was that baby."

He laughed and I could hear Julie giggling in the background. Rather than bring Joe down to my planet, I told him, "I've been busy, but I'll catch you up when we speak tonight."

We exchanged coast-to-coast kisses and had just clicked off when Gloria Rose called out, "Here I am." Martha began some fancy woofing and dancing, and I handed her leash to Mrs. Rose.

Fifteen minutes later, after navigating the morning rush, I parked in the shade of the overpass on Harriet Street. I walked the long block to the Hall's main entrance, showed my badge, passed my gun alongside the metal detector, then took the four flights of fire stairs to the Homicide division.

There's a hinged wooden gate about three feet high just inside the doorway, and just beyond it is the front desk and our gate-keeper. That's retired court officer Bobby Nussbaum. Bob's job is to field incoming calls and block walk-ins and random intruders.

As I passed his desk, I waggled my fingers "hello." He waggled back. Our squad room is a no-frills, forty-by-forty-foot space lit by overhead fluorescent tubes, dampened by frustration, and lifted by the cohesion of our team, respect for our lieutenant, and the sparkling occasions when we closed cases and crossed them off the board.

I walked past the two rows of gray metal desks toward the workstation Conklin, Alvarez, and I had staked out as our own. Our three desks form a square U-shape with my desk bridging the other two. My two partners were on their phones, but Alvarez said "Hey" as I approached.

Inspector Sonia Alvarez is in her early thirties, a leggy brunette recently relocated from Las Vegas MPD, where she used her street smarts working undercover in Vice. She's funny, brilliant, and can hold a tune. Now she's with the SFPD, getting an on-the-job degree in Homicide.

Rich hung up and said, "Boxer, check your email."

We three partners shared passwords to our work accounts so as never to miss a break in a case.

"Morning. Coffee first," I said while stowing my handbag in my bottom desk drawer.

Alvarez had also ended her call, saying to me, "You're going to want to see this."

"Right after coffee."

"Tell you what," Alvarez said. "You open your mail; I'll get the coffee."

"Jeez," I muttered. "What's the rush?"

"You two, stay," said Conklin. "*I'll* get the coffee."

Okay, then. Whatever. I booted up my refurbished Dell and hit "new mail." I was skimming my inbox when I saw "Ralph Hammer" in a subject line.

I jammed on the brakes, tapped a key, and the email opened. It read, "See the attachment." And it was signed, "Blackout."

I was still reeling from kissing my family goodbye, my turbulent session with Dr. Greene, and now Ralph Hammer's name was hauling me back to Saturday night.

It was a night I'd happily forget.

CHAPTER 15

RICHIE PUT A hotel-style china mug of black coffee and four packets of sugar on my desk.

"Who's 'Blackout'?" I asked.

"No spoilers," he said.

I clicked on the video attachment and a window opened taking up the whole of my screen. It was as if I were sitting in the back seat of a car, my eyes inches from the back of a man's head. Ralph Hammer's head.

How was this possible?

A leather-gloved hand gripping a stun gun came into view. The man with the weapon spoke, his voice digitally enhanced, but clear.

"Your time's up, buddy."

The driver turned his head forty-five degrees and I recognized Cindy's heckler in profile. And Ralph Hammer saw his would-be killer.

He pulled away, squealing, *"No. Don't."*

The hand pressed the stun gun to Hammer's neck. I knew what was coming but couldn't drag my eyes from the screen. I heard the electric burr of the weapon, saw Ralph Hammer go rigid before the stun gun disappeared and gloved hands slipped a loop of wire around his neck. It was a garrote, a wire affixed to two wooden handles; a cheap and efficient tool used by killers all over the world.

I was fixated on the gloved hands as they gripped the handles, pulling the wire tight, cutting off blood flow to Ralph Hammer's brain. Hammer made inhuman sounds as he lifted off the seat, grabbing at his neck as he fought certain death.

The screen went black. I turned on my partners.

"Hey. Warn me next time, why don't you?"

"It's not over," Alvarez said.

Damn. I like Alvarez, but this blindside pissed me off. I had more to say, but a gloved hand was back on my screen, this time gripping a Ruger Mark IV with suppressor. There were two quiet pops. Blood sprayed on the lens, but enough clarity between the streaks to see Hammer's body slump out of sight.

The angle changed. I saw day's end in the Bayside Shopping Center through the assassin's eyes; cars and pedestrians streamed by singly and in groups, no one looking at the killer.

Then, he spoke—to me.

"Good form, right, Sergeant? A quick, bad, death. This is Blackout, signing off."

The video went black.

I closed my mouth, looked at Conklin, turned to look at Alvarez, then, asked, "Has Brady seen this?"

Conklin said, "We agreed you should be the one to do it."

Brady's office is a small glass-enclosed space at the far end of the bullpen. Looking down the center aisle and the length of the room, I could see Chief Clapper sitting across the desk from Brady.

I typed a message to my boss: "This is a video of Hammer's murder. Urgent." I attached the murder tape and pressed Send.

CHAPTER 16

I WAITED FOR Brady to read my note, look at the hellacious clip of cold-blooded murder, and give me a sign. But five long minutes after I'd sent him that appalling video, he and Clapper were still deep in conversation.

I was about to go to his office when Claire texted me. "Important, Lindsay. Can you come down?"

Instead of rapping on Brady's door, I buzzed Brenda, Brady's assistant, who is stationed outside his office.

"Bren. I'm going to the ME's office for a few minutes. Call if you need me."

Brenda said, "You got it."

Conklin and Alvarez had accessed the video from our shared account and looped it on their screens. I asked them to scour all databases for anything on Hammer and on the alias "Blackout."

"We've already run Hammer through VICAP and AFIS crime databases," said Conklin. "Nothing to add to what Fama told us. Hammer was a small-time loser. 'Blackout' comes up a hundred different ways; end of a scene, loss of consciousness, power outage—all are apt, but not a name. I have a computer tech who can take a deeper dive."

"Good. If possible, we want to trace the video to a phone or an ID and ask if he can figure out how this sick footage was recorded. I'll be back in a few."

Leaving the squad room, I jogged down the fire stairs, exited the lobby through the rear door, then fast-walked along the breeze-way that connects the ME's office to the Hall. I pulled open the door and stepped up to the front desk. The new receptionist was about twenty, wearing amber-tinted glasses and a very serious look. I badged her, told her that I was expected.

She said, "Please take a seat."

An elderly woman sat in one in a line of chairs, her hands over her eyes, her shoulders heaving with sobs. Someone she cared about was inside with Claire, before, during, or after the autopsy. The door beside the receptionist opened and Claire waved me in.

Dr. Claire Washburn and I have been close since I was on patrol and she was a junior pathologist with the coroner's office. Best friends through all those years, there were no secrets between us. Now, I was burning out in Homicide and Claire was at the top of her game.

"I've got something for you, girlfriend," she said.

We walked down the inner corridor to the cold storage room. There, Claire pulled out a drawer and turned down the blue drape uncovering a seventy-something man with a bullet hole in his forehead. There were two more holes in his chest.

Claire said, "Name is Jacob Johnston."

She filled me in: that the body had been found on Taylor Street yesterday, that Central Station was turning the case over to South-ern Station. Central's homicide department was thin, and only took night-shift homicide cases. I guessed that even their night shift—from eight to eight—was shorthanded.

Claire was saying, "You'd kill me if I didn't bring you in on this."

My attention was on Johnston's body. He'd been physically fit for his apparent age and the bullet to his forehead sure looked like it had been the kill shot.

"Look here," Claire said.

She pointed to two holes in his throat. I leaned in to get a better look. Adrenaline lit me up but it took a few more seconds for my brain to connect Johnston's stun-gun burns to the video of Ralph Hammer's murder.

Claire was saying, "Theory only. Stun gun knocked him down but not out. I'm guessing Johnston fought back."

Re-draping his neck, Claire continued.

"Hypothesis. Mr. Johnston refused to die so his attacker shot him. First to the head and then to the chest."

"Reminds me of someone else," I said, then filled Claire in on the video of Ralph Hammer's murder, that the killer put two gunshots into Hammer after he was dead.

The receptionist pushed through the swinging doors.

"Doctor. Mrs. Johnston says she *must* speak with you. She's hysterical."

Same time, I got a text from Conklin: "You're needed up here."

I said goodbye to Claire and made the return trip to the squad room, fast. As I walked, my mind circled a widening ring of questions. *Were Johnston and Hammer murdered by the same killer? If so how were the three of them connected? And why had that killer sent evidence to me, evidence that would be exhibit one in a murder case against him?*

I had just reached my desk when Lieutenant Jackson Brady and Chief Charles Clapper came up the aisle.

Brady said, "Boxer, you're with me. Conklin, Alvarez, check out a car and follow us."

Clapper said to all of us, "Meet you there."

While we waited on Bryant Street for Conklin to sign a car out of the pool, I asked Brady where we were going.

"To the last place I ever expected to go again. Ever."

CHAPTER 17

BRADY'S VOICE WAS barely audible over the crackling police band static and the rumble of traffic coming through my open window. I buzzed up the window and dialed down the radio.

I said to Brady, "Talk to me."

He said, "This is what Clapper told me. Some kid on spring break was walking along the beach this morning at around nine. He saw something big riding the waves. Kid thought it was a seal or a bag of garbage."

"Bodies? What do you mean?"

"A woman in her twenties with a baby in a carrier strapped to her chest."

I clapped my hands over my mouth and kept them there, but Brady had finished talking. He drove and managed his job by phone and radio, while I unpacked memories that I'd put away but hadn't forgotten. Baker Beach. A red-haired baby. Murdered. Her mother, dark haired and murdered, her body found on China Beach. Last names Burke. Evan Burke's granddaughter and daughter-in-law.

Beside me, Brady turned the car first onto Bowley Street and then onto Gibson Road and slowed as we approached the parking lot on the bluff above Baker Beach. Several National Park Service cars had preceded us and two SFPD cruisers were restricting parking lot access to law enforcement only.

A uniformed officer handed Brady a clipboard. He signed the log as did Conklin, who'd just come up behind us. I didn't wait for the team to come together. As soon as Brady set the brakes, I got out and walked to the edge of the cliff. The big surf roared. I took deep breaths and stared out at the panoramic view: the Golden Gate Bridge, the Marin Headlands, and the seamless sky and seascape rolling out past Lands End Lookout. But the beauty of the place couldn't lift my mood.

It's common for an unsolved case to haunt homicide detectives even after retirement. Those cops have framed pictures of those victims and bring their murder books home. They scrutinize current news wondering what they'd missed before the case went cold.

The deaths of Lorrie and Tara Burke were like that for me with one glaring exception: their case had been solved. Their killer was in prison. Still, the pain of their deaths had never left me.

I told myself to snap out of it and lowered my eyes to the mile-long crescent of sand below the ridge. Patrol officers and a CSU van had driven down to the beach. Police had cordoned off a large section of it and were standing by to protect the scene. Gene Hallows, our crime lab director, gestured as he briefed Clapper. CSIs in hazmat suits stepped down from the van. Beyond them, the tide gently shifted a body within the margin of foam between the sand and sea.

An officer who'd been stationed at the parking lot came up behind me and saw what I saw.

He muttered, "Jesus, God. It's déjà vu all over again."

I felt light-headed. Pin lights sparked in front of my eyes, but before I could drop, someone gripped my left arm and put a hand behind my back. Brady.

"I'm okay," I said.

"Let's sit down."

"I'm good."

"I'm not," he said. "When you're ready, take a good look."

This time when I stared down at the bodies I couldn't miss it. Like Lorrie and Tara Burke, the deceased baby was a redhead, and her mother was a brunette.

Brady said, "We can't go down until Hallows says so."

I took Brady's arm and returned with him to the chaos in the parking lot.

CHAPTER 18

FROM HER PREFERRED back-of-the-courtroom seat, Cindy watched Yuki question Barbara Sullivan's neighbor Carol Linnert. She was making notes when a text came in from Henry Tyler, the *Chronicle*'s publisher and editor in chief. He'd written, "2 bodies on Baker Beach. Call me."

"Stand by."

Cindy grabbed her heavy carryall and edged her way to the exit, where a court officer opened the door. Once she was in the hallway, she called Henry on his private line.

"You're going to want to check this out, Cindy. Baker Beach. Woman with child washed up two hours ago. Peretti is on his way to pick you up."

Michael Peretti was Cindy's favorite photographer and videographer. A foot taller than Cindy, Mike could both shoot over the heads of a crowd and muscle his way through them.

Cindy took the elevator down to the lobby and when she reached Bryant, she looked for Mike. A horn honked and she followed the sound with her eyes, leading her to spot a green Jeep Comanche double-parked on the far side of the street. Cindy crossed against the light, pulled open the passenger-side door and hauled herself into the Jeep. Cindy always kept her police scanner with her, and now she took it out of her bag and set it up on the dash.

"Mike. This is spooky."

Peretti said, "Hang on, Spooky. Buckle up."

She did it.

As Mike pulled out into traffic, Cindy flipped on the scanner and tuned it until she got a clear signal. SFPD dispatch was fielding an armed holdup in a liquor store on Mission.

Peretti said, "I'll tell you what I know."

By the time they'd safely reached their destination, Cindy was up to speed; a woman and infant had been discovered in the surf off Baker Beach, which was well-known for being unsafe at any time. Heedless daredevils had died in those waters.

She and Peretti discussed the possibility that this could be a drowning, but the word "baby" alarmed Cindy.

"It's possible," she said, "that a clueless young mother took her baby in for a dip, but my gut says 'no.'"

Mike agreed for the same reason Tyler had pulled Cindy out of a trial that was being covered by reporters across the country. This incident on Baker beach was too reminiscent of Lorrie and Tara Burke.

And these days no one knew their killer better than Cindy Thomas.

CHAPTER 19

IN THE BRIEF time I'd spent bracing myself for what was to come, the rowdy crowd that had gathered at the entrance to the parking lot had gotten rowdier. Patrol officers were holding the line, waving cars off. Some of those cars parked on the road, and mavericks broke free from the herd and made for the beach on foot. Patrol cars sped down the access road and cut them off.

I joined the police line behind the tape, but when Cindy stepped out of the jostling mob, I broke rank.

I was that glad to see my friend.

But she hadn't seen me. She called out to Conklin and he shook his head, *no, no, no.* Meaning, no, he wouldn't give her a quote. Rich was right, but I heard her say, "You *want* me to write something, Rich. I can *help.*"

Cindy had broken cases before.

Brady stepped up to the tape with a bullhorn in hand.

"Listen up, alla y'all. Quiet down."

An imposing figure, muscular, with platinum-blond hair and the trace of a Southern accent, Brady spoke his name and rank.

The crowd did quiet down, eager to hear what the lieutenant had to say.

"Everyone, this is a fresh situation and we do not know what has happened. Even if we did, we still would not comment on an ongoing investigation. Ladies and gents of the press, I'm asking you personally, kindly do not publish pictures of the deceased. They have not been identified. Families have not been notified. If someone has information, please call the tip line. We will get back to you promptly."

Brady gave out the phone number and lowered the megaphone. He was heading toward me when Cindy called my name.

I reached her and grabbed her hand.

"Cindy, I can't…"

"Lindsay, this is freaking me out."

"Me, too.

"I keep thinking about Evan Burke. He confessed to killing Lorrie and Tara, right? We did get the right guy?"

"Of *course* we did," I said to Cindy.

Cindy was the undisputed expert on Burke, but her confidence was shaken. I worried that she was grappling with the effects of her Burke-induced PTSD.

She said, "I can put out photos with a request for information in about ten minutes."

"It's too soon, Cin. They may have been reported missing."

The police line parted and the ME's van drove through, taking the service entrance to the beach.

"Cindy. I gotta go."

Brady signaled to me, and together we headed down to the scene.

CHAPTER **20**

BRADY, CONKLIN, ALVAREZ, and I stood on the beach watching the CSIs do their work. The area had been scoured for anything that could be related to the victims, and nothing had been found. And then, as he'd done when the victim on Baker Beach had been Burke's granddaughter and he was the new chief of SFPD, Charles Clapper stepped into the undulating surf.

This time Gene Hallows, who replaced Clapper as head of forensics, joined him.

They worked as a unit, Clapper getting a grip under the dead woman's arms, while Hallows grasped her ankles. Together, they lifted the mother, the baby still strapped to her, and carried them up to dry land.

I was close by and saw that even waterlogged and wave-tossed, the woman had been beautiful. Now, water sluiced from her clothes. Her coat was open, exposing her red and white sweater, her dark gray pants. Without anyone to support her arms, they fell from her sides and hung below her torso. Seawater dripped from her fingers and her long dark hair. One of her boots had come off and her bare foot looked swollen and all too human.

But it was the baby's face that just killed *me*. I couldn't look away. She was just about a year old and I had a clear image in mind of Julie at that age. Impish. Feisty. Giggly. In those ways, Julie hadn't changed, but she had grown. Now, she was nearly five, could do new things every day, things that this little girl…

I watched as Clapper and Hallows placed the bodies on a sheet-lined gurney and with Claire and her team slid the gurney inside the van. With Claire's okay, I gowned and gloved up and I climbed through the rear doors and stood aside as a tech wrapped the bodies.

CSI had taken their photos on the beach. Claire would take photos in the morgue and both sets would be sent to Brady. Before the day was over, we would have a file on the unknown victims and our work would begin.

Claire said, "Linds. We have to go."

"Sure. I'll see you later."

"Give me the rest of the day to do the external exams."

We reached out to each other and even in that cramped space managed to hug. Then I climbed back out of the van.

Brady called to me. I discarded my wardrobe covering and got into the squad car beside him. On the road again, he conspicuously turned off the radio, but I had nothing to say.

He said, "Lindsay. Listen to me. I know how you feel and that's as it should be. But I want you to get mad. Can you do that? For that woman. For her baby? For me? I've known you since I came out here. You've closed more cases than me. You hold the record. I'm not saying get crazy mad. Get smart mad. The victims need you and this case is yours."

"Brady. Claire hasn't pronounced them homicides."

"Let me rephrase. If someone killed this woman and her child, we must get him. And I'll say it again. It's your case."

Got it.

Back in the squad room, I followed Brady to his office. When he snapped his head around and saw me, I saw that he was in pain. I expected him to bark, "What?"

I pressed on.

"Brady. I sent you a video of Ralph Hammer's murder. You have to see it now."

CHAPTER 21

CAPPY AND CHI were running late for our 6:00 p.m. task force meeting for Team Blackout, so, we three went to the empty corner office and started without them. Alvarez drew a timeline on the whiteboard, Conklin and I taped up the morgue photos of Ralph Hammer. We'd dragged chairs up to the well-used metal table and were ready to work when the door swung open and Cappy came in alone.

"Chi's wrapping up a few things. Be just a minute," he said and he dropped his 270 pounds into the seat next to Alvarez. Cappy McNeil is a storied homicide detective who even worked the Zodiac Killer case—he has an extensive network of CIs throughout the Bay Area and a great partner in Paul Chi. Chi has half the years on the job that Cappy has but is tireless and brings his Mensa-grade brain to our unit.

In partnership with Marin County PD, O'Neil and Chi had spent their day in Sausalito, tossing Ralph Hammer's apartment, looking for something, anything that might have gotten the guy killed. I couldn't read Cappy's expression. He looked worn out and as wired as the rest of us.

He began his debrief.

"Hammer was renting an apartment over a garage outside Mill Valley. He had full use of the garage, which was a dump. Half the space was floor-to-ceiling bags of found items which we inventoried: canned goods, old magazines, bubble wrap and T-shirts with the tags still on. The other half of the garage was for his car.

"Upstairs in the apartment we found more bags of junk, piles of screenplays on the floor, and we turned his computer over to the local PD. His landlord stated and I quote," Cappy flipped open his notebook and read, " 'Ralph sleeps all day, is out most nights, hasn't brought home any girls or friends. Thinks Hammer's a part-time bartender and a wannabe writer.' "

Cappy summed up by saying that he and Chi found no evidence pointing to why someone would have killed Ralph Hammer.

"But," Cappy said, impishly, "our friend, Chris Fama, gave us something. It's either a big fat zero or a red-hot clue."

Alvarez said, "Ten bucks says it's a clue."

If only. Even a small break would send me to the moon.

The door opened again and Chi came into the room, wearing a coat and tie, high-shined shoes, good haircut. He apologized for being late, then, picked up where Cappy had left us hanging.

He said, "Just got off the phone with Fama. A copy of Cindy's book was found in Hammer's car where Blackout popped him."

Conklin said, "Whoa."

Chi said, "Keep your expectations in check. There are a lot of brunettes in this state, and only one who washed up on Baker Beach."

CHAPTER 22

CLAIRE WAS WAITING for me in the doorway between reception and her offices. Something was up. She was scowling and had crossed her arms over her chest.

I said, "You look like you want to punch someone."

"Back at ya, babe," she said.

"Point taken."

Yeah, I was mad. Team Blackout had four open homicides, a mystery video of one, but no leads to the killer. And the worst of it was how much the unnamed woman and her baby brought to mind another young woman found on China Beach and her child found on Baker Beach. Coincidence? Or a connection?

"I'll be quick," I said. "I need your read on Jane Doe."

Claire relaxed her scowl and handed me a sealed packet of protective gear. I gowned and gloved up and followed her down the corridor.

She said, "You do understand that I haven't done the internal autopsies."

"Got it," I said.

Meaning, Claire would be giving me an off-the-record first look without her final conclusions. She strong-armed a pair of swinging doors and a cold breeze blew at my face as we entered the autopsy suite. Directly across the room was a wall of metal drawers. Claire went to one, pulled the handle and slid out a body covered with a blue cotton drape and lying on a stainless-steel tray.

Claire drew down the drape, revealing the nude remains of the woman who'd washed up on the sand this morning. I felt a fresh blow to my heart and couldn't turn away.

"Here's what I know. Jane and Baby Doe were in the water for about a day. Jane was a healthy, well-nourished Caucasian female, mid-twenties," Claire said. "She has an old appendix scar and abrasions on the side of her left foot and knee. Those injuries are postmortem and were probably sustained when she was dumped out of a vehicle."

"How'd she die?"

"Not there yet, Linds," she said. "I know you're thinking that we've seen this before. But unlike their doppelgangers, Jane's neck wasn't slashed."

"What then?"

Claire threw a sigh.

"Look here. Discoloration at the sides of her neck and swelling at the back. The perp held a strong young mother, probably fighting back as best she could, long enough to kill. Whoever did this was strong."

"Shit," I said, picturing it.

Claire put a gloved hand on my arm and kept talking.

"There was no sign of sexual activity. And. She was wearing these."

She held up a plastic bag containing a wedding band and an engagement ring with a large diamond solitaire.

"No robbery. These'll go to the lab tonight along with their clothes and the baby carrier," Claire said. Her phone buzzed and she pulled it from her pocket, tapped a message. Paused. Typed again.

"It's Edmund," she said, texting her husband. "I'm late."

I said, "Another minute, Claire. Marin's M.E. found a copy of Cindy's book in Ralph Hammer's car.

"It's a long shot, but I asked Hallows to run it for any prints not belonging to Hammer. I asked pretty please."

Claire looked at her watch, then at me. She said, "You want to know about the baby."

"Yes."

She lowered her chin and muttered, *unh, unh*. Dead kids come with the territory, but a mother of four, Claire always took young victims hard. I was right there with her.

"I don't have much else, Linds. The X-rays show no broken bones on either victim. Baby Doe was smothered. This is not unique, not a signature. Babies are killed this way. I'll show you the body tomorrow. Okay?"

I nodded, yes. I thanked Claire again and left her offices. I had just reached the Hall's back door when Brady phoned me.

"I have to run out," he said. "We got a hit from Missing Persons. Jane Doe's name is Catherine Fleet. Her baby is Josephina. The Fleet family lives in Russian Hill. The husband, Brad Fleet, is in Interview One with Conklin and Alvarez. They're waiting on you," Brady said. "I'll be back in fifteen minutes."

CHAPTER 23

I STOOD AT the glass in the observation room abutting Interview One. Conklin was questioning Brad Fleet, a fit man in his thirties with prematurely gray hair, wearing a rumpled tan suit. Even without sound, Catherine Fleet's bereaved husband appeared devastated.

I dialed up the audio and quickly got the gist. Fleet had no idea what had happened to his wife and child, and pleaded with Conklin, "Whatever you need from me. Whatever you can do…"

That was my cue. I knocked on the door and Alvarez opened it wide, showing me in. I said, "I'm Lindsay. Sergeant Boxer, Mr. Fleet. Very sorry for your loss."

He nodded his acknowledgment and said, "I still. Can't believe this is real. I just can't."

I took the chair beside Fleet, who threw a long sigh before lifting his eyes to mine.

Conklin said, "Mr. Fleet. If you could tell Sergeant Boxer what you told us about the last time you saw Catherine and Josie."

Fleet nodded, but he didn't speak. I let the silence play out. Finally, he said, "Yesterday morning. I didn't even say goodbye."

He whimpered, then said, "Are you sure it's them. I haven't seen their..." He took out his phone, showed me a picture of his wife and child. Vibrant. Laughing. Alive.

"It appears to be them. I'm very sorry," I said. "Then, what can you tell me about yesterday morning?"

Fleet spoke haltingly as he recalled his last living memory of his wife and baby.

"Like I said, it was a Monday. Cath gets up like always and takes the baby out for a walk in Ina Coolbrith Park. Every day they come back to say goodbye before I leave for work. Yesterday, they didn't. I had a strategy meeting..."

Fleet's face crumpled and his tears spilled from his eyes.

Conklin got a box of tissues from the supply cabinet and I told Fleet to take his time. I pulled the interview form over to my patch of the table and skimmed it.

Conklin had underlined Fleet's address and I knew why. They lived on Leavenworth, only a short distance from where Jacob Johnston's body was found on Taylor Street. I listened to Fleet and visualized Catherine on the last day of her life. I saw her layering on the clothes she had died in, strapping Josephina into the baby carrier. I thought if her habits were as regular as her husband said, her killer may have known her movements. I thought about Fleet saying he expected to see his wife and child before leaving the house, and when he didn't, he drove to work. Strategy meeting.

I asked, "Did you call her when you got to the office?"

"I had an early meeting. She goes for long walks, maybe stops to look at seabirds or something. I only worried when I got home at dinnertime and she wasn't there. That's when I called the police."

Alvarez said, "Mr. Fleet. I have to ask. How were you and Catherine getting along? You were married for, what, three years?"

"What are you asking? I loved Cath. I loved Josie. They were everything to me. We didn't fight. We didn't have affairs. This was real love. Do you hear me? Why did this happen?"

He dropped his head to the table and cried into his jacket sleeves. I reached over and touched his shoulder.

"We're on your side, Mr. Fleet. We're with you. The whole SFPD wants to find whoever is responsible for this."

Fleet cried harder, then lifted his head. With his voice breaking at times, he told this story; he and Catherine worked at the same advertising firm, Ennis, Neiman and Bright. They'd met there, fallen in love.

He said, "Cath and I didn't work in the same department, but she was all business and really smart. And tough. But as I told Missing Persons, Catherine decided to take a break from work for a while when Josie was born, because she wanted to stay home with her. The police asked me, 'How do you know she didn't just take off with the baby?' For God's sake, people. I wish she had."

I asked, "Who can verify your movements yesterday?"

I passed a pad and pen to Fleet who scrawled some names and passed the list back to me, asking angrily, "Now what?"

I said, "There are a few more things we have to go over with you, Mr. Fleet. I'll be right back."

CHAPTER 24

I UNLOCKED THE empty corner office where we'd been meeting, pulled two photos down from the whiteboard, and returned to Interview One.

Fleet stared at me with bloodshot eyes.

"Mr. Fleet. I'm going to show you pictures of two deceased individuals. Tell me if you know them."

Fleet pushed back his chair, moving away from something he didn't want to see. I flipped Hammer's photo over first and watched Fleet take a look, then shake his head, no.

"Never saw him. Did Catherine know him?"

I said, "We don't know. Do you recognize this man?" I turned over the photo of Jacob Johnston. Fleet saw the bullet hole in the center of the dead man's forehead. He blanched, closed his eyes, then, some latent memory clicked in. He reached for the picture and pulled it toward him.

"I-I-I know him to say hello," he said. "He lives in our neighborhood. I've seen him out running. Who is—was he? What does he have to do…?"

I said, "This is Jacob Johnston. He lived on Taylor, a couple of blocks over from your home on Leavenworth. His body was found not far from the entrance to Ina Coolbrith Park. That's where Catherine goes for her walk, isn't it?"

"I don't get it. I don't get it. You think they were together? I would have *known*."

Fleet stared at me, at Conklin, back to me. "You people are crazy. Crazy."

I assured Fleet that we weren't suggesting that Catherine and this man were a couple or that she knew Johnston at all. We were just getting started. Putting pieces on the table. And I got down to it. I asked Fleet if his wife kept a journal, wrote a blog, had a Facebook page. Fleet answered *no, no, no*.

I wanted to ask, *Do you have any ideas at all?* But his shock was real. He couldn't get past the blinding truth that his wife and child were dead.

Pushing forward, I said, "If you have no objections, I'd like Inspectors Conklin and Alvarez to drive you home, take a look around your house, bring back any appointment logs or diaries Catherine may have kept..."

"I just told you she didn't have anything like that."

"She had a cell phone? A laptop?" I asked.

He nodded yes.

"We need to go through those, Mr. Fleet. See if she'd gotten any threats or had any admirers."

"And if I don't want her things tampered with?"

"You want us to find out who did this, don't you?" I said.

He nodded, and I asked if he was ready to go now. If he refused, given the hour, it might be another day before I could get a search warrant.

"Yes. Fine," said Fleet.

While my partners drove Brad Fleet to his empty home, I returned to my desk and made notes for the files. I was so absorbed I was startled when Brady dragged out Conklin's chair, sat down hard, and asked me, "Do you like Fleet for the murders?"

"Too soon to say, but my sense is no. I'll check out his alibi when his office opens tomorrow."

"What's bothering you the most, Boxer?"

"That it's too familiar. And that I haven't got a clue."

Brady said, "I'm putting every available body on canvassing the neighborhood and 24/7 surveillance on Brad Fleet. It's day one, Lindsay. We're just getting started."

I was driving home to my dog when I heard laughter inside my head. It was Evan Burke, psychopath of note, his disembodied guffaws coming to me from his solitary cell in San Quentin.

Today's events would have been his idea of a really good time.

CHAPTER 25

YUKI AND HER associate, Nick Gaines, were well aware that District Attorney Leonard Parisi was in the gallery. A large man, nicknamed Red Dog for his hair color and pit-bull personality, Parisi had been as invested in the Sullivan case as the press were since day one.

Parisi had agreed to an interview with *60 Minutes* at the conclusion of this trial, and today he wanted to watch the proceedings for himself. "No pressure," he'd said, but Nick and Yuki found it impossible to ignore his looming presence four rows back from the counsel table.

The Honorable Judge Karen Froman entered the courtroom through the door behind the bench. The jury was seated, the bailiff read the decree, and there was order in the court.

Judge Froman said, "Ms. Castellano, please call your witness."

Yuki stood. "The People call Dr. Michael Parker."

Dr. Parker came through the doors and down the center aisle to the witness stand. He was a fit man of fifty wearing a jacket and tie, pressed trousers, and he looked wrung-out. As if he'd been working all night and hadn't yet slept. An emergency physician, Dr. Parker had tended to Barbara Sullivan when she was admitted to St. Vincent's ER.

Parker was sworn in by the bailiff and took his seat on the witness stand. Yuki admitted the HIPAA release into evidence, the document signed by Barbara Sullivan, giving him permission to discuss her condition in court.

Yuki walked toward the witness and began her direct examination. She asked Parker, "How would you describe the job of emergency medicine physician?"

"In brief, we deal with trauma. Our jobs are to quickly diagnose our patient, stabilize them, resuscitate the dying, and know when to call in other experts. In short, an emergency doctor's job is to save lives."

"Thank you, Dr. Parker. Do you remember the afternoon when Mrs. Sullivan was brought into the ER?"

"Yes. I remember it well."

"Can you give the court your impression of Ms. Sullivan's condition at that time?"

Parker said, "I didn't think I could save her. I've been an ER physician for twenty years, and in that time, I've never seen a person who'd been beaten so badly and was so close to death. She had a pulse. She was breathing. But she had internal injuries, broken bones and external injuries over her entire body."

"Had she been beaten with fists?"

"Most certainly, but not exclusively. There was evidence that she'd been kicked with steel-toed boots, cut with a serrated blade, her head stamped on to the effect that her left orbital socket was broken and she had a fractured skull and a concussion, as well as three broken ribs, a punctured right lung, extensive damage to one kidney, and her right leg was broken in three places. She had more than three dozen knife cuts on her arms and torso, and she'd lost more than fifteen percent of total blood volume. Some of the superficial injuries had begun to heal, giving me reason to believe that Mrs. Sullivan had been tortured over twenty-four hours."

Gaines left his seat and went to the whiteboard set beside the witness where he posted two anatomically correct line drawings of a female body, front and back. There were X's, straight and zig-zagging lines standing for injuries. Callouts were printed beside the markings indicating the damaged areas.

"Dr. Parker, did you prepare this chart of Mrs. Sullivan's injuries?"

"Yes. But not even photos could represent what was done to her. Catastrophic injuries were made of that."

"Was your patient able to tell you what had happened to her?"

"She was in no condition to speak," said the doctor.

Yuki thanked Dr. Parker. Defense wisely had no questions. Parker stood down, walked up the aisle through the courtroom. When he passed the defense counsel table he did so without looking at Lewis Sullivan, passing him as if he didn't exist at all.

CHAPTER 26

WHEN THE DOCTOR had left the courtroom, Yuki called Stephen Sullivan to the stand.

Defense counsel Maurice Switzer shot to his feet. "Objection, Your Honor. Stephen Sullivan is eleven years old and per the Parent-Child Privilege Act cannot be compelled to testify. May we approach?"

The judge waved them in and Yuki and Mo walked up to the bench. Mo told the judge that Stephen was present and had overheard some of the events that had brought this case to trial.

"It's prejudicial, Your Honor."

"Sustained. Please sit down, Counselors."

When the attorneys were at their tables, Judge Froman asked Yuki, "Do the people have another witness?"

"We do, Your Honor. The people call Barbara James Sullivan."

A gasp traveled across the gallery as the front doors opened.

Yuki turned in her seat and watched as a court officer pushed thirty-six-year-old Barbara Sullivan's wheelchair into the courtroom. Barbara's right leg, encased in a plaster cast from foot to thigh, stuck straight out, pointing the way.

Barbara wore an eye patch over her left eye and a full brown skirt with matching long-sleeved top that covered most of her body. Her face and hands were mottled shades of purple, yellow, and green as the bruises metamorphosed toward pink.

As every person in the courtroom watched, the court officer pushed Barbara's chair slowly up the aisle to the witness stand. Gaines stood up, ready to assist, but the officer said, "I've got her."

Did he? Barbara's head lolled. She seemed utterly fragile and somewhat disoriented. Would she be able to withstand questioning? When they reached the stand, the officer turned Barbara Sullivan's chair so that she was facing the counselors, the jury, the gallery. She was sworn in.

Yuki walked over to her witness and greeted her.

"Can you do this, Barbara?"

"I can try," she said.

Yuki said, "If you need a break at any time, just tell me, okay?" Barbara nodded slowly and said, "I'm glad to be here."

Yuki said, "Okay, good." After asking her witness to say her full name, she said, "Barbara, please tell the court. Do you remember how you became injured?"

"I have some memories," she said.

Yuki felt weak when she heard "some memories." Barbara had remembered a great deal of the events when they'd last spoken, but the effects of pain drugs on top of the heavy antibiotics and other medication she was given at the rehab facility could easily have caused memory loss.

"Barbara, please tell us what you do remember."

She said, "I see what happened in...flashes. I remember my head throbbing. It hurt so badly I couldn't think. I heard Stephen calling for me."

"Stephen is your son."

"My older son. I couldn't answer him. I couldn't sit up. I could wiggle a little bit, but I was tied. Taped. Chained."

Barbara Sullivan stopped speaking. Her mind was turning inward and she was not focusing her good eye on anyone. Then, "I remember waking up, lying in my blood. My hands were chained over my head. I was looking at the moon."

"The moon, Barbara?"

"It was the underside...of the sink in the laundry room.

"My head. My eye. My leg. Oh, my God. Stephen calling me, calling me, and then he stopped. Everything stopped."

"Barbara?"

Yuki wasn't sure if Barbara was frozen in her memories or if she was having a mental block.

"Barbara, are you all right?"

She seemed to awake from sleep. She said, "Yuki, right?"

"That's right." Yuki resisted the urge to reach out and hold Barbara's hand. "Is there anything else you remember from that day?"

"I woke up inside an ambulance. I woke up again in the hospital. Flashes now. Lights in my eyes. Deep sleep. Waking again. Asking for the children. That's all."

Yuki needed more. She had taken Barbara to this point. She needed the name of who had done this to her. And she could only ask questions without hinting at answers or Mo Switzer would object that she was leading the witness and shut her down.

Yuki had to play it right down the center line and pray that Barbara could answer the question.

"Barbara. Who hurt you?"

Barbara lifted her arm in the direction of the defense table. "Him. Lew."

"Can you say his full name?"

"Lewis Sullivan. My husband," said Barbara.

Yuki thanked her witness, looked up at the judge who was say-ing, "Mr. Switzer. Do you wish to cross?"

"Not at this time, your Honor. But I reserve the right to recall this witness at a later time."

Returning to the prosecution table, Yuki caught Len Parisi's eye. He nodded and smiled. She took her seat and she watched Barbara Sullivan's slow rolling exit from the courtroom.

CHAPTER 27

CINDY ENTERED VROMAN'S, the largest independent bookstore in Southern California, and was instantly bathed with well-being. The space was open, bright, suffused with music. There were miles of bookshelves and the ineffable aroma of new books. Life-sized posters announced that the author would be speaking at five, that refreshments would be served, and that she would be signing books at six. Folding chairs had been arranged in a deep semicircle facing the podium.

She gave the store's owner, Joel Sheldon, a genuine smile as he welcomed her and told Cindy that he was a fan. Together, they toured the premises while he took her through Vroman's hundred-year history. As the time closed in on five, he escorted her to the podium set on a dais against the backdrop of the floor-to-ceiling windows. Once the audience had packed the available seats, Sheldon delivered an effusive introduction and turned the room over to Cindy.

Adjusting the mic and smiling out over the audience, Cindy began her speech.

"Writing this book with Evan Burke has been the most harrowing experience of my life," she said and was sucked back into her time with Burke: the revolting research, the in-person meetings in his cell, sitting close enough to smell him, writing in Evan Burke's voice as he leered at her. She cut off the thoughts before they could bloom.

To do this well, she had to be in an author's state of mind. Faces turned up to her and she felt the connection with the audience, their empathy for how hard the work had been. They were leaning in, soaking up her well-informed history of a monster as told to her by the monster himself. When she'd concluded her speech to rolling applause, Cindy opened the floor to questions.

At first, there were queries about the process, why she'd written the authorized biography and how she'd been able to handle this intimate work with Burke. And then, as at Book Passage, the questions about Burke increased and came at her like flights of darts.

How could she stand being with him? Had she been afraid of him? What had made him a killer? Had he shown remorse? Was there any chance he would get out of jail?

"None," Cindy said. "He was sentenced to six life terms without possibility of parole. His permanent address is San Quentin State Prison."

As a fresh wave of applause washed over her, Cindy was glad she'd fought off her fear of hecklers but sorry that Richie wasn't here to share this with her. She gave and received a few laughs before a woman dressed smartly in black pants and cardigan over a white silk blouse raised her hand and stood up.

She said, "I'm Marge. It's my turn."

"I'm sorry?"

"You should be," Marge said. "How long do you expect us to listen patiently to your flagrantly insensitive talk?"

"I don't understand."

"Understand this. One of Burke's victims lived on my street, went to school with one of my daughters, and was killed by that beast."

"I'm sorry to hear that. But I didn't use real names. I disguised—"

"I don't give a flip how you disguised names or hair color or anything else. She was a girl with a curious spirit, a future, and was brutally murdered, but to you it's just a book. It's disgusting. You're disgusting."

Cindy blinked and as the woman edged out of the row and headed to the exit, she realized that Marge had a point. Burke was a beast who didn't deserve fame or approbation. But surely, there were lessons to be learned from Evan Burke. The facts of his killings, for one. For another, she'd endangered her health in order to write it and paid dearly for it.

Members of the Pasadena press pushed in from the sidelines. Cindy ignored the requests for an interview and looked blindly for Mr. Sheldon. And then he was at her elbow, helping her down from behind the small, raised platform while telling her, "Sorry, Cindy, let's get you out of here. We'll do this again and it will not be like this, I promise you. I'm so sorry."

Cindy was halfway to LAX before realizing that she hadn't signed a single book. This was regrettable and she didn't know how to fix it.

CHAPTER 28

THE SUN HAD dropped below the horizon, leaving a band of light under a charcoal-gray sky. Cindy asked her driver to tune a good music station on the car radio and her sadness slowly ebbed away. She was making good time even in rush hour. The traffic was thick but moving. Then it was congested and then it stopped dead. *Damn.*

Getting out of the car, standing on the median strip, Cindy saw a red star field of taillights up ahead, no end in sight. Car horns blew discordant notes behind and ahead of her.

Back in her car, an announcer cut into the music programming to say that a tractor-trailer on the I-105 West had jackknifed, propelling a car into the guardrail and closing off the freeway.

Motorcycle cops streamed between the lanes and a detour opened at the next exit. Cindy's chances of making her return flight seemed slim.

The driver turned onto the I-105 West off-ramp and Cindy called Melanie, her publicist.

A flurry of calls between the publisher's office in New York and

Delta Airlines had Cindy sure she'd heard wrong when Melanie dropped a bomb: SFO was fogged in. All flights to San Francisco were cancelled.

"Wait. It's been years since we've gotten fog like that."

"I'm sorry, Ms. Thomas. There are still two open seats on the eight a.m. flight. I suggest we book one plus a room for tonight at the Skyways Hotel."

Cindy agreed and then she dialed Richie.

"Cin. How did it go?"

"I'll tell you when I see you," she said, staring into the eyes of a little boy making faces at her through the rear window of the car in front of her. "But my flight's been cancelled. SFO is fogged in. Can you believe that?"

"Can't remember the last time that happened," Rich said. "I'll book you a room near LAX."

"My publicist has done it. I'll be on the eight a.m. flight tomorrow."

"Call me before you board. I'll pick you up."

Cindy told Richie that traffic was moving, that she'd call him later from the hotel. She sent a kiss over the 5G network and received one back. Mercifully, their call ended before she'd told Rich that her PTSD from her time with Evan Burke had been reignited by a verbal assault. That she'd frozen up, lost her nerve, and no longer knew who she was.

CHAPTER 29

CINDY HUNG THE DO NOT DISTURB sign outside her door at the Skyways Hotel. Once inside room 202, she double-locked the door, turned on all the lights, and inspected the place. It was decent. The bed was large and the spread looked fresh. The carpet was clean enough. She was encouraged by the muffled whine from the airliners landing, taxiing, taking off. She would be on a plane home soon.

Parking her backpack on the desk chair near the window Cindy charged her devices and checked the time. It was seven forty and she was hungry. Now, Plan B.

Flicking her eyes over the menu for the hotel restaurant, Cindy phoned in a salad, a small bottle of chardonnay, and chocolate cake. While she waited for her dinner, she opened her laptop and skipping the hundred and fifty-eight emails from people she didn't know, she opened the *Chronicle* website hoping to read that the fog would lift in time for her morning flight.

She scanned the headlines, then shifted to the *Los Angeles Times* online. Like a punch to the heart, she read, "Woman Killed in Pasadena."

Cindy stabbed a key with her finger and the article filled her screen. A map inside the article showed a section of town including both the Fuller Theological Seminary and the stretch of East Colorado Boulevard where Vroman's Bookstore was located.

That couldn't be.

Cindy speed-read the short article posted one hour ago.

"A woman wearing a red tracksuit was found on the grounds of the Fuller Theological Seminary in Pasadena. Witnesses told this reporter that the body was lying in plain sight on a path. The victim has not yet been identified, nor have the police stated her cause of death..."

Shoving her laptop aside, Cindy switched on her scanner and tuned it to the local police channel. When the staticky reception cleared, she could make out the voices of cops speaking with dispatch. She caught the words, "Late twenties to early thirties. No ID. Body is still warm."

Cindy had left Vroman's at around six and now she leapt to an unprovable but inescapable theory. Someone who'd come to Vroman's had walked to the seminary campus and killed the woman in red.

Cindy redialed Richie, and when her call went to voicemail, she called Lindsay, who picked up.

"Linds, can you talk?"

"Sure, Cindy. I just got home. How'd it go?"

"Another nightmare, Lindsay. But something worse just happened—"

"Where are you?"

Cindy said, "The Skyways at LAX. SFO is fogged in and I'm flying back tomorrow morning..."

"Are you okay?"

"Lindsay, a woman was murdered within walking distance of

Vroman's where I just spoke. There was a heckler. Named Marge. It's like Ralph Hammer all over again."

"You're going too fast…"

"I'm trying to gauge if I'm paranoid. Or if some killer is trying to freak me out. Can you call Pasadena PD? Find out what the hell happened? They'll never talk to me."

"They may not speak with me either," Lindsay said.

"You're a *cop*. I'm a *reporter*."

"Okay. Okay, I'll give it a shot. Text me your flight info and Rich or I will pick you up at SFO. Call any time if you need to talk. I'm here."

"Thanks. I love you, Lindsay."

"I love you, too. See you tomorrow."

When delivery knocked, Cindy shouted, "Please leave the bag outside."

She moved her police scanner to the nightstand. The machine chattered with radio calls requesting officers to a fender bender, a drunk and disorderly, a holdup in progress.

Cindy was still monitoring radio calls when she fell asleep.

CHAPTER **30**

I WAS AT work before seven that morning. Rich had gone to the airport to get Cindy and would be coming in ASAP. By eight, I'd spoken with Joe and left messages for everyone on my to-do list. Alvarez and I were having coffee at our desks when an email hit my inbox and blew it all to hell.

I stared at the subject heading: *News Flash from Blackout to Boxer.* And there was an attachment. I said, "Oh, shit," and Alvarez wheeled her chair around and looked over my shoulder.

"Open it," she said.

I clicked. The email was blank so I downloaded the video. Like the one Blackout had shot from the back seat of Hammer's Camry, this was also as seen through the killer's eyes.

"Body cam?" I said.

"Video glasses," said Alvarez. "So says Rich's tech."

"There," I said, putting my finger on my computer screen just above a woman in a red tracksuit jogging toward the camera. There was sound: birds, wind through leaves, then, Blackout's digitized voice, which was pulsing but clear.

He said, "This is the kind of girl we like. Twenties. Limber. Strong."

I said, "We? Who is we?"

Blackout called out to the runner, "Excuse me. I think I'm lost."

The young woman stopped running a few yards from Blackout, caught her breath, walked closer. She had chin-length, wavy brown hair, a pretty face.

She asked Blackout, "Where do you want to go?"

"Brooks Avenue," said Blackout. "Where'd I go wrong?"

Behind my shoulder Alvarez was watching as I reacted to the scene playing out on-screen.

"Oh-my-God, oh-my-God," I said. "This is last night's victim."

The runner was looking at a map on Blackout's phone, pointing out that he'd passed Brooks Avenue, tracing the correct direction on the screen. Our view changed. Blackout was looking up and around, as if he was visualizing the route, giving us a panoramic view of the Fuller Theological Seminary campus. There were lawns. Winding paths. Park benches. Sabal palms. But this was not a sightseeing tour for my benefit. Blackout was making sure the way was clear.

His gloved hand dipped into the pocket of his black windbreaker and came out clenched around a small canister. The runner looked at it, puzzled. She didn't know what it was. The gloved hand aimed the nozzle at her eyes and pressed the lever with his thumb. The woman shrieked, tried to clear her eyes with her hands and sleeves, but she had no chance against this man who reached for her. She backed up, stumbled, and dropped to the pavement.

I gripped the edge of my desk as she cried out, but all I could see of the scuffle that followed was Blackout's right hand clapped over her mouth, his left arm angling her into a carotid restraint hold. He formed a right angle with her neck in the crux between his forearm and biceps. He used his full weight to subdue her—and he squeezed.

Alvarez and I watched in shock as the woman's writhing and kicking stopped. The leather-gloved hand came off her mouth and she didn't cry out. She was lifeless. Dead.

Blackout stood, and again panned the campus before walking out the way he came. Sound came up, classical music I recognized as "Adagio for Strings." Soft. Mournful. A dramatic bass line. Blackout's view shifted upward as if he were looking through palm fronds overhead.

In his digitized voice he said, "Dedicated to you, Mr. Burke."

The image of palm trees backlit by an indigo sky froze. Then faded to black.

CHAPTER 31

AT TEN THAT morning, the squad room was loud with ringing phones and homicide cops shouting to each other across the aisle. The interview rooms were full. Brady was in his office with Brenda. I was on the line with Jacob Johnston's widow when Conklin arrived with Cindy.

I explained to Mrs. Johnston that finding who'd killed her husband was top priority, that we still had no suspects, no witnesses, and agreed with her that Mr. Johnston had no known enemies. And I promised to call her day or night if there was a break or even a crack in the case. She was crying when I said goodbye. By then, Cindy and Conklin were crossing the room toward our square horseshoe of desks under the overhead TV.

The morning anchor was talking about the murder in Pasadena when Cindy slipped into Conklin's chair and glanced up at the TV. I looked her over, asked her how her flight had been, how she was feeling.

"I had a crappy night's sleep at the hotel, but otherwise I'm, uh, perfect."

I said, "Okay, good," and squeezed her hand, but honestly she looked tense and pale. Conklin dragged a chair over to our desks and I told him that Chi and Cappy were at Ennis, Neiman and Bright Advertising checking out Brad Fleet's alibi.

Rich said to Cindy, "Coffee, hon?"

While he brought Cindy to the break room, I forwarded Blackout's newest production to Brady, waited thirty to forty seconds, then told Alvarez I'd be right back.

Brady was watching Blackout's video when I opened his office door. He was swearing softly, making notes with a red grease pencil on a yellow legal pad. When "Adagio for Strings" came up under moonlit palms, he said, "This guy loves himself. He wants to be famous."

He clicked off the video and looked up at me. He said, "Boxer, let's talk."

We covered a lot of ground in five minutes. We both had unproven theories and one common certainty: that Blackout had killed at least two, and maybe five, people in less than a week. In addition to the two videos he'd sent us—Ralph Hammer and this unnamed young jogger—we also liked him for Catherine and Josie Fleet, given the Evan Burke connection, with Jacob Johnston as possible collateral. Brady said, "Grab Conklin and Alvarez, Chi and Cappy, and ask Cindy to join us in the corner."

Copy that. Quickly, the seven of us assembled in the empty corner office. It hadn't been cleaned since our last meeting. Coffee containers were in the trash. Morgue photos were still taped to the whiteboard. Cindy stared at Hammer and Johnston's dead headshots and Brady came in with more faces of the dead; Catherine Fleet, Josie Fleet, and a screenshot printout of the unnamed woman from Pasadena.

Brady taped them to the board and drew a timeline down the left-hand side starting with Saturday and Ralph Hammer to last night's murder of the woman in Pasadena.

Putting down his red pencil, Brady turned to Cindy. "You know what I'm going to say?"

"It's off the record. It is. Girl Scout's honor."

"Good. This killer is running the show and clearly wants attention. We don't know shit. Not who, why, or if he's going to do it again. Press could get him giddy enough to step up his game."

"Copy that," said Cindy.

Laughs rounded the table. Richie kissed Cindy's face, and when the light moment had passed, Brady said, "Boxer, tell the team what you said to me when you showed me Blackout's videos."

"I said, Blackout's taunting me.

"Why me?" I continued. "Don't know. Why these targets? Don't yet know. But, based on Joe's copy of the FBI Guide to Serial Killer Pathology that we keep on the nightstand," I joked, "Blackout's MO is unusual. He doesn't sexually abuse his victims. He doesn't collect souvenirs. He films them with sound. He's clearly experienced at this bloody game. He likes to choke out his female victims. He uses weapons to kill the males. He likes to watch them all die."

Alvarez rocked back in her chair and then she said, "The music is thoughtfully chosen. He's an intellectual. And smart. The films are homemade, but he edits the footage. He adds the music, frames the ending. I half expected him to roll credits."

Conklin said, "If only."

Brady looked up from his notepad and said, "How does Cindy fit in? At the end of his latest video, Blackout dedicates the murder to 'Mr. Burke.' Two of the five killings occur after she does her book signing of Evan Burke's bio."

Cindy said, "Why would this guy take out people around me when I'm an unarmed, unguarded target?"

"Effective when I leave this room, you'll have undercover security 24/7," said Brady.

Rich said, "Thanks, Brady."

Brady carefully placed the grease pencil at the top of the page, closed the pad, and folded his hands.

"Cindy, we need your help."

"Absolutely, yes. What do you need?"

"Tell the team everything you remember about the two people who confronted you, Hammer and this woman, Marge. No detail is too small. And then y'all watch surveillance tapes from both bookstores. I know Rick Martinez, homicide lieutenant at Pasadena PD. I'm sending him the Blackout's video and the bookstore surveillance."

When Brady left the room, I switched my phone to record, slid it to the middle of the table, and said, "Ready, Cin? Picture Ralph Hammer. What do you remember about him?"

CHAPTER 32

YUKI SLIPPED INTO her chair at the prosecution table moments before court was called back into session.

She whispered to Gaines, "What'd I miss?"

Her second chair shrugged his right shoulder in the direction of the defense table and Yuki looked across the aisle. Switzer and his client, Lewis Sullivan, had swiveled in their seats. They were facing one another and whispering vehemently behind their hands. Yuki couldn't hear them, but their body language was loud and clear. There was disagreement between attorney and client and the client was winning his point. What was up?

The bailiff intoned, "All rise for the Honorable Judge Karen Froman." The hundred people inside the courtroom got to their feet, as Her Honor entered the courtroom from her door behind the bench. The judge asked them to sit and they did.

Switzer stopped his whispered confab with his client and resumed his normal calm demeanor.

Judge Froman quieted the rustle of bags, shuffle of feet, and murmurs into cell phones with the bang of her gavel. When the room was still, Froman said, "Mr. Switzer, your first witness?"

"Yes, Your Honor," he said. "We call Mr. Lewis Sullivan."

Yuki and Gaines exchanged surprised looks. Sullivan was going to testify? It was a very risky strategy, but it appeared that Sullivan had demanded to take the stand.

Yuki watched as Lewis Sullivan stood up from his seat at the counsel table. He was wearing a blue suit, white shirt, and businessman's striped tie, tie clip. His haircut was jailhouse style, cut with blunt scissors, shaved high and short on the back and sides. Still, he looked presentable and almost pure as he walked across the blond-wood floor to the witness stand.

When Sullivan had been sworn in and was seated, Switzer asked his client, "How are you holding up?"

"Bad," Sullivan said. "I hadn't planned on being put up at the city jail."

Juror number four, Pierce Rodman, a retired restaurateur in his fifties, laughed at Sullivan's joke.

Sullivan thought he was funny. But Yuki had a different thought. Something she had learned long ago in law school. a laughing jury is an acquitting jury.

She started making notes for her cross-examination, but now she heard Switzer asking Sullivan the very same damaging questions she was planning to ask. A legal tactic known as "drawing the sting."

Switzer asked, "During three days in January of this year, did you have occasion to chain your wife to a sink pedestal and restrain her in other ways?"

"Yes. I did."

"Did you injure her with your fists and shoes and a number of other implements including a bread knife?"

"I did that, yes."

"Can you tell the jury why you committed these acts against your wife?"

Sullivan's face reddened and his lower lip quavered. He had a handkerchief in his breast pocket and used it to now dry the sweat from his face, dab at his eyes, and possibly buy a few moments of time to think.

Switzer stood by patiently until Sullivan was composed.

"I can't give you an easy answer," Sullivan said. "I—We—"

Yuki stood, "Nonresponsive, Your Honor."

"Mr. Sullivan," the Judge said. "Answer the question."

"Could you repeat it, please?"

Switzer said, "Lew. Very simply, why did you beat up your wife?"

"I did it for Barbara."

Gasps come from the gallery and the jury box.

Sullivan explained himself. "I mean, she has issues. She introduced me to rough sex. I wasn't trying to kill Barbara. And I didn't. I love her, even now. She knows that and loves me, too. If I could just *talk* to her…"

Yuki was prepared to object again, but Sullivan's shoulders heaved, he began to sob loudly, saying "Sorry, sorry," but kept crying.

Switzer said, "Your Honor, may we have a ten-minute recess?"

"No," Sullivan said. "I'm still going to be like this in ten minutes or whatever. My heart is fucking broken."

Switzer said, "Take a few breaths, Lew."

"She seems like a victim, I know," Sullivan said. "But she liked to get me going. She flirts with other people to egg me on. One of our neighbors, Tom, is in love with her. This time, she was tormenting me and I was ready for sex. Then she lunged at me with a knife, like this," Sullivan continued, thrusting out his clenched right hand.

"I was defending myself. I got the knife away from her. And she kicked me in the balls. I snapped. I wanted to teach her a lesson, but she kept calling me names. I wanted her to apologize, and she wouldn't give in. She wouldn't say, 'I'm sorry.' I hurt her. But still, I never, ever wanted to kill her."

Switzer thanked his witness and said, "I have no more questions."

CHAPTER 33

LEW SULLIVAN WAS blowing his nose and otherwise mopping up when Yuki addressed him in her cross-examination.

"Mr. Sullivan, do you feel well enough to answer a few questions? Or would you like to take a break?"

"I want to get this over with, if it's okay with you."

"Sure. This isn't the first time you've beaten Barbara, is it?"

"Like I said, she liked it rough, but this time was the worst."

"She's called the police some of those times, isn't that right?"

"Objection," said Switzer. "Prejudicial."

"Showing a pattern of behavior, Your Honor," Yuki shot back.

Sullivan said, "I'd like to answer that, Your Honor."

"Go ahead," Froman said, as if to say, *It's your funeral.*

"Barbara liked to pull the sympathy card," said Sullivan, "and then change her mind at the last minute."

"So, that's a 'yes,'" Yuki said. "Your wife has had to call the police on you in the past."

"Yes, she called the police a few times to scare me but always dropped the charges. Until now."

Yuki said, "As I understand your testimony, Barbara was goading you with a knife. You snatched it. And she kicked you in the testicles."

"That's what happened. And that's why I snapped."

"By 'snapped,' do you mean that you bound her hands and feet to free weights, sliced her up, kicked her to the point of destroying one of her kidneys, broke three ribs and punctured her right lung, broke her right leg in three places, as well as fractured her skull, resulting in a severe concussion and possible brain damage. And you blinded her in one eye. Do I have that right, Mr. Sullivan?"

"It was like someone else took me over. I didn't know what I was doing. I wish I could take every bit of that back."

"That's a 'yes'?"

"Yes. Apparently, I did that."

"In order to wreak this damage on your wife and mother of your children you had to assemble your arsenal of instruments in advance, correct?"

"Most of it was already in the basement. She brought the knife."

"Isn't it possible, Mr. Sullivan, that Barbara brought the knife to protect herself against your abuse?"

"No. It isn't."

"Emergency Medicine Doctor Michael Parker testified that from the partial healing of her superficial wounds, it was evident that you'd worked Barbara over for twenty-four hours, is that correct?"

No answer from Sullivan.

"Your Honor, please direct Mr. Sullivan to answer the question."

"Mr. Sullivan. You must answer."

"Yes, Your Honor. I spaced out just now. What was the question."

"Ms. Castellano, please restate your question."

"Did you chain and restrain and beat your wife for a period of twenty-four hours?"

"I didn't keep track of the time."

"And did you know that your children could hear their mother calling out to them and knew that you were hurting her?"

"Objection, Your Honor," Mo Switzer said. "Prejudicial. No foundation for this line of question by the prosecution."

Froman sustained the defense objection and told the jury to ignore the prosecution's question.

Yuki said, "I just have one more question, Mr. Sullivan. You maintain that you had no intention of killing Barbara James Sullivan, your beloved wife. And yet, when you saw her semiconscious, bleeding profusely, soaked in blood, you didn't call for an ambulance, did you?"

No answer from Sullivan. Yuki continued, "The reason you didn't call the police is that you wanted her to die, isn't it?"

When Sullivan didn't reply, Yuki let the silence gather like a storm over the courtroom, then said, "I have no further questions."

"Mr. Switzer. Redirect?"

Switzer rose to his feet and walked over to his client who had gone red in the face. Sullivan said to Switzer, "Who does she think she is?"

Switzer said, "Is there anything else you'd like to tell the court?"

"Yes. I love Barbara. I've loved her since we were in the eighth grade. I haven't been permitted to speak with her but if I could, I would tell her how sorry I am and that I love her with all my heart."

CHAPTER 34

LOOKING SHELL-SHOCKED AND sleep-deprived, Cindy sat beside me in Alvarez's desk chair. I taped her with my phone as she described Hammer's appearance as well as the tone and content of his verbal attack on her.

"He looked to be in his thirties. He dressed in well-worn casuals: khakis, a black leather bomber jacket, and glasses. Thick ones. He looked, ummm, artistic.

"He seemed friendly at first," she said. "His opening line was, 'I come in peace.' But then he launched into a tirade, not peaceful at all. He said that I was a 'man-hater.' Me?"

I asked, "How'd he get that?"

"I advised women to be on guard with men they don't know. I was referencing Evan Burke. He stabbed the air with his finger to make his points. So, he was quite aggressive. And he said that my book 'rewarded an unrepentant killer.' That pissed him off. About then, he was hustled out by security and you guys. He had a limp. Left leg."

I hadn't noticed a limp. Cindy's memory of Hammer was impressive. He'd been standing thirty yards away from her. We ordered pizza and went on to watch surveillance video. First, Book Passage, then Vroman's. We were looking for similarities, anomalies, a suspicious someone who after leaving Book Passage killed Ralph Hammer. We were looking for the same person who after leaving Vroman's killed a female jogger in the park, the woman Lieutenant Rick Martinez identified as twenty-eight-year-old Beth Welky. Would we recognize a serial killer in the crowds? It was unlikely, but still within the realm of possibility.

We rolled the video tape.

Both stores were crowded, and there was both too much and too little to see. But going back and forth throughout the next three hours, one person stood out. At Book Passage, a man stood to the left and a few yards behind Ralph Hammer, as if watching him. Someone who appeared to be that same man also left Vroman's with Marge, the woman who had told Cindy she was insensitive for writing about Burke's victims.

Rich said, "What about this guy? He's the only one I see who's at both locations."

Conklin isolated the image of the man who may have been Marge's companion and was also at Book Passage standing behind Hammer. Cindy hadn't noticed him and neither had I. Now, I assessed him. He was maybe forty, five ten, brown hair, lightweight tweed jacket and brown trousers. His clothing was loose, disguising his frame.

A sprint through the DMV database came up with his name, address, and phone number. He lived in a one-family house on Page Street in the Lower Haight, San Francisco, California. No points on his license.

I said, "I didn't imagine Blackout looking like this. We just keep digging."

CHAPTER 35

CAPPY ENTERED OUR war room with Chi right behind him. He peered at Conklin's monitor and at the man who'd been matched by the software.

He said, "Man looks like a baked potato."

I agreed. "Excellent look for a serial killer. How'd it go at the ad agency?" I asked.

Chi answered in four words: "Fleet's alibi checks out."

Cappy added, "He signed in at the front desk at eight fifty-seven a.m. and signed out at seven ten p.m. We spoke to fifteen people from top boss to the mailroom guy and Fleet's assistant. They all confirmed that our man was at work on Monday and in meetings all day. Doesn't seem possible he could've killed Catherine and Josie Monday morning, dumped their bodies, changed his clothes, and still gotten to work on time.

"Plus," Cappy added, "He couldn't have killed them over the weekend either. We spoke to the Fleets' neighbors. Brad was seen with Catherine and Josie, bringing home pizza on Sunday night.

"But here's the clincher. We talked to a Mrs. Krauss who was friends with the Fleets. She was walking her dog Monday morning and spoke to Catherine as she was walking on Macondray Lane. The baby was crying, but mother stopped to pet the dog."

I said, "Good job, you guys. Ninety-nine-point-nine percent certainty, Brad didn't do it."

I crossed Brad Fleet off our list and filled Chi and Cappy in on the lady in red. I divvied up the assignments, leaving Cappy and Chi to bring a man named Marvin Bender in for questioning, and wrapped up the meeting.

"We'll continue to meet at six every evening unless we're in the field," I said. "Cindy, you're on book-tour leave from the *Chronicle*. Please work from here for now."

"Okay, Linds. By the way, I'm booked to do a signing in Vegas this Friday."

"Take a pass," I said automatically. Then again, I know Cindy.

"It's a very good store," she said. "And I'm committed to this tour. Look, I understand your reasoning, but I've dealt with killers before, you know. I'll have security—"

Conklin said, "Cindy, no. Our cops can't protect you in Vegas."

"The store has security," she said, miffed.

"To be discussed," said Richie. "In private."

CHAPTER 36

SERGEANTS CAPPY O'NEIL and Paul Chi waited in an unmarked car outside a grubby apartment building on Page Street in the Lower Haight. Marvin Bender, senior sales rep at J&P Pharmaceuticals, appeared to be home. Lights were on inside his third-floor rental and his dusty Ford sedan was parked at the curb.

Chi and O'Neil had decided that if Bender didn't leave home in five minutes, they would buzz up, identify themselves, and tell Bender they needed a few minutes of his time. They had no warrant, no probable cause to arrest the man, but Chi had called for backup in the event that they needed eyes on Bender's car if he was uncooperative.

The front door opened and Bender, wearing brown trousers and a backpack over his unremarkable sport jacket, exited 231 Page Street and locked the door. He didn't look around, just came down the front steps into a hazy morning in this gray neighborhood at the tail end of the morning rush.

O'Neil and Chi got out of their SFPD unmarked car and met up with Bender as he reached his vehicle. Cappy had his jacket open, showing his Glock parked in his shoulder holster and his badge hanging to mid-tie from a chain around his neck.

Bender stopped at his car door with his key in his hand. Cappy introduced himself and his partner and said, "Mr. Bender, we'd like you to accompany us to the Hall of Justice. You're not in any trouble, but you may be able to assist us in a homicide investigation."

Bender said, "What? Me? You have the wrong guy. Wait, is Blauner complaining about my garbage cans again? I'll deal with them later. I'm late for work."

"We're being polite, Mr. Bender," Cappy said. "If you don't cooperate, we'll get a search warrant this afternoon. We'll stop by your office and not just bring you to the Hall, we'll search your premises, impound your car and your devices while we detain you as a material witness."

"You're nuts. I'm a salesman. I don't know any criminals and no dead people, either."

"Listen to me, Mr. Bender," said Chi. "Your refusal to cooperate is going to turn a simple conversation to a probable arrest on suspicion of homicide."

"No, you've got nothing and you're bluffing. But thanks for the advice."

Bender called Chi a few choice names, unloaded some expletives about cops in general, then pushed past the detectives and opened his driver's-side door. He shrugged out of his backpack and tossed it into the passenger seat, slid inside, slammed his door hard and put the car in drive. By the time the engine turned over, Chi had pulled the SFPD unmarked car around so that it was parked crosswise in front of Bender's front end.

Bender showed little concern for his ride. He stepped on the gas and plowed hood first into the squad car, crushing the passenger-side door. Bender shifted into reverse as a backup cruiser, responding to Chi's radio call, blocked the gray sedan from behind, squeezing it hard against Chi's car so that Bender couldn't move his car at all.

Just to be sure, Cappy, who'd been watching this automotive cha-cha, pulled his Glock and shot out two of Bender's tires. Then he leaned into Bender's window.

"That's it, Mr. Bender. You're under arrest. The cops coming toward us on foot? They're going to give you a free ride to the Hall."

CHAPTER 37

CINDY HAD PROMISED Lindsay she'd work from the squad room, but she needed information she could only get from her office at the *Chronicle*. Her desk faced a glass wall with its view of the bustling City Room but her eyes were on her computer. She'd sped through news feeds searching for recent unsolved homicides and found only one that sang out Murder by Blackout.

That one was the Pasadena victim, Beth Welky. The twenty-eight-year-old from Seattle had been killed during or after Cindy's reading at Vroman's Wednesday, two days ago, but no connection had been drawn from Welky's death to the unsolved murders in San Francisco and Marin County.

There was a story here circling around her, but Cindy couldn't spend more time on this right now. Her flight to Vegas was departing soon and she had to go. She emailed her editor and publisher, Henry Tyler, and repacked her devices and her scanner. She was headed out the door when she noticed a plain white envelope in the inbox used for interoffice memos.

Cindy plucked the envelope from the tray. Her name was typed in capital letters and there was no return address. Probably an anonymous tipster had dropped it off at reception. She slipped the envelope into her bag to read in the car, but the need to know won her over. She retrieved the envelope, slit it with a nail file, then dumped out the contents—a flimsy paper ribbon, a receipt from the San Quentin commissary for three cups of ramen noodles, a box of mac and cheese, and a six-pack of Coke. On the reverse side, penned in small block letters, was a note addressed to her.

Cindy skimmed it, then started over from the top.

Dear Cindy,

I heard you had a wall-to-wall crowd in Pasadena. Good for you. I wanted you to hear this first from me. You've only got half the story. I'm writing a book of my own. The Last Face You'll See: The Life of Evan Burke. The book is loaded with surprises, things I've never told you and I really think you'll be impressed. In particular, the book's ending is a real killer—and you're part of the ending.

Love, Evan

CHAPTER 38

CAPPY PHONED ME as he and Chi were leaving the Lower Haight.

"We picked Bender up outside his apartment," Cappy said. "Told him he needed to assist us with a couple of homicides. He was highly PO'd, gave us a boatload of crap and tried to evade us. Did some damage to our car. We cuffed him and stashed him in the back of a cruiser. We're about ten minutes out."

Ten minutes crawled by followed by another twenty until Alvarez and I stood behind the glass watching Cappy and Chi interviewing Marvin Bender. The subject wore old cheap clothes and a sour attitude. He bitched for several minutes about the outrage and that he would sue us for false arrest.

Then Bender demanded coffee. Cappy said, "In a bone china cup? With heavy cream and a biscuit? Earn the damned coffee, Bender."

"You're a putz, you know that?"

Cappy said, "Are you done now? Or do you want to chill in holding while we get an estimate on repairs on the PD's car and fill out a formal arrest form. Now we have you on felony reckless evading and vehicular assault on a police officer. Mandatory prison sentence. I wonder why you tried so hard to get away. And I will find out."

"How many times have I got to say it? I know nothing about any homicides. This is police harassment and you should know this, you jerk-off: my brother is a great attorney."

Chi cracked a smile. He had a short stack of papers facedown in front of him. He said to Bender, "I'm going to show you some pictures."

He flipped over a printout of a moment from the Book Passage surveillance footage. It was a shot of the audience during Cindy's speech. In this photo, Ralph Hammer was standing behind the folding chairs, his finger stabbing the air as he made a point. Behind him and a few yards to his right was Marvin Bender, just looking on.

Chi took a pen and circled Hammer's head, asking, "Do you know this man?"

"No. Who is he?"

"Ralph Hammer. Do you remember this?"

Chi flipped over another screenshot, this one of me, Rich, and an armed security guard moving Hammer out of the store.

"I remember now. But I don't know the guy."

Chi flipped over the third photo, this one from Vroman's surveillance tape. "Marge" was standing and had a look of disgust on her face. Bender was sitting beside her.

Chi said, "Mr. Bender, is this you?"

"Yes. I went to Vroman's with Marge Warner." He tapped her image with his forefinger. "We belong to an online book club."

"Talk to me about Ms. Warner, the woman you drove six hours to meet."

"I'm sure you've already vetted her."

Cappy and Chi waited until Bender said, "I only met her this one time at Vroman's. We'd gotten advance reading copies of *You Never Knew Me*. She wanted to go to the signing, and I knew she was going to be critical. She's pretty negative as a rule. She told me she owns a boutique called Dress Express in Pasadena and that she's married with children. That's it. That's all I know. Personally, I liked the book. I'm working on a true-crime book myself. Maybe you'll give me some help with it."

Chi flipped over the last picture and showed it to Bender.

"Do I know her, you're asking?"

"Yes."

"No," Bender said, looking at the photo of the woman in the red tracksuit, sprawled out on a path in the Fuller Theological Seminary campus. "Who is she?"

Chi collected all the photos and said, "Mr. Bender, you were seen leaving Vroman's with Marge Warner around six. Where did you go?"

"I walked her to her car. Then I got in mine and drove home."

"You must have been tired after driving twelve hours round trip. What did you do when you got home? Around midnight?"

"I ate a bowl of Dinty Moore stew, washed it down with a Sam Adams, and watched a film on TV. *Mr. Brooks*. Kevin Costner plays the Thumbprint Killer. I love that film. I had another beer, then I went to bed. Alone."

Chi said, "Here's what I'm thinking. You were within walking distance of the murders of Ralph Hammer—"

"Me and a few hundred other people."

"No, see," said Cappy. "You were the only person who went to both bookstores. Where did you go after the Book Passage reading?"

"I don't have a life, chief. I went home."

"Anyone see you? A neighbor, for instance?"

"I don't know Ralph Hammer."

"He's dead," said Cappy.

"I don't know nothing about none of this. You've got nothing, nothing on me. It's not against the law to go to book signings, is it?"

"We're arresting you for vehicular assault on a police officer with a deadly weapon—"

"What? What are you talking about—?"

Chi read Bender his rights, then said, "Destruction of municipal property, felony reckless evading, assault on me with a deadly weapon and incidentally, suspicion of murder. You get one phone call. I suggest you call your brother, the lawyer."

Back at my desk beside Sonia Alvarez I said, "My gut says he's not the guy."

"No," said Alvarez. "He didn't blink. But he plowed into a police car. What's with this guy?"

"He's guilty of something. Something else. And he's a hard-wired malcontent in my humble opinion."

"I'll help Chi and Cappy do background checks."

"Good. Thanks, Sonia."

I turned on my computer, checked my email, ran my eyes down the list. While we'd been listening to Bender, I'd gotten another message from Blackout. My heart started galloping before I could focus on the subject line: "Blackout to Boxer."

"What's wrong?" Alvarez asked me. She came around the desk and looked over my shoulder as I opened the email. She read out loud, *"Heads up, Boxer. I'm working on an idea for a new video. I think it's going to be a masterpiece."*

CHAPTER 39

DR. SAMUEL HOYT, Lewis Sullivan's psychiatrist, was on the stand, testifying for the defense. For several minutes he had explained to the court that he had been treating Mr. Sullivan for paranoid tendencies and explosive anger disorder.

Attorney Maurice Switzer asked, "Dr. Hoyt, is it possible that Mr. Sullivan was in an altered state when he inflicted injuries on his wife?"

"I wasn't there, and I haven't seen Mr. Sullivan since that incident or series of incidents. However, when in the middle of a rage, he could be irrational, another way of saying 'altered state.'"

"Is it fair to say that if angry, if irrational, he might not have known what he was doing?"

"That's possible."

Switzer said, "Thank you," and turned Dr. Hoyt over to Yuki for cross-examination.

Yuki said, "Dr. Hoyt, does Mr. Sullivan know right from wrong?"

Dr. Hoyt said, "Yes, with exceptions."

"I'll ask that a different way. Does Mr. Sullivan know that tying someone down, beating that person with fists and kicking that person with work boots, making twenty cuts in her torso and extremities with a serrated knife, stomping on that person's head to the effect that the skull was fractured and an eye popped out of the socket—would he know that these actions are 'wrong,' doctor?"

Hoyt said, "Mr. Sullivan would have known that what he'd done was wrong, and still, he's easily provoked and easily angered and when angry, he loses control."

"So even if he's feeling paranoid and angry and out of control, you agree he knows right from wrong. He's legally *sane*, correct?"

"That is correct."

"Is it likely that Mr. Sullivan could be in this angry, paranoid, or so-called altered state for three days without cessation?"

"In my opinion, that's unlikely."

The judge asked Switzer if he wanted to cross-examine his witness, and Switzer cut his losses and said "no." However, as he had reserved the right to cross-examine Barbara Sullivan, he asked for her to be called to the stand.

CHAPTER 40

FOR THE SECOND time this week, Yuki watched as Barbara Sullivan was wheeled into the courtroom, her leg still extended straight out and encased in plaster. There was a thick bandage over where her eyelid had been sutured closed. She wore a long over-blouse, a dark purple tunic with sleeves that covered her wrists so that almost none of her skin showed, and black pants, one leg slashed along the side seam to accommodate her cast.

Barbara was wheeled over to the witness stand but remained in her chair. She swore on the Bible to tell the truth.

Switzer addressed Barbara Sullivan kindly, asked how she was feeling and said he hoped she'd be walking soon. Then he began his cross-examination of his client's wife, victim, and the person who could put Lewis Sullivan in jail for life.

Yuki had spent an hour with Barbara preparing her for today's testimony and she had seemed vague about the beatings. There was nothing Yuki could do but watch, listen, and hope that Barbara would stay focused.

Now, Switzer was asking her, "You like what is termed rough sex, isn't that right, Barbara?"

"There's fantasy and there's over the line."

"Which is this?"

Defense counsel read a journal entry by Barbara in which she wrote, "I had another rape dream. I couldn't see the man's face as he was hurting me. He said he knew that I liked my hair pulled hard. I woke up in a sweat."

Switzer showed the small black canvas-covered book to Barbara and asked, "Did you write this?"

Barbara said, "I don't remember. That's my dream diary."

"If not you, who would write in your dream diary?"

Barbara said, "I don't remember if I wrote it, but if I did, it was about a dream. It says that, doesn't it?"

"How about this? Is this your handwriting?"

Switzer showed Barbara an enlarged photo of the basement wall taken after the time Barbara was tied down and tortured. The photo clearly showed the words in slanted block lettering, 'I love you,' written in blood. Switzer said, "Looks like the handwritten entry in your journal."

Yuki stood. "Objection, your honor. Handwriting is an unreliable indicator when used to match with other samples. This is especially true when one sample is written with a pen on paper and the other, written on wallpaper with a finger dipped in blood. I move to exclude."

The judge said, "So ordered."

Switzer shrugged off the objection and continued his cross-examination. "You're comfortable in the role of victim, isn't that right, Barbara? Wouldn't you say that you actually crave victimhood?"

Yuki objected on the grounds that counsel was leading the witness. Badgering her, too.

The judge sustained the objection and cautioned Switzer not to put his thoughts into the witness's mouth.

Smooth as ever, Switzer stepped over to his table, looked at a note and returned with an object in hand.

"If it pleases your honor, the defense wishes to introduce this bread knife into evidence as Exhibit X."

Yuki recognized the bread knife recovered from the Sullivans' basement. It had been processed by the crime lab, had Barbara's blood and fingerprints on the handle. Lewis Sullivan's prints were also on the knife.

Switzer said, "This is your bread knife, isn't it?"

"It looks like one of our kitchen knives."

Switzer said, "So, it would be yours, isn't that right?"

Barbara said, "That looks like our knife, but I'm not sure. I have brain damage. From what he did."

Switzer said, "Thank you, Mrs. Sullivan," and to the judge, "We have nothing further for the witness."

Yuki thought, this cross-examination has been a big nothing for the defense, but the jury has had another look at Barbara, who looked pitiful. Still, Switzer had drilled down on Sullivan's defense. *My wife made me do it.*

Yuki said, "Your Honor, redirect."

"Go ahead, Ms. Castellano."

CHAPTER 41

YUKI HOPED BARBARA Sullivan would be able to handle another round of testimony. Given her condition, antagonistic questions from the opposition had surely disturbed her.

Yuki got up from the counsel table and crossed the well to the witness stand.

Barbara looked dazed. Yuki smiled and asked her how she was doing. After hesitation, the injured woman said, "I'm okay. Considering."

"This won't take long," Yuki said, hoping that she wasn't over-promising.

"Barbara," she said, "do you remember if Lewis ever beat you before the incident that hospitalized you?"

"Yes," Barbara said in a soft, sibilant voice. "I was allowed back into our house last night. It was the first time since...what happened. I got some clean things from the closet and memories began to come back to me."

Switzer objected to the introduction of new testimony.

Before the judge could rule on Switzer's BS objection—meant

only to break Yuki's rhythm and interrupt Barbara's distractible train of thought—there was a disruption from an unexpected source. Juror number three, Mrs. Doris Caro, clapped her hands to her chest and slid from her seat onto the floor of the jury box.

The court officers went directly to the fallen woman, one of them calling 911. Judge Froman adjourned the court until Monday morning and ordered the courtroom cleared. Yuki and Nick Gaines went to the witness stand and, assisted by the bailiff, carefully helped wheel Barbara out of the courtroom.

Yuki knew that a car and driver were waiting for Barbara outside the Hall in the All-Day parking lot across the street. Lew Sullivan called his wife's name. She turned her head in his direction and Yuki leaned down to Barbara's ear.

"Not now, Barbara. You can't speak to him while the trial is ongoing. It's not part of our strategy. Nicky, let's get Barbara downstairs."

Yuki was thinking that, in a minute, the paramedics would be coming up the elevator with a stretcher for Juror number three. She had to get Barbara into her car before anyone—the press, another witness—spoke to her client. She stabbed the call button and pictured getting Barbara into the elevator without banging her leg against the wall.

She would get Barbara safely into the elevator and then into the car across the street before Switzer called for a mistrial. With Nick's help. So help her, God.

CHAPTER 42

CINDY WAS PLEASANTLY exhausted. It was 9:30 p.m. and she'd had a wonderful event at the Writer's Block.

Now she stood in the hall outside her room at the Legend Hotel, just off the strip. She'd asked Stefan the bellman if he'd mind going through her room before her, and he'd said, "Not a problem." He checked the bathroom, pulled open the curtains, looked under the bed and inside the narrow closet.

Cindy chattered as Stefan secured the room, saying, "I'm a writer, you know. I have a vivid imagination."

"It's okay, Miss. Happy to do it."

She thought about Blackout and how Richie and Lindsay had worried her and pleaded with her not to go on any trips, pointing to the killings after her speeches. Damn. She wished they could have seen her today.

When the bellhop finished checking every conceivable hiding spot, he showed her the wine cooler and the temperature controls and that to reach security she'd only need to call 05 on the land-line. She thanked him and gave him a twenty-dollar bill. Secure in her room with its very mid-twentieth-century furnishings, Cindy found a news station on the TV and got ready for bed.

Only when she was wearing her nightgown and ensconced in the Cal King bed with a lot of pillows did she call Richie. He didn't answer, which was odd. At this time of night, he was usually falling asleep in front of the TV. She left a message saying she was going to sleep and would see him at the San Francisco airport tomorrow morning at ten.

Cindy set the alarm and called the desk for a 7:00 a.m. wake-up call and texted her driver to make sure he would be on time. She got out of bed to double-check the door locks and memorized the directions to the fire exit and brought back a glass of ice water before turning out all of the lights again.

Outside her window, raindrops fell and the neon-lit strip made a silent, blinking light show through the curtains. Very quickly Cindy fell sound asleep.

And then she was awake.

There had been a sound, not very loud, maybe someone in an adjacent room had closed a door or bumped against the wall. She listened and the sound came again. It was a knock at her door. And she heard a man's voice call her name.

Cindy took the receiver off the hook and felt for the zero five buttons that would call help when a man's voice called out.

"Cindy, it's me."

Oh, my God. It was Richie.

Or was it?

"Rich?"

"Let me in, Cindy, before security shows me out."

She peered through the peephole. Richie was outside her door, alone, his hair falling over his eyes.

"Hang on," she said.

Leaving the chain in its track, she cracked the door and looked into Rich's big brown eyes.

"Surprise, honey. Do you know me now? Or do you want to see my badge?"

She opened the door fully and once Richie was inside the room and had re-locked the door, she threw her arms around his neck.

"You okay?" he said between kisses.

"Feel my heart. Feel it. I'm fine except that between you and Lindsay, I'm a freaking scaredy cat like never before."

"Well, I'm really happy to see you."

"I think I'm mad at you for scaring me."

Rich swooped Cindy up into his arms and she tucked her head between his neck and shoulder as her lover carried her across the shag carpeting to the bed. He put her down and kissed her again.

"We're just begging you to use common sense."

"I *am* using common sense and also keeping my commitment to my publisher. I'm doing great. I wish you could have seen me tonight."

"God, you're frustrating," he said sitting on the side of the bed. He took off his shoes and socks, stood, shed his jacket, tie, shirt, and pants, then got into the bed in the dimly lit room. He turned to Cindy and their arms went around each other.

"You're so crazy," she said, her voice cracking running her hands down his body. "I had to do this, you understand?"

"Don't stop," he said.

She laughed and he handled her in the ways he knew she loved. There was so much adrenaline streaming through her and at the same time there were clashing images in her mind of strangers knocking at the door, and then, in a rush, all of her fear was replaced by this man she loved.

She told him. He told her. They made love with flashing neon signs lighting the curtains and Cindy, breathless, managed to say, "I've never—I love you. Richie."

CHAPTER 43

I'D SLEPT IN short bursts broken by bad dreams featuring Blackout's Ruger pointed between my eyes. The last time my eyes flashed open, it was 5:10 a.m., and there was no sleep left in me. I got myself and my good dog, Martha, ready for a Saturday workday. I made oatmeal with bananas for me and left Martha and a box of dog biscuits with my neighbor, Mrs. Rose. Then I drove to the Hall.

Blackout's trailer of "coming attractions" had jacked up my anxiety and I couldn't do a thing about it. He was somewhere in his cycle, about to make a kill or he'd already done it.

I texted Cindy and got no reply. Presumably, she was on the flight from Vegas on her way home.

I was at my desk by seven thirty, grousing to Alvarez about Blackout's damned email teasing us about a murder on his to-do list without a hint of who he had in his sights, where or when this killing would happen.

She said, "He's a ghoul, Lindsay. Insatiable. With special powers."

"Got any ideas, Sonia? I'm wide-open to even the wildest theories."

"I'll keep you posted."

"Coffee?"

"Thanks, no. I'm good."

I went to the break room, returned with a full mug, a couple of Cappy's homemade peanut butter cookies, and Cappy himself.

"Where's Richie?" I asked.

Cappy shrugged and took Conklin's chair.

I told him, "Blackout's working on a new video."

Cappy said, "Brady was just filling me in on his take. That Blackout's a classic malignant narcissist."

"Exactly. He says he's creating a video masterpiece but provided no details. He's keeping me in suspense, hanging me upside down from the rafters."

Cappy said, "So, it's all about making the videos and getting a reaction. What's the story on the lady in red?"

I pushed a sheet of paper over to him that had Beth Welky's particulars: married Seattle homemaker with two children under five, food-bank volunteer with no connection to books or bookstores or Cindy. She had been vacationing in Pasadena, jogging through the Fuller Theological Seminary, where she was killed.

Cappy said, "Murder of convenience?"

Alvarez said, "Maybe he was meeting a quota."

I said, "I see a connection to Cindy or through her to Burke. Killings happen after she makes a speech about the Burke book. The Burke book was found in Ralph Hammer's car. The Fleet murders mimicked the murders of Tara and Lorrie Burke. Cindy is the world expert on Evan Burke. I can't help but worry about her."

And yet Blackout had not contacted Cindy, nor sent her a video.

Burke had done that. And the last time I'd checked, he was securely confined in maximum security at the Q.

CHAPTER 44

BY SATURDAY NOON Team Blackout was working hard and in concert. Brady had drafted Inspectors Billy Michaels and Tyler Wang to the task force, and I assigned them to Jacob Johnston's case, the only murder I could not tie to the rest.

I spoke with Tom Mancuso, lead investigator in Corte Madera, who was doggedly spinning his wheels on the Ralph Hammer case. Brad Fleet called twice asking for an update on the murders of his wife and child. The second time, he was crying.

I had nothing for him.

Lieutenant Rick Martinez, primary on the Beth Welky homicide, checked in. "Her killer left nothing on her body," he said. "The bastard lured her in and killed her, leaving not a trace. No witnesses, no prints, no saliva, nothing under her nails.

"I interviewed her friends and family. There were no reports of a stalker or an abusive husband. It was unanimous. Beth Welky was a bundle of goodness. Good mother, devout, made sandwiches for the homeless and handed out five-dollar bills to them, too. I've got no leads beyond your video and that takes me nowhere."

We worked through lunch and I checked my email again and again. At around four, Cappy gave his report on Marvin Bender, the dude who'd been caught on surveillance tape in two book-stores where Cindy had given a reading.

Cappy said, "Bender's coworkers say he's an SOB. He's touchy and mean, divorced with no friends and locked in an ongoing dis-pute with a neighbor about parking and garbage-can placement. Neighbor hates him. Otherwise, Bender is an average Joe."

An average Joe now awaiting arraignment for attempting to flee the SFPD. Still in jail. Still a suspect.

I turned to my screen as I'd done a hundred times today.

This time there was an email with the subject line reading, "Sergeant Boxer. Are you ready?"

I told Cappy who said, "I'll get Brady. Alvarez is in the break room."

When I entered the break room, Alvarez looked up from the Mr. Coffee machine.

I said, "I've got mail."

Alvarez said, "I feel sick," and followed me back to our desks where she and Cappy walked two chairs-on-wheels over to mine, pinning me in on both sides.

"Hit it," said Brady.

I had the same hollow feeling I got whenever entering a blood-spattered crime scene. Dread. I braced, feeling faint at the thought of watching another murder through Blackout's eyes.

CHAPTER 45

BLACKOUT'S UNTRACEABLE EMAIL came with the "Are you ready?" subject line and a video attachment. I pressed Play and without preamble, my partners and I were peering through a windshield into a dark and hazy night. The car's parking lights lit up the broken yellow line in the center of what appeared to be a secondary road. Raindrops fell intermittently on the glass and the wipers came on. Blackout saw no streetlights or road signs or traffic so neither did we.

Blackout glanced at his dashboard. We saw mileage, speed, and the time: 63,072 miles, fifty mph, 9:32, and the gas tank was half full. Was he in California? None of us could tell.

Blackout's eerie electronic voice came over the speaker. He said, "I don't understand what happened."

Our view changed as a flashlight switched on inside the car and Blackout rotated his head to look at the passenger sitting beside him. I started making screenshots of the video, capturing the image of the passenger. He was white, looked to be in his mid-twenties, with dark, medium-length hair. It was hard to judge his height and build, but I guessed him to be an average six-footer, 180 or so. He wore a dark sweatshirt with a hood down on his shoulders.

"He looks pissed," said Cappy.

Blackout's eyes swung back to the road. His gloved hands were in the "9 and 3" position on the wheel.

We watched raindrops and a broken yellow line as the passenger spoke, his voice also digitized.

"I was walking home after work. I hitched a ride from a guy in a pickup truck but when I opened the door, I didn't like his looks, so I changed my mind and got out."

"Didn't like his looks? Were you working?"

"You mean…? No, no…What do you take me for? But he thought so. Actually, I'm in college but I have a part-time job at the diner. I just wanted a ride home, so then, I didn't. I said 'Sorry, I need to take a piss.' I was backing out of the truck…"

"And then?"

"And then that whacko *shot* me. I don't think the bullet hit the bone, but it hurts like hell."

Blackout swung his head and looked at his passenger.

"Did you call the police?"

"No. I just ran. I didn't want him to shoot me again. Thanks for the lift, man."

Blackout's view dropped to where the young man was holding his right arm with his left.

Cappy said, "He's putting pressure on the wound."

"There," Alvarez said. "You can see blood seeping between his fingers."

Blackout said, "How far to the hospital?"

"Five miles. Something like that. Go straight and I'll tell you where to turn."

"I've got an ace bandage in the glove box," Blackout said. "Use your good arm. Be careful."

The young man said, "Sure."

He bent to the glove box and by the sound of the latch, he opened it. Alvarez shouted, "Noooo," as Blackout's gloved hand lifted off the steering wheel and came back into the frame holding a suppressed Ruger Mark IV.

"Aw, shit," Brady said from behind me. A soft, muffled pop sounded from the speaker of my boxy old Dell. The passenger turned disbelieving eyes to Blackout. His face stretched in shock before going slack. His eyes closed and he slumped against his window.

"Not your lucky night, buddy," Blackout said. He fired a second shot into the victim's head, then, put the gun down on the seat and wrenched the steering wheel hard to the right. He pulled the car onto the disabled vehicle lane and braked. I heard the click of his seat belt separating from the latch, then, Blackout's arm snaked out across the passenger's body. He reached over and lifted up on the door handle.

I strained to see anything of our killer. A patch of skin above the cuff of his sleeve, a flash of his face in the rearview mirror, but that didn't happen.

The vehicle was parked so that the passenger side was lower than the driver's side. When the door swung open, the dead man rolled against the seat belt's shoulder strap. Blackout unlatched the strap and started to drive. Momentum caused the body to fall out under its own weight.

Blackout braked the car again. We saw the victim's clothes, a darkened view of the glove box, Blackout's gloved hand pulling the passenger door shut. As he accelerated into driving speed, orchestral music came up and raindrops quickened, falling heavily on the windshield.

The piano notes were soft and slow.

"Satie," said Alvarez.

"What? Who's that?"

"Say-tee. That's the name of the composer. Solo by Ciccolini."

I was concerned by the increasing force of the rain. A downpour would cleanse the victim's body of trace evidence, obscure tire tracks, and lessen the chances of anyone finding the body that night.

In the remaining seconds of the video, we stared at a blurry black road. As before, there were no landmarks, no other vehicles or crossroads. The syncopation of the windshield wipers crossing the glass in time with the music was almost hypnotic — and then the show was interrupted by the electronic voice.

"Sergeant Boxer. You have no jurisdiction here, so just call it a gift. You're welcome. More and better to come."

The music became louder just before the picture faded to black. Tears came into my eyes. I was wiping them away when Cappy handed me a paper napkin.

"He's never going to stop," I said.

No one contradicted me.

CHAPTER 46

IT WAS SATURDAY evening, and I was at my desk, tidying up my submission of Blackout's criminal profile to ViCAP, the Violent Criminal Apprehension Program unit of the FBI.

I was suddenly aware that I hadn't yet spoken with Joe and Julie today and that it was getting close to our call time, the heart of my day. So when my cell phone rang, I grabbed it.

"Joe?"

"Linds, it's *me*."

"Cindy? Are you okay? Where are you?"

"At McBain's. Richie's with me. Where are you?"

"At my desk."

Rich got on the line. "Can you come over, Lindsay?"

"Is Cindy all right?"

"She's fine but she has a lot to say. Dinner, beer, and chocolate mud pie is on me."

"I need ten minutes."

I called Joe to tell him I was running late, made a similar call to Mrs. Rose, and five minutes later, I was wading through the boozy crowd at McBain's Bar and Grill. I was shown to a table at the back of the restaurant. Cindy and Conklin stood up. Cindy reached out her arms and Rich pulled out a chair for me between them.

"Tell me everything," I said, hugging Cindy.

"Beer?" Richie asked.

"Bring it on," I said. "I have to order at the same time."

We ordered the specials and gave Cindy the floor.

I leaned in to hear her say, "Before flying to Vegas, I stopped off at my office to check my mail, grab a couple of things. As I was walking out the door, I found this in my inbox."

Cindy held out an opened white envelope with her name printed on the front.

"Read it," she said, handing it to me.

I glanced at Conklin. He looked bummed.

I upended Cindy's envelope and a slim strip of paper fluttered into my hand. It appeared to be a receipt for food and soda from the San Quentin commissary. I turned the receipt over and saw a handwritten note to Cindy from Evan Burke about a book he was going to write.

"Burke says there's going to be a killer ending?" I said. "And you're going to be part of it?"

Cindy said, "I don't know if that's the point. I think he just wants me to know that he's writing a book on his own. That doesn't exactly stir me up, Linds. I wouldn't work with him again for — anything."

Rich said, "So, Cindy leaves the office and flies to Vegas as planned."

I looked back to Cindy.

"The Writer's Block and Artificial Bird Sanctuary."

"What did you say?"

"That's the name of the bookstore. They have an 'artificial bird sanctuary' with cute fake birds hanging from the ceiling. Never mind. The reading went great. No one hassled me. My driver came into the store and watched out for me. There was extra security, and get this: Adam Levine—yes, that Adam Levine—asked me to sign his book. He said that he loved *Fish's Girl*. Couldn't wait to read about Burke."

"What fun," I said.

"I got applause and whistles," said Cindy. "Then I got into the car, spent the night at the hotel, and did not order room service. Lights out at around nine thirty or so and then I wake up. There's a knock-knock at the door. Lindsay. I was scared."

"I carry a gun," Rich said.

"You went to Vegas?" I laughed at the thought of it.

Cindy said, "The rest is off the record."

"I swear I won't tell," I said, mimicking Cindy.

She gave me a little punch to the arm.

"Anyway, I felt great about the reading."

Suddenly, I was worried again. *What now, Cindy? No more suspense, please.*

She went on. "In the morning, Rich and I get into the limo and the driver is kind of upset. He tells me that a dead body was found on a back road. The dead guy was shot to death."

I felt faint. There were spots before my eyes. The waitress served dinner, and the smell of food brought me halfway back to myself. And now I knew why Richie had been looking like this was his last meal. Another person had been killed after Cindy had done her reading.

Rich said, "I checked out the driver," he said. "Michael Brill. He's been with First Call Limos for ten years. Maybe he's the doer.

Maybe not. I ran his name through everything. He got three traffic tickets. Two for speeding. One for a busted taillight. I'll check his trip ledger with his boss tomorrow."

Cindy said, "I've made Rich paranoid."

"Me, too. Cindy, tell me every word your driver said."

"He only knew what he heard on the *radio*," Cindy said. "We just need to do a little police work to find out about the victim: who, what, when, where, and why."

She was using the "we" word because Brady had invited her in. I'd just watched Blackout shoot a man to death inside a Ford on a secondary road, apparently outside Vegas.

Blackout knew Cindy's schedule. He'd been within shooting range of her last night. He was making little films and to me, the shooting in Las Vegas felt like the middle of the second act.

I called Brady between the burger and the mud pie.

CHAPTER 47

I COULDN'T JUST sit home on Sunday while Blackout had taken possession of my mind, so I drove to the Hall.

The bullpen was teaming with the swing shift. I greeted old friends and moved my laptop to the war room. There, I ran a new ViCAP search for a strangler who sometimes used a Ruger Mark IV who seemed to have a high IQ, video glasses, and a cloak of invisibility. I was awash in serial killer profiles when Brady found me in the corner office.

I'd told Brady about the homicide in outer Las Vegas and he'd forwarded my screenshots to Chief Belinky of the LVMPD. And now Brady had an idea that might lead us to the killer. He leaned against the windowsill and laid it out for me. I felt conflicted about his plan, but it would be good to partner again with my friend Jackson Brady.

I said, "Count me in."

I left the Hall before six and picked up noodle soup and a pickled radish salad at the Chinese restaurant two blocks from home sweet home. I took the elevator and when I got to our floor, I rang

Mrs. Rose's bell. Her door opened, Martha yipped happily, and Mrs. Rose's smile spread extra wide. I handed her the noodle dinner, her favorite TV meal.

"You didn't have to do this, Lindsay."

"Thank you, Gloria. For everything."

Martha and I took a nice long walk to the park and with her leash looped around my hand I sat for a while on a bench with a view of the lake. I thought of the many times Joe and I had occupied this very bench, his arm around my shoulders, Martha pulling against the leash, Julie naming the ducks and making up songs.

In twenty-four hours or so, my family would be home and life would be in balance again. Or would it? How would I ever scrub my mind of Blackout's close-up, eyeball view of cold-blooded murder? I couldn't shake it but was saved by the bell.

I answered my phone. It was Claire.

"Is this a good time?" she asked me.

"Totally. You okay?"

"Yeah, yeah. I want to release the bodies of Catherine and Josie Fleet to Brad Fleet before he drives me to suicide."

"Tell me what you found," I said to my best friend.

"Very little news in the autopsy reports, Lindsay. Both were dead when they were dumped into the bay. Catherine was choked out. She had pepper spray in her eyes and on her face, so I think that's how her killer got control. Josephina was smothered. Hand over her nose and mouth. I found finger marks on the left side of her face."

"Toxicology?"

"Nothing there."

"Let them go with Brad," I said. "I'll tell Brady."

"Good. How're you doing, girlfriend?"

"Never better," I chirped.

Claire laughed. "Liar. When's Joe coming back?"

"This time on Monday. I hope to God."

"Oh, damn," said Claire. "I'm getting a call. Gotta go. I'll call you tomorrow."

Once the sun had fully set, Martha and I went home to 23 Lake Street.

I made dinners for the two of us and after I'd showered and changed, the phone rang.

Yes, dear God, it was him.

CHAPTER 48

I PICTURED JOE on his mother's flowered sectional, Julie charming Grandma while eating cookie dough in her large prewar kitchen. I heard Joe's brothers laughing and a ball game on a TV in the background. I wished I was there.

Joe said, "How's it going, sweetie?"

I said, "On a scale of one to ten, ten being horrible—"

"Nine," he guessed.

"Twenty," I said. "How're you and Jules?"

Joe told me that Julie was starting to get homesick—for Martha. I got a laugh out of that and told Joe to tell Julie that Martha had put on a couple of pounds since Mrs. Rose was pretty much cooking for her all day long.

Joe swore to tell her.

Then, he asked, "What news on Blackout?"

"Same and worse," I told him, then, filled him in on the latest video by Blackout.

"He shot the new victim in Las Vegas, where, by the way, Cindy was continuing her book tour. She's okay, thank God. Glowing a little, to tell the truth. But this killing in Vegas isn't a coincidence. You're a psychology pro. Cindy is doing another book signing next week in Scottsdale. Why is she doing this? Is she sticking her tongue out at Blackout?"

"I'm not a real shrink, you know."

"What's she doing, Joe?"

"Ahh, wild guess. She's restoring her self-esteem. That year with Burke would have depressed anyone. I think despite the murders, she's getting back up on the horse."

I was quiet, thinking about that, Cindy getting her courage on. And I thought about the dark street all around my empty apartment. I wished that Joe was here in his big chair wearing his blue striped pajamas, that Julie was in her big-girl bed with Martha, and that Team Blackout held the key to his identity.

That's when a thought I'd been hiding from myself jumped out and said "Boo."

Blackout was making plans for Phoenix.

An incoming call beeped. It was Brady.

I thanked my husband for his input, told him I loved him, and missed him. We exchanged I love yous and after confirmation of flight details tomorrow, I switched over to my incoming call.

Brady's sober voice was in my ear. Tomorrow, Monday morning, we'd be surrounded by razor wire and tiers of concrete cells meeting with a convicted killer imprisoned for six life sentences, a man who hates me for what I'd done to put him there.

CHAPTER 49

BRADY AND I were in the maximum-security wing of San Quentin State Prison. We sat together outside a wire mesh cell the size of a shower stall. Inside the cell was the notorious Ghost of Catalina, Evan Burke, who claimed to hold the record for most kills of anyone in the last hundred years. That was his ego speaking. I could name two other psycho-killers, Pedro Lopez and Harold Shipman, who topped his number, but Brady and I hadn't arranged this meeting to debunk Burke's tally. We'd come prepared to deal for information: a lead, a hint, a clue that would throw light on Blackout's ID and with extreme luck, his contact information.

Burke sat in a metal chair bolted to the floor of his cage. His hands were cuffed and he'd lost a few pounds since I'd seen him last. His hair was now shoulder-length, the salt outweighed the pepper, he had a two-day beard and the lenses in his glasses had an amber tint used principally to block blue rays from the computer screen Burke had been granted as one of his prison privileges. Burke smiled when he saw us take seats across from him, outside the wire-mesh walls.

Cocking his head he asked me, "Do I know you?"

It was a put-down. I'd arrested him and testified against him. If not for me, Burke would be haunting dark places from California to Nevada and adding to his body count.

Burke knew me but he didn't know Brady.

I introduced them, and Brady said to Burke, "Have you heard you have a copycat?"

"Really? You see, chief, I don't watch the news. I like reality shows. *The Bachelor. The Real Housewives of Orange County.*"

He grinned. He had that serial-killer charm. That psychopathy.

I said, "Do you know Ralph Hammer?"

"Nope. Cool name, though."

"A week and a half ago, he was in the driver seat of his parked car when he was garroted from behind. Then he was shot through the back of his head."

Burke mused, "I don't like the garrote much. I like a straight-edge razor. Well, you know that, don't you, Sergeant Boxer? Your girlfriend, Cindy, right? She did an in-depth study of my MO. How is she, by the way? She doesn't call. Doesn't write."

Brady removed an envelope from his breast pocket, opened it and one by one pressed a few 4" x 6" photos against the wire cage wall. Burke leaned closer and asked, "Got any more?"

"Tell me what you think of these," Brady said. "I might leave them for you."

"Is that supposed to be Tara and Lorrie on the beach?"

I said, "What do you think?"

Burke said, "I think someone is trying to give me a shout-out. Is that what you mean? Because I don't know that girl. Or her babe. How were they killed?"

I said, "Have you heard from a fan bragging about kills, or asking

for advice, or anyone trying to copy you? Is someone outside trying to compete with your record? Have any thoughts that would
help us?"

"And what's in it for me?"

Brady said, "Let's hear what you've got."

I was thinking, *God, if you're listening, let this human waste of oxygen
lead us to Blackout.*

"I've got nothing," Burke said, grinning, showing me his big yellow teeth. A violent thought came into my mind and evaporated
before Burke saw that murderous impulse on my face.

Brady said, "Nice meeting you, Burke. Let's go, Sergeant. The
warden is waiting for us."

"Wait," said Burke, getting to his feet, still safely locked behind
the walls of his narrow interview cell.

Brady and I turned to face him.

"Speak," said Brady, as if he were addressing a dog.

CHAPTER 50

"SHOW ME THE pictures, again," Burke said. He took off his glasses and wiped them with the hem of his blue shirt. Then, he looked expectantly at Brady.

Brady removed the photos from the envelope and pressed one of them against the wall of the cage. It was an image that I would never forget: the body of Catherine Fleet, lying face-up on the beach, her coat sleeves and long skeins of her dark hair being lifted by the outgoing waves.

Josephina Fleet looked almost alive. Attached to her mother by the straps of the front-facing carrier, her pale eyes were open, as if looking at seabirds flying overhead.

Burke asked the victims' names and Brady shook his head "no." He returned the pictures to his pocket.

Burke said, "Well, I see why you showed that to me. I guess there's a similarity to Tara and Lorrie. But I give the killer a B minus. You spoke of a garrote. No ligature mark on this girl, so I'd say it was manual asphyxiation. Which I think is more personal and therefore better, though these two were put down fast and with no style. That lowered his score."

Burke scratched at a cheek and said thoughtfully, "Do I know whodunit? Nope. I wish I could take some credit—but you know, I can't. Actually, I'd do anything to be this guy for a day."

Brady called the guards.

They came, removed their prisoner by the rear door of his cage. Burke turned his head and called back to us. "Lieutenant? If you want me to consult for you, you know where to find me. I think we can make a deal."

I heard his laughter as he was escorted roughly out of our view. A buzzer sounded. A metal door clanged shut. Brady said, "He doesn't know Blackout. He would've baited the hook."

"He's going to hate that someone is trying to steal his thunder."

"Let's go see the warden," said Brady.

Warden Hauser's office door was open. He had a small, one-window office with a bay view. His desk was tidy, file cabinets taking up much of the floor space, nothing on the walls but a picture of the warden transferring Charles Manson to a prison van marked California State Prison-Corcoran, where Manson was incarcerated until he died.

The warden looked up and, recognizing me, stood to greet me. I introduced Brady and we were invited to sit down.

I said, "Warden, we have a serial killer on a spree. We believe he's killed six people in under two weeks. A man, woman, and infant in San Francisco. Another man in Corte Madera, a woman in Pasadena, and a third man on Friday night in Las Vegas."

"It's the same doer? You're sure?"

Brady said, "He makes videos of some of his kills and pretties them up with classical music and lighting effects before sending them to Sergeant Boxer."

Warden Hauser expressed shock, had many questions, including, "And you came to see Burke why?"

Brady said, "The recent Baker Beach double homicide resembles Evan Burke's MO, and there's something else. Half the time, the killings seem to revolve around Cindy Thomas, the journalist who wrote Burke's authorized biography."

"What did Burke say?"

"He sent Cindy a letter, told her he was writing a book. He told us he knows nothing about the recent killings," I said. "He might be telling the truth."

"Figures," the warden said. "He has a TV but his laptop is no better than a typewriter. No internet connection. He does get mail and some visitors, hucksters, his attorney, true-crime fans."

Warden Hauser leaned back in his chair and said, "He's a nonstop headache, that guy. He's disruptive. We have a 24/7 watch on him to protect him from death threats. It would be a big deal to be the one who takes him out."

Brady said, "That mail that he gets. Maybe Burke knows something. You think you could put the screws to him a little? Monitor his mail a little more closely. Nothing illegal. If we see him again, I'd like him to be in a negotiating frame of mind."

Hauser said, "Well. There've been some security breaches lately, including cyber. We'll have to confiscate his computer for a while."

I said, "He'll say he can't access the web."

The warden smiled, rocked his chair to its upright position. "He's a lifer. What's he gonna do?"

Good deal.

CHAPTER 51

FOR THE THIRD time, Barbara Sullivan was on the witness stand. Yuki greeted her witness Monday morning and reminded her that she was still under oath.

"I understand."

"Very good," Yuki said. "On Friday, you told the court that you'd recently visited your home for the first time since your husband beat you. Going home refreshed your memory of that beating?"

"Yes. I remembered that the fight started when Lew and I came back from the grocery store with the kids. Tom Watkins, our neighbor, had offered to help me unload the groceries from the car. I'd said, 'No, thanks, we've got it.'

"But Lew didn't like Tom even talking to me. By the time we were inside, he was boiling mad. He called me names. He said he wanted to kill me. I didn't take him seriously. I went downstairs to run some laundry. Lew came down after me. He said something like, 'This is it. Say your prayers. Do it fast.' He had a knife."

Barbara covered her eyes with her palms, finally accepting a packet of tissues from Yuki, holding a wad of them to her eyes.

A few uncomfortable moments passed, as Barbara's muffled sobs filled the courtroom from wall to wall. She coughed, apologized to the judge, then continued her narrative.

"Lew grabbed me by my hair, pulled my head back, and pressed the blade to my throat. I knew then that he really might kill me. I kneed him in the balls and he dropped the knife. He let go of me for that one moment and so I grabbed the knife off the floor and held it out in front of me, gripping the handle with both hands."

Yuki urged Barbara to go on.

"The standoff ended when Lew held his hands up, his palms facing me and said, 'Okay, okay, you win.' I asked Lew to please leave so I could do the laundry. I turned back to the washer and felt a blow to the back of my head. When I woke up, I was tied to the laundry sink by my wrists. My ankles were taped to free weights and Lewis was kicking me in the ribs. He said, 'Wake up,' and called me a name. Then he—raped me. I passed out."

Barbara broke down again. Yuki asked if she was able to continue.

"I'll try. I must have been out for a long time. When I woke up, it was night. I can't describe the pain. I hurt everywhere inside and out. I couldn't see. I touched my…eye. God help me. I called out but there was no answer. When I woke up again, it was morning and I was throbbing everywhere. Every breath was like shards of glass in my lungs. I heard my seven-year-old, Kevin, calling me. I called back, but my voice was scratchy. A whisper. I tried to break free. The pain was too much. I was having out-of-body waking dreams, Ms. Castellano. When the police came, I felt that my soul was leaving my body. That's what I remembered from when I went home recently."

"Thank you, Barbara. I have just a few more questions to ask you. Do you remember the times you called the police prior to this event?"

"Yes. Once after a bad fight. And once when I was afraid to go into the house."

"And did you drop the charges? If so, why?"

"Yes. Because I was afraid of Lewis. He threatened me and called me names and hurled the most horrifying insults in the world at me for days. He was careful to hurt me without leaving marks. So it would be my word against his. All the time telling me what he would do to me. Above all, there were the children. I didn't want him to lie about me and somehow get custody of the children. That would be an endless hell for them."

Tears spilled down Barbara's cheeks. She put a hand on her chest to steady her heaving.

"Thank you, Barbara. I have no more questions."

Yuki took her seat at the counsel table. Gaines had pushed a note card over to Yuki's place. It read "Brilliant."

The judge asked if defense would redirect and Switzer had the good sense to say "No, Your Honor."

Court was adjourned for lunch break. Yuki stood as the judge left the bench.

As Barbara was rolled out of the courtroom, Yuki hoped she'd made every man and woman in the room feel as trapped and as close to death as that poor woman had felt. Had the jurors believed Barbara? Yuki couldn't think of anything she would have done differently. At this minute, everyone in Courtroom 6A was thinking about Barbara Sullivan.

CHAPTER **52**

WHEN COURT RECONVENED, Her Honor Judge Froman asked the defense counsel if Mr. Switzer was ready to make his closing argument.

"Yes, Your Honor."

Maurice Switzer stood, walked to the jury box and addressed the jurors. He looked attractive, honest, and made good eye contact with the jurors. Switzer didn't bother with a preamble. No warm-up lines. He got right to it.

He said, "This is what happened one terrible afternoon in a homey house in Alamo Square. Barbara Sullivan antagonized her husband by giving the time of day to a man Lewis thought was a competitor for his wife's affections. He picked up a bread knife from the kitchen counter and followed his wife to the basement laundry room where he threatened her. In her own words, Barbara didn't take his threat seriously, which further inflamed her husband. When he stepped up his threat with the knife, Barbara kicked her husband in the testicles, causing intolerable pain. She could have left the basement, called the police, or gotten into the car with the children.

"Instead Barbara picked up the bread knife and threatened Lewis, already fired up, furious, and in pain.

"Barbara's memory may be challenged in this regard. She called Lewis names that no man could handle. He remembers. She told him that he was a loser, a failed husband and father, and that she couldn't stand to look at him. She knew how to push Lew's buttons. She was good at it.

"Over the course of that evening, we maintain that Barbara wrote 'I love you' on the basement wall. Yes. With her own blood and her own hand. Was she baiting him? Offering an olive branch? We don't know. But we know that she didn't leave the basement. She remained there for twenty-four hours.

"As mentioned by the defendant and alluded to by Mrs. Sullivan, she liked rough sex and was Lew's mentor in this activity. She encouraged it. If things went too far, Barbara told us that there is 'fantasy and there is over the line.' This is not a tangible line. This is an arbitrary distinction that Barbara alone made.

"In my opinion, Mr. Sullivan can be pardoned for not seeing that line. Historically, if Barbara called the police, she dropped the charges before ever giving a statement. She says she was afraid of her husband, but she didn't leave him. She didn't file for separation or divorce. She stayed.

"Barbara Sullivan knew the game she was playing but—combined with his own failure to read the situation—she pushed her husband too far. He loves her. He maintains that she loves him. Lew never intended for their sex game to result in the physical pain Barbara suffered and he is remorseful and repentant.

"But Lewis Sullivan did not attempt to murder Barbara.

"He could have done it, but he did not."

Maurice Switzer thanked the jury and returned to his seat.

CHAPTER 53

I DROVE FROM the Hall to the southern edge of the Financial District in about ten minutes without using sirens and flashers. I parked on Jackson, not far from Susie's front door. Susie's Café is a Caribbean-style bar and restaurant and all are welcome, but Claire, Cindy, Yuki, and I thought of Susie's as our clubhouse, the Women's Murder Club HQ.

The plate glass windows were alight and when I opened the front door, a wonderful spicy aroma turned my mind toward dinner. The bar was full at 6:00 p.m. Fireman was manning the bar taps, the Yellow Bird Quartet was tuning up their steel drums, and the ochre sponge-painted walls added a glow to the front room. Old acquaintances waved, called out, "Hey, Sarge," and I returned greetings. Susie, a limber and athletic woman, stopped me to say that the limbo contest was slated for six thirty and did I want to sign up?

"Sorry, Suz. I'm out of shape."

She politely disagreed but I told her maybe next time and as I made my way to the back room, I was singing to the Yellow Birds' warm-up; *"Down at de market you can hear people cry out while on their heads they wear/Hot tea, rice, salt fish is nice and de rum is fine any time of year..."*

Claire was in the corner of "our" booth talking to Yuki, I slid into next to my BFF and asked to be brought up to speed. Claire was in her listening mode. She put her arm around my shoulders and said, "Yuki can bring you up to speed faster and better than I can."

Yuki has a high metabolism, is a fast-talker with a melodious laugh and a low tolerance for alcohol—tequila being her juice of choice. This evening she was drinking tea and seemed subdued.

Claire said, "Yuki, tell her."

"You've heard this before."

"Go ahead," I said.

"Defense made a stellar closing argument. Really."

Lorraine brought a pitcher of beer and said she'd be back for our order when Cindy showed up.

Yuki said, "He blamed the victim! Here's the victim, battered to a pulp and defense counsel is saying she flirted with the neighbor. She calls her husband names. He's sorry.

"Sorry?" Yuki continued, knocking her teacup with one hand, catching it with the other, never losing a beat.

"The husband tied her down for twenty-four hours without sustenance or a wet cloth or anything. He rapes her. And while her kids are screaming for her, he breaks her ribs, her leg, steps on her head, and pops out an eyeball. All because, according to the defendant, she flirted with a neighbor in full light of day.

"So, Switzer said, 'Barbara went too far and because of that, her husband lost it and retaliated, and things got out of hand. The defendant is sorry, really sorry. He loves her and she loves him.'

"Mo Switzer has that cool masculine authority, you know? His closing was elegant in its simplicity."

I asked, "There are women jurors, Yuki?"

"Six," she said.

Claire said, "They're not going to buy what Switzer's selling."

"Hope you're right," Yuki said as Cindy plopped into the seat beside her. Our friend and author reached across the table, sipped from my beer mug, and said, "So? What'd I miss?"

"You first," said Claire.

"Sure thing. *You Never Knew Me* is likely to hit number one on the *Times* Best Seller list this week," Cindy said. "And I'm flying to Phoenix in the morning for an event at the Poisoned Pen in Scottsdale."

"No," Claire said. "You're joking."

Cindy shook her head, no, and sang a few words of a Glen Campbell oldie. *"By the time I get to Phoenix, she'll be rising…"*

Claire said, "You, Cindy. Are incorrigible. I know I'm laughing but I'm not joking, girlfriend. I love you so I'm telling you the truth. It's not a day in Phoenix. It's dangerous. Like walking across a line strung between two skyscrapers, blindfolded and without a net. That's what I'm saying."

I followed Claire's image and saw Cindy doing exactly that.

And I didn't know anyone who could stop her.

CHAPTER 54

LORRAINE CAME OVER, saying "hi" to Cindy, who asked, "What's good tonight?"

"Everything. Point me in a direction." Lorraine took her pen and pad out of her apron pocket.

"Seafood something," said Cindy.

"Good choice. Trust me. And can you sign this for Rinaldo?" Lorraine had an ad for Cindy's book leaved between pages of her order pad. She presented it to Cindy.

"To Rinaldo?"

"That's it and sign it, 'Love, Cindy.'"

"Haha."

Rinaldo had a crush on Cindy. She signed her name for the chef and said, "Rum and Coke?"

"Coming up."

"Cindy," Claire said, genuinely concerned. "You don't see a link between your book signing in Vegas and that boy who was killed that night?"

"I did hear, and Rich showed me Blackout's nauseating video. It was horrible—beyond words or comprehension. But here's the thing, Claire. *I* haven't received any threats, or emails, or videos, or texts, or anything. I was terrified until I put it together. I didn't know any of those people who were killed. And I don't know why they were killed in the same city where I was on tour. So, I have a question," she said, taking in all three of us.

"Weren't other people killed in cities where I wasn't signing my book?"

I leaned back in my seat.

I said, "You're saying, you think these particular killings are unrelated to you and the book?"

"Exactly," she said.

Lorraine has the ability to be invisible when she wants to be. She placed some kind of savory seafood stew in front of Cindy along with a basket of bread and her cold drink. I thought about Cindy's point.

Yes, people had been killed in other cities on the days Cindy had done book signings. Dozens. Hundreds. And three of the victims we were considering part of Blackout's tally—the Fleets and Jacob Johnston—were killed in San Francisco. No book signing. And no videos, either. And to her point, Blackout had never mentioned Cindy. Pieces of the puzzle did not fit neatly together. It was maddening. Blackout was maddening.

I wanted to say Blackout's spree had something to do with Burke. He'd dedicated the video of Beth Welky's murder to him. But even though Cindy was signing books in Pasadena that same night I certainly couldn't prove the connection. And now Cindy was going to continue her book tour in Phoenix.

I knew no one in the Phoenix PD.

With a shock, I became aware of the time. It was past six, and

Joe and Julie were going to be home by eight tonight. I had to eat fast and drive home. Lorraine set my jerked beef and rice in front of me, same for Claire, plus a salad for Yuki, who said, "A watermelon margarita, please, Lorraine."

Yuki said, "Cindy, did you know Burke has a new lawyer working on an appeal of his sentence?"

"On what grounds?" Cindy said. "He confessed. He gave me all the proof anyone could need to convict him many times over. He wanted people to know his score because he's an egomaniac. And because of his confession, he *only* got six consecutive life sentences. He's done."

Yuki said, "That's all I know."

Claire said, "In my professional opinion, Evan Burke has surpassed all categories of criminally insane. He needs a new category."

Cindy agreed. "A class of his own. Call it 'All Burked Up.'"

There was laughter, booze, yummy food, sounds of applause from the front room as the limbo competition ended. I checked my phone. Seven fifteen.

"Cin, when's your flight tomorrow morning?"

"Ten twenty-two."

"Stop by my place at eight thirty," I said. "I'll drive us to the airport. Please don't fight me, Cin. I'm going with you to Phoenix."

CHAPTER 55

I WAS IN bed with Joe when Julie climbed up over the foot of
the bed, crawled northward, and wedged herself between us. She
fell straight to sleep on top of the blankets. My head was on Joe's
shoulder. His left arm was around me and we held hands, speaking
softly so as not to wake our little girl. Martha was snoring on the
rug beside the bed, the four of us filling the available sleeping
space in our blue-painted bedroom, which for me was the center
of the universe.

Joe was telling me about his visit to his childhood home.

He said, "It was crazy. Like a cross between *Leave It to Beaver* and
Animal House," he said. "And Mom. She says, 'Seventy-five is the
new ninety.'"

"She meant seventy-five is the new fifty?"

Joe laughed. "Nope. She never sat down. She vacuumed every
morning, did laundry every other day, and cooked every night. Our
first night there, the whole table was lined with my brothers. So, she
made four kinds of pasta and sides, all different sauces...and everyone was tossing cracked jokes and bread.

"Mom said, 'Are you kids ever going to grow up?'

"'Noooooo,' from the whole pack and it just kept going."

I laughed thinking about that and said, "But tell me about Julie. I'm trying to picture her at that table."

"She sat on a big pile of cushions between me and Mom. Her head swiveled from me to Mom to Petie, to Aldo, to George, back to me, and then down the table to Greg and Paul, and then straight ahead to Dad's picture over the sideboard. I think she was trying to process how we all looked almost alike."

Joe laughed again and I smiled into his shoulder. Julie adjusted her position, spooning against me. I tucked my arm around her and kissed the top of her head.

"It was good for her to get all those uncle horsie rides, play 'Go Fish,' and just be with her Grandma."

"I need some of that horsing around and time with your family, myself."

"You sure do. Next time, you're coming."

I said, "I ditched Dr. Greene this morning. Didn't remember. Didn't even call him."

"I believe that's called unconscious resistance."

"Like I don't want to face something? Well, that would be true." I told Joe that my week had been like his week only upside down and inside out and on speed. That for my peace of mind and Cindy's safety I was going to Phoenix with her in the morning. "I'll be home tomorrow night."

"Is that just a good idea or a necessity?" he asked.

"Necessity. She's determined and unarmed. I want to see if someone's watching her."

"Try to have some fun, will you?"

I said I would try just before Joe's hand went slack. Soon, he and

Martha were both snoring. I nudged our little one and carried her to her bedroom with Martha padding behind us. I put her to bed asking, "How's my girl?"

"I missed you, Mommy."

"I missed you, too, Jules."

Martha hopped up into bed with Julie. She circled, put her head on Julie's pillow, and closed her big brown eyes. I stood watching them sleep by the night-light shaped like an angel.

Julie hadn't said the Lord's Prayer tonight, and come to think of it, neither had I — not in a long time. I knelt beside Julie's bed and did it for her. After "God bless..." I included everyone in the Molinari and Boxer families and Mrs. Rose. I requested blessings for the Women's Murder Club and their men and my friends and colleagues at the SFPD. I tucked Cindy's name in once more, just before "Amen."

I turned to leave Julie's room with an idea to wake my husband accidentally on purpose. But he was already up, standing in Julie's doorway after watching and listening to me pray.

"And God bless you," he said.

He hugged me tight and walked me back to bed.

CHAPTER 56

WE WERE ON the Tuesday morning flight to Phoenix when Cindy told me that the book tour was driving sales far beyond expectations.

"You know what they say? 'Books are flying off the shelves.'"

We both grinned at the image and actually I liked how she sounded. The Cindy who'd had too much contact with Evan Burke, who'd been steeped in souvenirs of his decades-long murder spree, was nearly back to her old self: enthusiastic, daring, fully alive.

When we exited the Phoenix terminal, Cindy's driver was waiting to take us to The Poisoned Pen Bookstore in Old Town Scottsdale. The store had an impressive exterior with corkscrew columns flanking the front door. Even more impressive was the line of customers stretched out the door to the street in advance of the afternoon signing. I badged the security guard, but before crossing the threshold, I stopped to admire Cindy's beautiful face on a larger-than-life-sized poster in the window. We each took pictures with Cindy as a backdrop, and she took a selfie of us together. And then we were welcomed inside by the Poisoned Pen's owner, Barbara Peters.

Barbara wore red, had a short blond bob, and was so glad to meet us both. She showed us the layout of the store, and where Cindy would be speaking. I met the retired cop she had hired for security and asked to be positioned so that my chair was angled toward the audience. Within a half hour, Barbara Peters introduced Cindy Thomas, best-selling author and crime reporter of note, to rousing applause. I clapped, too, and at the same time watched the room for anomalies, sudden movements or a face I'd seen in previous bookstore videos.

Once Cindy engaged the audience, she was encouraged to speak longer and answer more questions, while the book signing line grew longer. We had planned to have an early dinner with Barbara Peters at Café Monarch, a five-star restaurant with a four-course menu that even one-star foodies like me would remember forever. But it was clear by the time we finished at the Poisoned Pen that we could have dinner or catch our return flight, but not both.

Barbara recommended Chelsea's Kitchen, an airport restaurant that was so popular, non-travelers drove out to the airport to eat there. We took her advice and had hot tacos and iced tea. And I told Cindy how proud I was of her.

"My God. That was such a great event. And you were so good, Cin. How'd you learn to do public speaking like that?"

"Well, I've had practice—"

"You're a natural, Cindy. And you know your subject—"

"Don't I, though?"

"You practically materialized Evan Burke into the store. The audience couldn't get enough of you."

"Thanks, Linds. I have to enjoy it while I can."

"While you can, what? You're scaring me."

"No, no. I mean, someone else's book will be top of the list in a couple of weeks. But still. This is almost like a first-class vacation. In Paris."

I laughed, paid the check, and waited for the waiter to bring back my card. There was a long pause as Cindy pulled at the hem of her flippy jersey dress and then asked, "Did you see anyone who looked wrong?"

"No. And I was watching while everyone else was looking at you."

"Hah," said Cindy. "So, we don't have to get into a fight when I go to Portland in a few days."

Quoting Claire, I said, "You're incorrigible."

"And I'm right. Let's go, Linds. They're calling our flight."

I exhaled. Cindy and I were both going home tonight.

Thank God. We hugged and boarded the plane.

CHAPTER 57

YUKI WAS WRAPPING up her summation, her left hand resting on the rail of the jury box.

She'd stood there since word one, making eye contact with each of the jurors and alternates. She stopped at Sam Winsted, moved on to Pearl Harvey, lifted her eyes to Mary Savino, moved on to Doris Caro, who'd recovered from her collapse in the courtroom during distressing testimony from Barbara. She felt that she'd reached them all, even Pierce Rodman, juror number four, who seemed to enjoy the hell out of Switzer.

Yuki said, "Did Barbara call Lewis names? Say she did. Did she threaten him with a knife in the laundry room, as Lewis claims? It was self-defense. Barbara and Lewis have different recollections of the altercation with the knife. That's common in traumatic situations. And while we can't know what went through the minds of these two people, we do know that Lewis Sullivan suffered no injuries, not a scratch. And we can look at the evidence, which is not in dispute. Lewis Sullivan incapacitated Barbara and beat and kicked and tortured her until she blacked out. Without police and medical intervention, Barbara would have bled out and died on the basement floor.

"We know this from the police officers who arrived at the scene and gave their testimony. We know this from the EMTs who kept Barbara Sullivan alive until she was delivered to the emergency room. Dr. Parker, the ER attending physician, testified that he had never seen injuries like Barbara's on a living person."

Yuki turned and signaled to her number two.

Nick Gaines brought a long cardboard tube to the whiteboard and withdrew a five by eight color photo. He unfurled it and taped it to the whiteboard that was angled so it could be seen throughout the small courtroom. The image was of Barbara Sullivan, half nude, bleeding from every part of her body, restrained by chain and tape.

Yuki thanked Gaines and gave the jurors a long minute to take it in. There were gasps and quiet "oh, my Gods" from jury and gallery alike. Lewis Sullivan lowered his head and Switzer put an arm around his client.

After a minute of silence, Yuki continued. "This photo was taken by Sergeant Birney. It was entered into evidence. We've had it enlarged, but it has not been enhanced in any way.

"As you've heard and can see, Barbara Sullivan was immobilized. She was raped and suffered severe vaginal tearing. The DNA from her rape kit matches one man and one man only. Lewis Sullivan. You've heard the litany of her injuries, internal and external, including eight broken bones, cranial factures, a concussion, and the loss of her left eye.

"Where was Barbara's husband at the time this photo was taken? Lewis had taken the boys out to lunch. If the police and EMTs had reached Barbara ten minutes later, she would have been dead.

"What was his intent? Lewis Sullivan spent twenty-four hours cutting, punching, raping, and kicking his wife. Did he intend to kill her?

"He denies this, but then here's what Lewis Sullivan *didn't* do. He *didn't* call the police. He *didn't* call an ambulance. He *didn't* ask his neighbors or anyone for help. He *didn't* untie his wife or attempt to give her succor. No. He took the kids to Arby's."

Yuki turned to the photo, giving the court another uninterrupted look at the gripping image of Barbara Sullivan's battered and broken body with a large pool of blood spreading outward from her head.

Yuki asked the jurors, "Did Lewis Sullivan want his wife to live?

"No. He did not. The people rest, Your Honor."

CHAPTER 58

YUKI'S PULSE WAS still pounding when she returned to the prosecution table. She was also winded and filled with a feeling of deep satisfaction. Gaines muttered, "I want to be you when I grow up."

Yuki patted his hand in acknowledgment. She was aware that eyes were on her from all sides, but she looked only at the judge.

Judge Karen Froman, both stern and patient, took her time charging the jury with their duties. Court was adjourned pending the return of a verdict. The gallery emptied and two court officers went to the defendant, each taking one of his arms. They were about to escort Lewis Sullivan back to his cell when he pulled an arm free and turned to Yuki, shouting, "I have something to say!"

The judge instructed the bailiff to accompany the jurors to the deliberation room. After they'd left through the side door, the defendant stood in the aisle between the guards and spoke to Yuki in a determined tone of voice: "Against advice of counsel, I will plead guilty to the charge of child endangerment. I admit I was oblivious to the kids hearing us fight and the effect of that. I'll take the hit for aggravated assault. I was aggravated. I did assault Barbara and I seriously hurt her. She may have permanent physical and mental damage and I'm going to suffer for that for the rest of my life.

"Ms. Castellano. Right now, I will plead guilty to the lesser charges if you drop 'attempted murder.'"

CHAPTER 59

DA LEONARD "RED DOG" Parisi was wearing a charcoal-gray suit with a red tie that highlighted his wild red hair. Three hundred fifty pounds of prosecutorial muscle, Len had been in the courtroom's back row all morning and was now waiting in the corridor for Yuki and Nick.

"My office," Parisi said when they came through the doors.

Although Yuki was dying to know his thoughts, Len had an unbreakable rule. Don't discuss the case in public areas.

The prosecution team didn't speak during that short walk to their department. The District Attorney's offices, as well as the courtrooms, were on the second floor. Press crowded and surrounded them, pushing mics and cameras forward, shouting questions, but Parisi was like a bulldozer, shoving rubbish off the road.

At times like this, the big man's office was a refuge. Furnished in dark leather, carpeted in Oriental rugs, with heavy curtains closed against the glare and noise of Bryant Street just below, it was dimly lit and quiet.

Yuki took a seat on the tufted love seat opposite Len's large hand-carved desk. Nick sat in a matching armchair at right angles to the sofa. Yuki glanced at the clock on the wall above Parisi's desk. Its face was a graphic design of a red pit bull, a reference to Parisi's nickname, earned by his ferocious prosecutions before he was promoted to the corner office.

Len's chair wheezed as it took his weight. Katie, Len's assistant, brought in a folder of phone messages. He thanked her and without looking, put the call sheet on the stack of memoranda.

Looking at Yuki, Len said, "Great job, Yuki. You, too, Nick. I know this case was painful for all concerned. Your star witness was outstanding. Your summation was letter-perfect. Your voice broke during your closing, Yuki, if you didn't know. A goddamn great touch."

Yuki said. "That picture…I hadn't seen the enlargement."

"I know your emotion was authentic," Red Dog said. "That's what notched your closing up to one of the best I've heard in this Hall."

Yuki thanked Parisi. Still, a "but" hung in the air. The "but" was a question: Should the prosecution let Sullivan plead guilty to the lesser charges and drop "attempted murder"?

The answer would be a calculated guess. Having heard the evidence, the testimonies and the arguments, what did the jurors believe? How would they decide their verdict?

Parisi said to Yuki, "What's your gut tell you? Make the deal on a sure thing? Or roll the dice on attempted murder?"

Yuki said, "Intent is the sticking point. Does the jury believe that Lew Sullivan meant to kill Barbara? If there's doubt in one juror's mind, we could lose on attempted murder and still get a conviction on assault and for scaring the kids. The lesser charges will still get Sullivan forty years in prison."

"On the other hand," Parisi said, "if we've proved intent to kill Barbara and he's guilty on all charges, he could get life, no possibility of parole."

Parisi asked Gaines for his thoughts. Gaines had grown up under Parisi and Len respected him. Nick was a notetaker and knew every word spoken during trial. He was not afraid of grunt work and not afraid of the DA.

Nick said, "It's that old saying, 'Half a loaf is better than none.'"

"So," said Parisi. "You'd drop 'attempted murder'? Tell us why?"

"Forty years in jail is a substantial term," Nick said, "I'm comfortable there. If we *lose* on attempted murder, it might have a cascading effect. Jurors raising issues. Other verdicts of not guilty on the lesser charges."

Parisi said, "I see. Yuki?"

"I'm thinking about bread. Half a loaf. Whole loaf. Or none."

Nick was nodding. Len was looking at Yuki.

Yuki said, "You know what? I'm going to take what's left of the lunch recess and give myself some air. I'll be ready when Froman reconvenes."

CHAPTER 60

IT WAS TIME to meet with Judge Froman, and Yuki was swamped by a monster wave of anxiety.

Red Dog had said, "Your case. Your decision."

He held the door for her and Yuki entered the Judge's cramped chambers with Parisi behind her. Mo Switzer had preceded them and was already seated at the mini-sized meeting table. Parisi stood with his back to the wall, his hands in his jacket pockets, his XXXL size dwarfing Froman's chambers to dollhouse proportions.

The judge was behind her desk, signing papers. She looked up and smiled as Yuki took the chair across from Switzer.

"Are we ready, people? We have fifteen minutes."

Both attorneys said, "Yes, Your Honor," but what was keeping Yuki on the fence was a technicality. She'd told the jury that to be guilty of attempted murder, Sullivan's near-fatal attack on Barbara had to be *intentional*. There had to be *intent* to kill her, even if his attempt had failed.

Had they understood that they had to infer intent from Lewis Sullivan's *actions*?

She had brought those actions into the courtroom with expert witnesses and implements of torture: the chain that lashed Barbara to the sink; the knife, Gorilla Tape, bolt cutter, and other paraphernalia Sullivan had assembled prior to the assault.

Yuki had stated emphatically in her closing that Sullivan hadn't called for help, hadn't given his wife food or drink during his three-day aggravated assault, that this proved that he intended to cause her death. And she'd produced the enlarged photo of Barbara Sullivan, beaten to the verge of death.

That police photo was a witness like no other.

But it was complicated. Jurors were not lawyers, and she'd asked them to grasp a legal concept. Sullivan intended to kill Barbara. Here's what he did. Here's the proof.

The judge put down her pen and looked at Yuki.

"Ms. Castellano. What have the People decided?"

This was it. Yuki had to speak. She said, "Your Honor, after due consideration, we've decided to reject Mr. Sullivan's offer and let the jury decide all three charges."

Switzer turned his smug face to Yuki and said, "We'll inform our client."

Judge Froman said, "All right then. Please remain available to answer juror questions. You'll be contacted when they return with a verdict. Thank you, all."

The room emptied. Without exchanging pleasantries, Switzer took the elevator to the holding cells on the seventh floor where his client waited, while Yuki and Len walked past the elevator bank to the DA's offices, a hundred yards away.

When they were alone, Len asked Yuki, "You feel okay?"

"Is anxious 'okay'?"

Parisi grinned. "It's completely appropriate. I'm going out for a half hour. Watch the phone?"

"No problem."

Yuki sat at her desk with a bag of vegetable chips and a glass of iced tea. Her laptop was open and she was reading email from concerned citizens while waiting, waiting, waiting for the phone to ring with a call that the verdict was in.

Yeah, she was anxious. Juries were notoriously unpredictable, and she was making herself crazy trying to predict the unknowable. It was in their hands now. There was nothing more to do, and no point in looking back. Yuki sipped tea and quieted her mind with an affirmation:

I've done my very best for Barbara Sullivan.

CHAPTER 61

SONIA ALVAREZ AND I were tidying up for the day: scanning, printing, sorting, filing. We were talking about Evan Burke, and about Michael Brill, the college kid who'd hitched a ride in Vegas with a man who fired a .22 bullet through his head.

Alvarez said, "Where did Conklin go? I need his notes."

I called Rich from my phone and he answered on the first ring. "I'm on the way up," he said.

Alvarez and I looked over the scant data we had on Michael Brill. Now that Brill's corpse had a name, there was some information on him. He was twenty-six, attending a community college, and working late shift at a deli. He made enough money to afford a small rental apartment on Promenade Place. He had decent grades and good relationships with his parents. As far as LVMPD knew, he had no known enemies. He also didn't have a rap sheet. No drugs, no prostitution, no misbehavior of any kind. His parents had called the police the day after the big rainstorm when they couldn't reach him by phone.

I shook my head. The images of Brill's last three minutes as documented by Blackout Productions were still alive in my head.

"Brill is a dead end," Alvarez said. "I'm not making a joke."

"You spoke to the police chief?" I asked her.

Alvarez had lived and worked undercover in Vice in Vegas until she moved to San Francisco not long ago. She knew half the police force in the LVMPD, including all the cops in narcotics and homicide.

She said, "I spoke to Chief Belinky and the primary on the case. Detective Lee Kogan. I know him. Lee told me that they picked up the first guy who shot Brill. It happened just like Brill tells Blackout in the video—the guy with a truck thought Brill was a streetwalker, and when Brill realized that he backed away. And the trucker just—" Alvarez made a gun with her hand, fired off a *pyeww* gunshot.

"And sent him running right into the worst guy in the world."

Alvarez said, "As I said, a dead end. And a videotape."

That's when Conklin came through the gate.

I lifted my hand in greeting and about two seconds later, I saw from his expression that his mood had nosedived since I'd seen him earlier. When Alvarez turned, saw him, and called out, "Hey," Conklin didn't seem to hear her. He pulled out his chair and dropped into his seat.

I said, "Rich. What's wrong?"

"I can't find Cindy."

I said, "Can't find her since when?"

"I left her in bed at seven this morning. I called her after we all had coffee. She didn't answer."

"That was eight or so?"

Richie nodded.

"She went for a run," I said.

"Right. So I didn't call her again for a few hours. I thought she might have gone back to sleep."

"You called her office?"

"I called Tyler, also Barnett, also Peretti."

"Her photographer?"

"Right," said Richie. "Nobody has seen or heard from her. It's what now, six thirty-eight p.m.? She ought to have called me by now to check about dinner. Even if she left her phone in a cab, she would have called me."

I said, "Or she would have called me."

Now I was alarmed, too. Rich hadn't heard from Cindy since leaving home nearly twelve hours ago. Cindy lived on her phone. Where was she? Rich was trying her number again right now. He looked at me and held out the phone so I could hear her outgoing message. I was already weighing whether or not to put out a BOLO for Cindy with a photo we'd taken yesterday in Phoenix, when I was stopped by an email that just popped up on my screen.

The subject heading read, "Sgt. I've got Breaking News."

It was from Blackout. There was a video attached.

CHAPTER 62

CONKLIN ROLLED HIS desk chair up to mine, crowding me on my right side while Cappy squeezed me in on my left. Alvarez's fierce look warded off any attempt to take her seat and the rest of Team Blackout packed into the narrow space between the back of my desk and the wall behind it.

Brenda's voice came over the intercom.

"Lieutenant Brady is on a call. He'll be there in a minute."

Rich couldn't wait a minute. He shouted, "Damn it, Lindsay. Run it. We can play it again for Brady."

Cappy put a hand on my shoulder, a touch that felt like a hug. I was beyond terrified. When I rolled the video, Blackout would show us how he'd murdered Cindy.

The sour smell of fear radiated off Conklin—or maybe that stink was me. My hand shook as I reached out to press the key that would launch the video. By force of will, I did it.

As had happened before, my fellow travelers and I were transported to an unknown place through the eyes of a highly intelligent and sadistic killer. This time, Blackout's video glasses showed us a vast, dimly lit interior that might be a warehouse. As he glanced around, I saw two banged-up metal desks, a desk chair, stacks of cardboard cartons, iron girders overhead.

What was this place, and where was it? Ten seconds into the video, I heard the muffled sound of a woman crying. Conklin gripped the sides of the monitor and angled it toward him. Blackout's view, our view, shifted from straight ahead to around behind him and down to the floor.

There was Cindy, lying on her back wearing jeans and a baby blue sweatshirt. Her wrists were tightly cinched together with flex ties and so were her ankles. She was barefooted. Her mouth was duct taped and she struggled as Blackout gripped her wrists and pulled her behind him across the floor.

That bastard, that killer, had Cindy. I said, "Richie." But he didn't hear me. Rich was watching the room on the screen, watching Cindy. He had last seen her at their apartment this morning. This video had been made sometime in the last twelve hours. How had Blackout gotten his hands on her?

"Where is this?" Rich asked the screen and the cops clustered around the computer. No one knew.

"She's fighting back," said Cappy. "She's alive."

"We don't know that," said Conklin. He didn't look anywhere but at the screen.

Chi said, "Pause the video."

I did it.

Chi said, "What time was this made? I see no windows. No lights. Maybe there's an open door providing natural light…"

I restarted the video and watched Blackout's view close in on Cindy's face. He spoke to her in his unearthly mechanical voice.

"Don't fight me," Blackout said. "I just want to talk."

Blackout's glove entered the frame and moved toward Cindy's face. He ripped the tape from her mouth revealing a cloth gag. He dragged the gag down to her chin.

Cindy screamed, "*Let me go!*"

I knew Cindy had faced psychos before. The last time, she'd been armed. Shot a killer. This time, she was tied up. This time, she *was* the story, and if she didn't flip the script fast, Blackout would do to her what he'd done before.

Rich was riveted to the screen. He was muttering, "Talk to him, Cindy."

On-screen Blackout said to Cindy, "Shut up. No one can hear you, but I will not put up with resistance. I can kill you faster than you can yell 'help.'"

Blackout leaned down to within inches from Cindy's face. Her mascara had run down her cheeks and her mouth was white, bloodless from the lingering pressure of the gag Blackout had only just removed. Her two front teeth overlap slightly, a charming imperfection that makes her face even prettier. But now her features blurred together in naked fear. I dropped my eyes and moaned. I just couldn't take it.

Rich was panting, powerless to help Cindy, but he was a cop, my partner. I knew his thoughts. *Where was Blackout? What was he doing to Cindy right now? Was she alive? Where were they?*

I looked up again and focused on the images. Blackout's videos were typically less than four minutes long, limited by the size of the chip in his glasses. I guessed half of that time had been spent.

The killer said to Cindy, "You know Evan Burke. I want to hear all about him. Everything he told you about himself, all of your thoughts about him. Cindy, do you hear me? As long as you talk about Burke, you stay alive."

That's when Blackout dropped the camera. That is, his video glasses apparently fell to the floor.

There were dizzying seconds as the images swam free. The frames bounced as he fumbled with them, picked them up and repositioned them on his face. When they had settled, he stared at the dim light coming through the transom window, a pane of industrial glass about three feet long and one foot high. Reading the light, I saw it was dusk. Had this video been shot within the last hour? *Were they still in San Francisco?*

Blackout couldn't see us, that we were paralyzed by shock and anger, impotent, frozen in silence.

But here's what he said to me as we all stared at the image of the transom window above the latched metal door:

"Sergeant, our time is up. To be continued."

The screen went black.

CHAPTER 63

ALVAREZ SHOUTED AT my old Dell desktop, "To be continued *when?*"

Beside me, Rich kicked the desk, making the computer jump.

I looked for Brady. He came up the aisle and stopped at our desks, his eyes asking me, *What's happened?*

I briefed the boss.

"Blackout has Cindy. He sent a video."

"Has her where?"

"Don't know. But whenever he shot this, Cindy was alive."

I teed up the video for replay. Cappy made room for Brady and I stayed in my chair beside Conklin. I had to watch it again. Maybe on the second pass I'd see something we'd missed. A logo. A clock. A sign, either virtual or actual.

Brady said, "Roll it."

I tapped the arrow and the opening shot appeared. It was the dimly lit warehouse interior from Blackout's point of view. All I saw that would identify the location was that the building was not in use.

Richie rocked in his desk chair beside me. The chair had had never been oiled and the rhythmic squeaking of the springs was both apt and intolerable. He looked dazed, removed, beside himself. I wanted to do something for him, anything, but there was only one thing he needed, only one person he wanted to see.

Brady's eyes were fixed on the screen. He knew Cindy well and had always liked her. He stared, his knuckles white as he gripped the arms of the chair.

"Son of a bitch," he said.

In two minutes and thirteen seconds, it was over.

"Play it again," he said.

"Hold up, Brady. I need to check my mail."

Another untraceable email from "Unknown Sender" was waiting. The subject line of the email contained two words: "Part two." I hovered my cursor over the attachment.

I said, "Rich. You ready?"

He nodded sharply. I felt like I was cutting open his chest when I tapped open the video file. I hit Play. At first glance, the time frame appeared to have picked up from where the first video ended. We saw the large metal door. Light was still showing through the transom window, but the sky was a shade darker now. My gut told me that the video had been recorded only minutes ago.

But. There was a distinct difference between videos labeled parts one and two. Cindy wasn't in the second video. What had he done with her? Had he simply stopped looking at her? Had he moved her? The video had nearly ended and we had yet to hear from Blackout. And then the picture jumped to a new location.

Blackout was *outside* the building. I scanned the narrow wedge of his vision intently as he walked unencumbered and unimpeded at a quick pace down a narrow and empty street.

Inspector Tyler Wang said from behind me, "I know this place. It's a commercial alley between Yerba Buena Gardens and Market."

Brady said, "Wang. You and Michaels go there now. I don't know what or who you're looking for, but I pray that you'll recognize him or see a building that could be the location. Get backup from the uniform pool. I'm calling dispatch now."

My intercom buzzed: Bobby at the front desk.

He said, "I have a call for you, Sergeant. He says you're waiting to hear from him. Wouldn't give me his name and his number is blocked. He's on hold."

I said, "Have the radio room trace and record the call and then switch it over to me."

"They've got the line," Bobby said.

"Put him through."

The light on my landline console blinked. I paused for a few seconds to get my pulse down to high normal and pressed the red button.

"This is Boxer."

"Do I have your attention, Sergeant?"

The electronic wheeze was gone. It was a man's voice. To my ear, it was a generic American English accent.

"To whom am I speaking?"

"You know."

"I'm putting you on speaker," I said, trying to keep the panic below my larynx. "Please let me talk to Cindy."

"I've just sent you another video. See you in the movies."

He clicked off.

CHAPTER 64

CONKLIN FREED HIMSELF from the chair jam around my desk, then, picking up the aluminum trash can, he drop-kicked it and continued to kick it down the bullpen's center aisle. After he'd reached the far wall, I called him back.

When he was sitting beside me again, I said, "Ready?"

"Do it."

I downloaded the third video.

The on-screen location had changed dramatically. Blackout was neither in the warehouse nor the alleyway. He was in a living room at an unknown location, looking at a well-worn beige sofa. In front of the couch was a plank board coffee table with nothing on it, also no artwork or carpet or any sign that this place was occupied. There was no time stamp, no skylight, no clock on the wall. I had no sense of time or place. And if Cindy was in that room, I couldn't see or hear her.

And then Blackout did something completely unexpected and totally shocking. He took off his glasses, causing crazed zigzags and gyrations on my monitor. Then he turned the glasses around and pointed the lenses at his face. He was showing us his face! I took screenshot after screenshot, saving the pictures to a new file.

A hand fluttered in front of the lens. One of the fingers of the dark-haired white male was tattooed with the Marine Corps Eagle, Globe, and Anchor emblem, less than an inch wide.

My line rang again. Bobby, manning the desk outside Brady's office, called the radio room. He motioned to me, spinning a finger like a reel of tape on a spool. I understood. *They're on it.*

Blackout said, "Sergeant?"

"Yes." And I rephrased my last question to Blackout. "How's Cindy?"

"She's not talking," he said. It was an ambiguous answer, and I didn't like it.

I gave Conklin's arm a reassuring squeeze.

"She'll talk to me if you let her," I said.

He didn't reply. Instead, he talked about Cindy. "I read the book she wrote with Evan Burke. I read her first book, too. She was a remarkable writer."

Was? The past tense usage was either deliberate or unconscious. Or both.

"What are you saying?" I asked, as Conklin lunged toward the screen.

"I envied her, you know," he said. "I would have liked to be with Evan all those months she spent with him. What a lucky thing for her. Anyway. I've got to go."

There was the click of the phone hanging up, but the video still rolled. Blackout put on his glasses, looked at the shabby sofa. I caught a glimpse of Cindy but then she disappeared from the frame.

Music came up, a dressed-up symphonic rendition of a pop song

I remembered from childhood. My father sang it at odd times, in the car, around the house; singer Peggy Lee's version of "Is That All There Is?" The lyrics were about disillusionment after important personal events. House fire. Circus. Falling in love. The second line of each chorus: "If that's all there is my friends, then let's keep dancing."

I'm a literal person and I wanted a literal answer, not an enigma wrapped in an old-time tune. Was Blackout saying he'd killed Cindy and that it was a big disappointment? Or that every life is a disappointment and that included Cindy's?

I looked at Alvarez. She shrugged sadly as the video feed cut out. A title card appeared on-screen. It was in a large bold Arial font, white letters centered on a black ground.

It read, "Blackout out."

CHAPTER 65

IS THAT ALL there is?

Brady called out, sharply. "Boxer. Conklin."

We looked up. Brady had moved from beside me and now stood at the front of our three-desk work pod, his thumbs hooked into the belt loops of his jeans.

"Rich, I'm not gonna pad this. If you want, go down the hall and I'll find you after."

"I'm staying right here."

He said to us all, "Okay. We don't know what Blackout did with Cindy, but we do know this. In every one of his earlier videos, Blackout made his kill video for you, Lindsay. He made them to shock you. To show you his ruthlessness. To make you crazy with no-clue clues. Am I right?"

"Make this good," I said.

"Okay. I'm saying that he hasn't killed Cindy. He's fucking with us. My opinion, but I trust it. I've been saying all along, Blackout is in love with himself. If he kills Cindy he's going to send you the video, Boxer, all dressed up with his show-off music."

Bobby called out, "Lieutenant, Chief calling for you."

"I'll call him back."

Brady continued. "That's why I don't buy this 'Blackout out' sign-off. He's not out. He has her. He's playing a game but Cindy can play him back. And she will do it; piece out what she knows about Evan Burke a little at a time. He'll love that. He told her, 'Tell me about Burke. As long as you talk, you live.'"

I was nodding. I wanted Brady's take on Blackout to be right. Team Blackout gathered around Brady and our desk pod under the flickering fluorescent lights. The distant sound of traffic on the freeway filled the long pause as we waited for Brady to speak again.

"This has been about Blackout's fixation on Evan Burke all along," Brady said, "starting with the Fleets, who could've passed for Tara and Lorrie Burke. He wants Burke's attention and Cindy is the ultimate hook. We thought Cindy was his focus and now we know why. She's his connection to his so-called mentor. Blackout is not done with Cindy, not yet. But we have to work fast and smart."

"What next?" Alvarez asked.

"I'm getting to it. First, I return Clapper's call and tell him Cindy's been kidnapped. Chief has a meeting with the FBI and they'll be looking at Blackout's whole spree, starting with Hammer and the Fleets. They can't work as fast as all of us. So, we don't sleep, not yet. We have work to do."

CHAPTER 66

BRADY'S THEORY THAT Cindy was still alive brought us together and gave us hope. Rich sat up and squeezed my hand. I had no questions for Brady because I couldn't fault his reasoning. Blackout was all about his vanity and bravado. Why would he send videos of Cindy as his captive without making us witness her cinematic execution?

But it was still a theory. Cindy's body could be in a freezer, or a shipping carton, or just behind the sofa shown in Blackout's video.

Brenda went to the break room and put on a fresh pot of coffee. Brady issued orders as the night squad punched in. All twelve night owls spoke with Brady and all twelve volunteered to do whatever the lieutenant needed: man the tip line, patrol the streets, canvass Yerba Buena and Market with Blackout's photo, collect surveillance tape along the way. Brady accepted all offers.

I printed out screen captures for distribution. The warehouse interior. The transom window and the metal door. Blackout on his walk, the room with the sofa. Blackout's face, unmasked. The Marine Corps tattoo on his finger.

While Rich ran Blackout's image through all criminal databases, I called Henry Tyler at the *Chronicle* and told him that Cindy had been abducted. He adored Cindy and for good reasons, not all of them commercial. Tyler's young daughter had herself been kidnapped years ago and Cindy had brought her home.

I said, "Mr. Tyler. We need your front page."

"Whatever you need," Tyler said, "you've got it."

I asked him to please call his contacts at TV news stations and refer them to us.

I felt Richie's desperation as he uploaded Blackout's selfie into our facial recognition program.

Hit or no hit?

No hit.

A prolific killer with real competence and yet no image in the database. Why not?

Brenda set up a conference call with investigators in Marin, Pasadena, and Phoenix. Brady took the call in his office, and I texted Joe.

Late night on the Job. Don't wait up. xox L

I called Yuki to let her know that Brady and the rest of us would be working late tonight. She asked why. But I couldn't tell her. "Top secret," I said. I'd leave it to her husband, Brady, to break the news. "Hope you get a guilty, guilty, guilty verdict, Yuki. Talk tomorrow."

Team Blackout strategized. Cappy knew every cop over the age of forty in San Francisco while Chi, Wang, and Michaels knew the younger generation. They texted, sent photos to cops and CIs. Alvarez has deep roots in Vegas and Reno and she became our Nevada point person.

Brady went upstairs to catch Clapper before he left the Hall, and I went downstairs to the ME's office to tell Claire about Cindy.

She was shocked and horrified at all of it; our feisty friend, kidnapped by a killer who'd left videos without clues, not even letting us know if she was still alive.

Claire asked, "What can I do? Is there anything I can do?"

"Not yet."

I showed her the screenshots but none of them were familiar to her. Then, while looking at the photo of Blackout's face, she said, "His eyelids look tight. He's a young guy but he's had work done. I can't see the sides of his face but I'll bet he had a full lift."

"Good catch," I said. It wasn't a clue that led to a location or a suspect, but it might cinch it if we found a person of interest. I told her that I had to go back to work and to keep her phone charged. I hugged her hard before running out the door.

CHAPTER 67

BY THE TIME I'd returned to the squad room, Blackout's video with Cindy had been forwarded to police captains and homicide lieutenants up and down the state of California and beyond. A major network was broadcasting a live breaking news report with the familiar anchor looking authoritatively into the camera's eye. He said, *"Best-selling author and crime reporter Cindy Thomas has been abducted. Do you know this man? Have you seen Cindy? Call this number."*

According to Brady, Clapper had uploaded the execution videos and the latest of one of Cindy, added our notes, and sent the package to the local FBI section chief, Craig Steinmetz. I knew Craig through Joe. He was first-class.

I was buoyed by the energy of our squad, the determination to bring my dear friend home. At just after midnight, Brady thanked the day shift and said he'd see them in the morning. He called Rich and me into his office and turned on the desk light, motioned for us to sit down.

"Lindsay, you feel that you can objectively work this case?"

"Absolutely, Brady. I'm all in."

He said, "I've spoken to Warden Hauser. You and I have an early morning date with Evan Burke. Rich, I know you want to be on this case, but I'm using my best judgment here. You're too personally involved, gotta be. But I need you to manage the department while I'm out with Lindsay tomorrow. Coordinate between me and this crew and I promise to keep you looped in. Okay?"

Rich nodded his agreement, but he was scowling. I knew that for him to step off the case as it involved Cindy was killing him. It had been five hours since Blackout had emailed me the video of showing him dragging Cindy behind him, stopping to rip off her gag, giving her direct orders. *As long as you talk about Burke, you stay alive.*

Had she talked?

Rich and I left the Hall together. I asked if he wanted to come home with me, kick it all around with Joe.

"I need to go home," he said. "Thanks, Lindsay."

I walked with Rich to his car parked in the All-Day parking lot across from 850 Bryant and watched him drive off. He was going home to an empty house, an empty bed. This wasn't supposed to happen.

I got into my car and called Joe.

He stayed on the line with me as I drove home.

CHAPTER 68

AT SEVEN THE next morning, Brady phoned me from the
street. I geared up, kissed Julie and her stuffed cow toy, put my
arms around Joe, and pressed my cheek to his chest. He gave me a
long strong hug and told me not to be alone with Burke for even a
second. I promised. He kissed me goodbye.

I jogged down the stairs and ducked into the passenger seat of
the white late-model SFPD SUV parked in front of our building.
Brady told me to buckle up. He looked tired, which partly explained
the two coffee containers in the cup holders and the bag of
donuts on the console between us. This would be my second
cup, but the caffeine and sugar would rev my engine. The radio
was squawking out calls to and from dispatch. I dialed down the
volume and opened my container of heavily sugared black
Colombian.

It was thirty miles to San Quentin and I barely noticed the sce-
nic wonders of the bay, the bridge, the sea pounding the shoreline.
Light rain was falling as we boarded the Larkspur Ferry, and

within moments the rain picked up with a blast of wind, stirring up a strong chop on the bay.

Brady and I sat in a middle row, loosely scripting this hoped-for meeting with Burke. We had no other leads and the outcome couldn't be predicted. Burke could refuse to see us or rush to see us; play ball or refuse to leave his cell. We knew Burke was a master manipulator. A god in his own mind. A monster in ours.

I checked in with Richie before we reached shore.

His voice was hoarse. He told me he'd been on the phone with his parents and sibs in the hours after midnight.

I asked, "Did you sleep?"

He said, "Something like sleep. Somewhere between comatose and being hooked up to a car battery."

"Aw, geez, Rich."

Alvarez joined the call. She said, "I dreamed."

"Of shooting Burke?"

"You, too?"

Brady was on his phone, looking out over the bay as we closed in on the wharf. I took a mirror from my handbag, applied concealer under my eyes, and finger-combed my wind-whipped hair. And I thought about Cindy. I remembered my trip with her to Phoenix two days ago. The flippy jersey dress that she'd worn. How she'd laughed. How much she'd enjoyed the applause. I remembered our dinner at the airport, getting the plane that night. How happy I'd felt getting Cindy safely the hell out of town.

Brady came over and joined me.

He said, "Yuki's on jury watch today."

"I know. I didn't tell her about Cindy. I didn't want to throw her off her game."

"She knows," said Brady.

I nodded.

Brady said, "We're going to get Cindy back."

I looked at my knees and said, "I know."

If anyone could bring Cindy home, it was Conklin, Brady, and me.

CHAPTER 69

BRADY AND I sat outside the screened-in interview cage in the maximum-security wing. Burke was seated inside, handcuffs and shackles linked to a chain around his waist. Prisoners had a choice of uniform; denim and chambray, or a one-piece orange jumpsuit. Burke wore blue, the words "San Quentin State Prison" stitched over the breast pocket and stenciled down the left leg of the pants.

"My dress blues," he said.

He had shaved his head since we'd seen him three days ago. I saw the lines and angles of his features knowing that this wasn't quite the face he'd been assigned at birth. The cosmetic work he'd had done more than once had allowed him to slide unrecognized past CCTV cameras in stores, on the street, at highway toll booth cameras and cash machines. He'd legally changed his name to Jake Winslow, giving him another layer of invisibility.

Claire had seen signs of plastic surgery around Blackout's eyes. I wondered if, like Burke, Blackout had changed his face to thwart criminal databases and facial rec.

Both Blackout and Burke loved control over life and death. In our previous meeting with Burke, he'd said that he'd give anything to be Blackout for a day. *Dream on, buddy.*

Burke ran his twinkling eyes up and down my body, pausing at my Kevlar vest and SFPD windbreaker. I didn't wait for an invitation to speak and got right to it.

"Mr. Burke—"

"We're old friends, right? Call me Evan and I'll call you Lindsay."

That psychopathic serial-killer charm again.

"Evan. The warden says you get visitors. Gene Harris. Who is he?"

"He's some kind of ad guy. He wanted to take my picture as I remember. Run a clickbait thing online. I refused."

"Because?"

"Because it cheapens the value of *You Never Knew Me.* It's a bestseller, you know."

"How about Marvin Bender?" I said, referring to the pharmaceutical salesman known around the bullpen as the baked-potato man. "Do you know him?"

"No. Yes. Wait. I think I got some fan mail from him, asking for advice on a true-crime book he's trying to write."

"Did you write back?"

"Hell, no. I despise mail. The kind I get. And thanks for having my laptop removed."

Brady said, "We have no authority here, Burke."

"Tremendous coincidence, Lieutenant. You were here. End of day, there's been a security breach and my laptop with no Wi-Fi capability was carted out of my cell."

Brady said, "I know nothing about it."

"Moving past your lies, Brady. Jackson, isn't it? Jack. You want to find Cindy. I know she's been kidnapped. I may have lost my computer, but I still have my TV and radio, so I've been following the news. I might help you under certain conditions. Bulletproof conditions."

Brady said, "Keep in mind we cannot commute your sentence. We cannot give you freedom of any kind. We're cops, Burke. SFPD cops."

"How about dinner? Can you get me out of here for a real fine meal? With security, of course. Do that, and I'll take you to view Cindy."

I asked, "You know where she is?" I heard my voice. It was shrill.

"Little birds. This place is full of them. I could work my connections," he said, "but right now, I don't know if she's still breathing."

"We'll get back to you," said Brady.

"Don't take too long," Burke taunted.

Brady called for the guards and we walked away from the cage to the clanking sounds of cuffs and shackles behind us. I was beyond apprehensive. Could we get Burke out of prison for a meal? Would he take us to Cindy?

An image of Cindy came to me. Like many of Burke's victims, she was lying fully dressed in a shallow grave.

CHAPTER 70

BRADY AND I had a meeting in a hallway beyond Burke's hearing and agreed we needed proof of life before we could even try to negotiate a deal. We went back to Burke and Brady gave him the conditions. "Proof of life and you get a great meal."

Burke said, "I know what Cindy's wearing. Baby-blue sweatshirt."

That detail had never been broadcast on the news. I knew it. Brady knew it.

Brady said, "I'll give you some further incentive. Takeout from a five-star steak house, direct to the Q. What do you want to see on your tray?"

Burke replied as if he was speaking to a waiter.

"Steak, bleu. Potatoes au gratin. Field greens. Hot rolls. A bottle of a French cabernet. Chocolate for dessert. Chef's choice."

Brady and I took the ferry to Larkspur and from there, drove to Mario's Steakhouse. We ordered lunch for ourselves and takeout for Burke. When we returned to the prison, Burke was back in the cage, cuffed and shackled and looking pleased to see us. Guard

Tim Mitchell set up Burke's tray, tucked the napkin into the neckline of his blue shirt and said, "Bon appetit."

"Merci." Burke sipped from his cup. "Hey, what's this?"

Brady said, "I tried. Wine is not permitted. That's Coke, the real thing. I hear it's your beverage of choice."

"There is no substitute for a good cab," he said.

"Try the steak," I said.

The steak had been pre-sliced and the utensils were plastic. That was as far as we could go. Burke talked about his kills while consuming his meal. He was particularly proud of a woman and her teenaged daughter he'd killed in a parking lot and had buried together in the same grave.

"They looked like angels," he said. "I posed them so that she had her arms around her child. Very satisfying. You won't find that story in Cindy's version of my life, you know."

He was spooning up chocolate mousse while telling us about some of the famous prisoners still incarcerated at San Quentin.

"They won't let me talk with them, of course. But I know about them and I've added up all their kills. Who do you think has the most notches in his belt?"

He looked up and gave us a sicko wink.

"That's right. It's me," he said, delighted with himself.

He was an entertaining speaker but I wasn't amused. I was barely able to keep my fury in check while sitting across from him.

Burke was saying about Cindy, "I picked the right writer, for sure. But I didn't tell her everything."

Brady said, "Who'd you leave out?"

Burke laughed and said, "You're going to have to wait. If I get my computer back, I'll be finishing my book by the end of the year.

Let the victims' families try to sue me for the profits. There will be plenty to go around."

With cuffs jangling, Burke put his tray on the floor and called for the guard standing outside the cage.

"You can take me back now, Mitchell. We're done here. Lindsay, if you ever see Cindy, tell her I said hi."

Mitchell lifted Burke out of his chair by his armpits.

Brady and I turned our backs as we'd done before. We didn't call Burke names, didn't give him a card or offer another "incentive." We walked twenty yards to the door to the corridor. It beeped, opened, and we were escorted out.

Brady and I didn't speak until we were walking down the ramp toward the ferry slip. Brady looked at the schedule. "We're in luck," he said. "Next ferry in thirty-five minutes."

"Perfect," I said.

I couldn't read Brady, but as for me, I regretted not getting Burke out of the Q and into a restaurant. If we'd done the impossible, we might have a lead to Cindy's whereabouts.

So, I was depressed. Burke had played us and if he knew where Cindy was, he was never going to give it up. It had been a wasted trip, but as we walked out toward the ferry the rainy weather had cleared and the image of Burke being lifted up like a doll in chains felt a lot better than a kick in the butt.

I sent my mind back to Blackout. There was still plenty of day left. With about a hundred cops looking for Cindy, there might be news back at the Hall.

CHAPTER 71

AT NINE THURSDAY morning, Yuki had gotten the call that the jury had reached a verdict, and by that afternoon, Yuki and Nick Gaines were at the prosecution table across the aisle from Mo Switzer and Lewis Sullivan. Barbara sat in her wheelchair on the outside aisle. Judge Froman was at the bench and the room was quiet as the jury filed in and took their places.

Yuki held her clenched hands below the table out of sight, but her eyes were on the jurors. She studied their faces, looking for tells, anything that would give her a hint as to their decision. She particularly looked at the foreman, George Campbell.

Campbell was retired now, but he had been a high school science teacher for forty years. During voir dire, Campbell had told the attorneys that he always followed the facts. Had Campbell been satisfied with the prosecution case? As if he felt her eyes on him, Campbell turned his head to look at Yuki. Yuki didn't look away, didn't smile or frown, just met his gaze and for several moments they maintained their distant connection; her dark eyes fixed on his blue ones.

This stalemate was broken by Judge Froman's voice sounding through the small courtroom.

"Will the defendant please stand."

Lewis Sullivan did as requested and his attorney stood beside him. The judge addressed the jury.

"Mr. Foreman, has the jury reached a verdict?"

Campbell stood. "We have, Your Honor."

The bailiff crossed to the jury box, received the single page with the decision. Campbell continued to stand as the bailiff carried the verdict to the judge. Froman examined the single page with a small amount of hand printing, decisions that would impact Barbara Sullivan directly, as well as people all over the country who would take comfort or become enraged by the decision of these twelve men and women, good and true.

Froman passed the verdict back to the bailiff who returned it to the foreman.

Froman asked, "On count one, endangerment of the minor child Kenneth Sullivan, how do you find?"

"Guilty, Your Honor."

"On count two, endangerment of minor child, Stephen Sullivan, how does the jury find?"

"Guilty, Your Honor."

Judge Froman adjusted her glasses. "On count three, aggravated assault of Barbara Sullivan. How do you find?"

"We find the defendant guilty, Your Honor."

Yuki clenched her fists, her fingernails making half-moon cuts in the palms of her hands as Judge Karen Froman asked, "And on the count of attempted murder of Barbara Sullivan, how does the jury find?"

If a circus had entered the courtroom with clowns and acrobats and trumpeting elephants, they wouldn't have thrown Yuki's concentration off the jury foreman.

Campbell, on the other hand, seemed confident and assured as he said, "We find the defendant, Lewis Sullivan, guilty as charged, Your Honor."

That was it.

Everything that Yuki had been working toward had come home: guilty on all counts. Guilty.

Lewis Sullivan had a different reaction. Turning to face the gallery, screaming, "You bitch!" at Barbara, only a few lunges away from her husband.

Court officers moved in on Sullivan, cuffed him, and took him toward the side exit. As Sullivan was led away, he shouted, "We'll appeal! With what we have on you, Barbara, the verdict will be overturned. I'll see you soon, sweetie. Love you..."

Judge Froman dismissed the court. Yuki stood. Len Parisi appeared at her elbow and Nick pulled back her chair. Together they left the room. By pure reflex, Yuki looked for Cindy as she and the prosecution left through the rear doors. That's where Cindy usually positioned herself. Electrical outlet. Wide view. Easy exit. Cindy wasn't there, but Yuki's husband, Jackson Brady, was.

He reached for her, put his arms around her and pulled her to him. "Great job," he said. "Congratulations, honey."

Brady shook Len's and Nicky's hands as they cleared the doorway, then steered Yuki into a niche in the corridor.

"How do you feel now?" he asked her.

She felt light-headed, as if she might faint and float away.

"There's still the sentencing hearing," she said to her husband. "I can't read the judge at all."

Yuki heard someone call her name. She looked and saw the bailiff pushing Barbara Sullivan toward her in her wheelchair.

"Barbara, this is my husband, Lieutenant Jackson Brady."

After the greetings and handshakes and *nice to meet yous*, Yuki looked up into Brady's face.

"Thanks for coming, Brady. I've got to get Barbara out of here. I'll see you tonight."

CHAPTER 72

BACK AT THE Hall at two thirty Thursday afternoon, I found Rich sitting behind Brady's tidy desk. Rich got to his feet, and I asked if anything had come in while we were out.

"I eliminated some filters on the facial rec hoping we'd get an array of men looking something like Blackout. Didn't matter. He still doesn't exist," he said.

"And Burke?" he asked us.

"Gave us the middle finger," I said. "I'll fill you in."

Rich and I walked back to our desks. I greeted Alvarez and briefed her and Rich on our dead-end excursion to and from San Quentin.

"Steak and potatoes with Burke's usual BS for dessert. Burke knew one unreported detail—what Cindy was wearing when she was kidnapped—but no real news. We were prepared for the Burke shit show and still fell for it."

Richie's face sagged.

"No, listen," I said. "We've just begun to fight."

He nodded, but he was well aware that when it came to kidnapping, the clock was running out.

I said, "When we were with Burke, I remembered that he'd had work done on his face. Claire thinks Blackout took a page out of Burke's plastic surgery playbook."

"That might explain why I get no hits," said Richie.

Alvarez said, "Cappy got some surveillance tape from the Bay Pharmacy two blocks north of where Rich and Cindy live. Yesterday Cindy came in at eight thirteen a.m., bought some lip balm, and left. She was on the phone, had her computer with her, same jeans and baby-blue sweatshirt she was wearing on the Blackout tape. It's not much, but it's a time stamp."

Bobby brought over a call-in sheet saying, "I just got a hang-up from a no-name caller," he said. "I said, 'hello, hello, hello' and he terminated the call. Check your mail."

I turned on my computer, started at the top of my office mail inbox and the message at the top carried the subject line "Blackout."

Rich peered at my monitor, then scootched his chair closer to mine. I opened the mail. There was no message, but there was a video attachment. I hesitated. Rich was right beside me. God only knew what door to hell I could be opening. Rich reached out a finger, downloaded the video, then pressed Play.

The video bloomed on my monitor. Blackout was talking to the camera in his normal, undisguised voice. He was sitting in an armchair, holding his video glasses loosely by an earpiece so that the glasses swung in his hand, swooping past his face, showing us the ceiling light, beige sofa, dingy white walls, the bookcase behind the chair where he sat with one blue-jeaned leg crossed over the other.

Alvarez said, "Take screenshots, Lindsay."

I captured a nanosecond of Blackout fooling with his glasses. Then he put them back on his face and looked around the room. I kept saving screenshots, scrutinized every inch of the scene, boosted the volume, and still there was neither sight nor sound of Cindy.

And then Blackout spoke to me.

"Hey there, Sergeant. I hope you can see and hear me because I may have an offer for you. See this?"

He held up his cell phone, Apple variety.

"I'll be able to tell when you open my email, so expect me to call you soon after," he said.

The video went black. I looked over at Bobby and he waited for the call, with the radio room on standby. But it was my cell phone that rang. Blackout had my goddamn cell number. Must have gotten it from Cindy's phone.

My phone rang again. I noticed that the caller ID read, "spam?$"

I put the phone on speaker and said, "This is Boxer."

"I'm enjoying Cindy's company," Blackout said, continuing to use his normal speaking voice, "but I'm thinking of making a trade, but we might have to negotiate more. I don't like the deal."

"What have you done with her?"

"How much would you like to see her, Sergeant? I'm working on a plan in honor of my mentor, Burke."

I said, "Why don't you give me a hint?"

"Here's the hint," he said. "Keep your phone on. I'll call you. I don't know when."

As he'd done before, he hung up. The line went dead.

CHAPTER 73

IF THERE WAS ever the time for a Women's Murder Club meeting, this was it. But not at Susie's. Not without Cindy. There's a coffee shop near City Hall called Grumpy Lynn's. Claire, Yuki, Alvarez, and I piled into my Explorer and headed east on Bryant to McAllister. It was just five on Thursday when we arrived at Lynn's. The bell over the door dinged as we pushed our way inside the little diner, which was decorated with red linoleum-topped tables, customer artwork on the walls, and redolent with the aromas of French fries and bacon cheeseburgers.

The lunch crowd was long gone. A couple of men were seated separately at the counter having meat loaf and mash, watching a ball game. We took a table by the front window and Lynn pointed to the sign above the cash register: WE CLOSE AT SIX.

She swiped at the table with a rag and handed out menus. One after another, we ordered coffee.

Claire sat beside me. She was wearing pink, a good color on her, but she looked beat. She had autopsied several of Blackout's victims, including Baby Josie Fleet, in addition to a few hundred other dead people this year. But Claire never got numb to the fact of death.

She opened the photo app on her phone and showed Alvarez a group picture of the Women's Murder Club standing around me, with newborn Julie Anne Molinari in my arms.

"See Cindy, hogging the camera?" Claire laughed. "Look at her."

Having seen the last known images of Cindy being dragged across a cement floor by a murdering psychopath, I felt tears welling up, spilling over. Claire closed the app and took my hand. Then she pulled a half-inch of paper napkins from the holder and pressed them to her own eyes.

Across from me, Yuki looked like she'd fallen down a well. She was sleepless from championing a woman who'd been unimaginably tortured and had barely survived. I knew Yuki was second-guessing herself as she waited for sentencing. She's physically small, but as she always did, she'd put her whole self into this case. She was in the headlines again and had to win, whatever the psychological cost to herself. And now there was fresh worry over Cindy in captivity—or worse.

Yuki told Sonia about Cindy's fearless investigative crime reporting at the *Chronicle*, how she'd once shot a killer, herself.

She said, "I don't know how Cindy lived through writing that book with Burke, that monster, but I don't have to tell *you* about Burke."

Alvarez and I had been moments from being Burke's victims ourselves, an event that involved gunfire in the dark, an all-sensory memory that would haunt the two of us forever.

Grumpy Lynn offered cherry pie and Claire and Yuki were takers. I sipped coffee and looked at my friends, thinking how hard we all pushed ourselves. We were trained, tested again and again, and that made us feel invincible. But we surely weren't. I thought we were all measuring the infinitesimal space between life and death, and there were no good vibes to be had. We weren't at Susie's, and Cindy wasn't with us.

It was Sonia who shifted the mood, saying, "Blackout's thirst for the kill is so much like Burke's, I'm actually feeling like I know him."

Claire said, "Can you talk about that?"

CHAPTER 74

I WAS RELIEVED when Alvarez took the talking stick. She'd never known Cindy the way Claire, Yuki, and I did and yet she was as involved as we were in getting her back and in locking up the psycho who called himself Blackout.

"He's wicked smart," Alvarez said of Blackout. "I'm talking high genius. He killed six people in fourteen days. But did he have help? In the most recent video, he called Burke his 'mentor.'"

I said, "True. Our knowledge base is evolving by micrometers. But we know that Blackout is a fan of Evan Burke."

Alvarez took a folded sheaf of paper out of her jacket pocket.

"Okay, Lindsay?" she asked me.

I looked around. The diners at the counter had left. Lynn was in the kitchen. We had the place to ourselves. "Sure."

Sonia unfolded photocopies of the screenshots I'd taken this afternoon and put them in the center of the table.

My newest partner said, "We have no background on him. Nothing. But by assessing his methods, I can say with confidence he's an extremely careful SOB. Professional grade. He likes to kill with his hands, but he's not opposed to garrotes, stun guns, and handguns. And he's a braggart. Blackout has sent Lindsay hard evidence of him committing murder. Of half of his known victims, anyway. Who in their right mind has the balls to do that?"

Yuki asked, "Why only half?"

"Don't know," said Alvarez. "Maybe it was a late-breaking idea. Or he recorded them all and only started sending them once Cindy did her book signing in Corte Madera. His kills in Pasadena and Vegas were local to where Cindy had book signings. We were sure this freak had Cindy on his kill list.

"But apart from those signings, we never found a closer connection to Cindy until the day she disappeared."

Yuki had a well-honed prosecutor's ability to screen out all but the indictable specifics.

She said, "So, from what I understand, discounting the homage to Burke, you haven't found motives for any of the murders."

"Let's build on what we know," I said. "He called Burke 'his mentor' and wants Cindy to give him information about Burke like no one else. She's a direct link to Burke, and Blackout sent a video of himself threatening her. He said that as long as she talks about Burke, she'll live."

"When was this?" Yuki asked.

"Lindsay just took these screenshots this afternoon."

Sonia Alvarez is an exceptional cop and was as interested as Yuki in what she saw in these images. We all focused on the printouts.

"He could be keeping Cindy here—wherever 'here' is—or this could be a red herring location," Alvarez said. "He shoots his videos with his glasses, so this is his view of the sofa. Here, he's twirling the glasses in his hand..."

"That's him?" Yuki asked, pulling one of the photocopies closer to her.

"Yep," said Alvarez. "Claire thinks he may have had work done on his face. I'm interested in this," Alvarez said of the swooping shot of the bookcase behind Blackout's chair. "I enlarged it so I could read the book titles and they cover a wide range of subjects. Criminology, classical music, physics, calculus, military history. More books on music, and here, biographies of great creative geniuses of Western Civilization."

"He could have bought the lot at a tag sale," Yuki cautioned.

"I agree," said Alvarez. "And this room could be a rental or abandoned or who knows. But if it's his, Blackout's reading range is a full circle. He's a polymath."

"What's that?" I asked.

"He's knowledgeable in a lot of different areas of learning. If this is Blackout's library, it's a screenshot of his mind."

CHAPTER 75

IT WAS AFTER seven that evening and I was home with Martha. I'd set the table, thrown the whites into the wash, and taken a quick shower. Claire had gifted me with an extra-large lavender-blue T-shirt, and I'd pulled it on over sweatpants. I fed Martha, then got into my big chair and closed my eyes.

Joe was out with Julie, picking up takeout dinner from Lucky Duck Best Chinese Food. I wasn't even slightly hungry, but I could still push rice around my plate with chopsticks, distracting my daughter so that she didn't read my mind. I could no longer read my own mind. It was that freaking chaotic inside my head.

Cindy had been missing for three days and it had been five hours since I'd heard from Blackout as if his email, video, and phone call were a ticking box of roses delivered to my desk.

I dozed off in the chair and was awoken by a blast of exuberance: Joe calling me, Martha woofing, Julie singing "Mommy we are home" to the tune of "Dashing through the snow." I got up and hugged her, took the bags of food from Joe, and as he made tea, I dished up the shrimp with broccoli and chicken yat gaw mein. As we exchanged looks, I noticed that Joe's expression mirrored my own.

He looked confused, worried, and like he had something to tell me.

I asked Julie to wash up before dinner, please, and signaled to Joe that we should go to his home office. Once inside, I closed the door.

"What's up?" I asked him.

"Short version for now," he said. "Blackout posted a video on YouTube."

"No."

Joe took out his phone, tapped on the screen, and said, "Brace yourself, Blondie."

He handed me the phone.

CHAPTER 76

I DIDN'T KNOW how much more bracing I could stand. Was I about to watch Blackout murder Cindy? But the image on the small screen was not of Blackout at all. It was of a woman tightly tucked in a sitting position, knees up, head down, inside the kneehole of an old desk. This could have been one of the metal desks we'd seen in Blackout's warehouse videos.

Was it really Cindy?

What I could see of the woman's hair looked blond. She appeared to be wearing jeans and the baby-blue sweatshirt she'd worn when Blackout dragged her across the floor. Was she alive? I couldn't tell. Blackout appeared, unmasked and his natural voice came up under the photo. This is what the YouTube audience had seen and heard.

He said, "Heads up to Warden Hauser and Sergeant Boxer. Here's the deal. You spring Evan Burke and I'll tell you where to find Cindy Thomas. I'll call you, Sergeant."

Blackout's face was replaced with a close-up of Cindy at the Poisoned Pen signing. This was exactly as I remembered her;

sitting behind a card table heavily stacked with books, pen in hand, smiling up at a reader. She looked radiant.

Joe said, "This has gone viral. It's on TV news, too."

I found my phone on the sink in the bathroom, battery dead. I took it to the living room, plugged it in, and found missed calls. Oh, my God, oh my God, they were all worried. Henry Tyler, Brady, Alvarez, Clapper, Claire, and three calls from Richie.

Julie was at the table banging her fork against the side of her plate.

"You have to feed me. It's your job."

I did my best to eat fast while tasting nothing.

Cindy, Cindy, Cindy.

I kept seeing her at that table, signing copies of *You Never Knew Me,* smiling up at her fans. I'd seen no danger. Not a bit. Blackout must have taken this photo from Cindy's phone. Or had Blackout been inside the store, standing right next to me?

Twenty minutes later, Julie was in her daddy's chair watching the Disney Channel and I had Joe to myself again.

We spoke across the table.

Joe said, "Steinmetz is putting me on this case as a nine-to-five liaison between the bureau and your team. Blackout is radioactive and he will not stop until he is caught."

"Joe. Is she still alive?"

"I think so but who knows? He likes the attention. And he's slick. We don't know where he is, who he is, but we've got manpower to throw against him now that Steinmetz is on board."

That night, after I tossed, flopped around, kicked off blankets to the point of waking Joe, I took my phone into the living room. In between returning calls, I read stories about Cindy in news feeds and newspapers across the country. *All about Cindy Thomas. How had she been captured? Who was she to the fugitive Blackout? Police are turning over every stone.*

Dawn lit up Lake Street. I felt half dead, but I couldn't wait to get to work.

CHAPTER 77

BY TEN THAT morning, Brady and I—along with Team Blackout and two FBI special agents—were in our war room, that depressing corner office lined with dirty windows and morgue shots taped to whiteboards leaning against the southern wall.

The FBI liaisons were Joe and his former partner Mike Wallenger, both of whom had started their careers with the Behavioral Science Unit at Quantico. Mike was bearded, pushing fifty, and at six three as big as Joe. The last time I'd seen Mike, we were at the flash point of a major drug sting involving tunnels from Tijuana to San Diego, hundreds of kilos of fentanyl and a half dozen refrigerated trucks loaded with trafficked military weapons.

All told, six people had died.

But this was a different time and instead of drug mules and FBI sharpshooters, we were faced with one anonymous killer who was using me as his conduit to the cops, and Cindy as the bait.

As team leader, I began the meeting with a review of the Blackout tapes that had been combined into one horrible sequential reel. It started with Ralph Hammer getting his head blown apart, continued through the killing in Pasadena and inside the car outside Vegas. Then Blackout's warehouse and apartment series and closing with his offer.

Burke for Cindy.

On our demand for proof of life, Blackout was silent.

Wallenger asked me to run the video again, pausing when he and Joe asked me to stop the forward motion for closer looks. They noted Blackout's methods, checked off the murder locations of the scenes on maps. This was all old news to me, but Wallenger had fresh eyes on the victims and the crime scenes. There was a chance he would see something we'd missed, but our most current "lead" was yesterday's news: Blackout's worship of Evan Burke.

Today we had federal backup and Henry Tyler had offered a twenty-five-thousand-dollar reward for information leading to the recovery of Cindy Thomas, no questions asked.

All we needed was a plan of action. But until I heard from Blackout, we couldn't even draft one.

CHAPTER 78

BRADY SAID, "MIKE, Joe, I'd like to hear your thoughts."

Wallenger said, "Okay, sure."

He took off his jacket, hung it over the back of his chair, and I pressed Record on my phone.

The senior FBI special agent said, "We've got unimpeachable video evidence of Blackout committing multiple murders including one showing that he has or had Ms. Thomas in a warehouse, location unknown. From what I saw, this guy is strong, fairly young, and proficient with a number of weapons. That leads me to think he may have been trained in the military, any service and really any country.

"This series of unrelated kills, including an unarmed woman and particularly one with an infant speaks to psychopathy. We know that not all psychopaths are murderers, and not all murderers are psychopaths, but psychopathy is a hallmark of serials. In other words, he doesn't give a damn about human life. He gets off on the thrill of the kill."

Wallenger continued. "From watching Blackout do his murders, he doesn't have a preferred victim type."

"The Fleets were an offering of some sort to Evan Burke," I said. "From the autopsy notes on Johnston, he didn't die fast. His killer used two weapons to put him down. The woman in Pasadena and the man outside Vegas were victims of opportunity."

Joe added, "Blackout's been careful. Again that goes to a possible military background. There was little traffic, pedestrian or auto, when he's taken his victims. He wears gloves and leaves no forensic evidence behind.

"Taking life with his hands, with or without a weapon, is what turns him on. Getting Burke's attention seems to drive him. Does he want Burke's approval or is this a competition in Blackout's mind? Is he trying to demonstrate that he's worthy or *better*? That he's the man."

Wallenger and Joe made sense, but we had little to go on. Chi and Michaels found nothing in the alley where Blackout may have been spotted. The SFPD radio room was trying and failing to trace Blackout's calls, leaving his real name and location still unknown. And we had no leads to Cindy.

There was a knock on the door. Brady opened it for Brenda. I was expecting lunch but Brenda handed me a note that read, "Blackout just called. He's sent you another video."

CHAPTER 79

I CLICKED ON the latest email from Blackout, subject header "Blackout Calling." There was no note. With Joe beside me and the team looking over my shoulders, I downloaded the video.

I was in Blackout's head, looking through his eyes. The ambient light was dim. It was early. Before dawn. It took a moment for me to realize that Blackout was inside a car, looking into a rearview mirror. The reflection in the glass was of Victorian row houses behind and across the street from his car.

Blackout's gloved hand came into the frame and he adjusted the mirror so that it was centered on several flights of wooden stairs. A figure was descending them, a woman with long, dark hair. Joe reached out a finger and pointed, saying, "There's the baby."

Got it. This was Catherine and Josie Fleet. And they were coming down a path I knew. "Macondray Lane," I said of the picturesque tree-lined path down the steep hill from Leavenworth that joined with the stairs and ended on Taylor Street.

Now, Blackout was on the move. The driver's door opened and we watched from his point of view as he crossed Taylor on course to intersect paths with Catherine Fleet.

Blackout's view of Catherine on the staircase bobbed as he strode across toward her, reaching the steps and starting up. And then he fell. I saw Catherine's boots on the wooden treads. He looked up past her trousers and the baby in a carrier on her chest. He focused on Catherine Fleet's face. I saw concern there and heard it in her voice.

"Oh, my gosh, are you all right?"

Again the images swooped and jostled. Blackout was struggling to his feet.

"I'm good," said Blackout. "Embarrassed is all. I try to impress with finesse."

I thought, "*Don't fall for it*," even as I knew she had.

I didn't fully see what happened next because of the camera's choppy movement. And then I saw Blackout's gloved fist fill the frame. I thought he was going to punch Catherine until I saw the canister in his grip. He pressed the lever with his thumb, sending a fine spray into the woman's eyes. She cried out and sat down hard, asking what he had done to her.

Blackout didn't answer, and the camera view whipped from her face to the stairs above, to the street below and back to Catherine. He was checking for witnesses while she was trying to get the pepper spray out of her eyes. The baby screamed and the video kept rolling.

Blackout was behind Catherine now, his left biceps were a vise around her neck. He spoke softly, gently. *Don't fight me, Catherine. It'll all be over soon. Shhh, shhh, I've got you.*

He brought his right arm around and pulled on his left fist, tightening his grip around Catherine's neck and pressing on it with his full weight as the baby wailed. All the life drained from Catherine.

Blackout picked her up, carried her in his arms with the crying baby still strapped to her chest. He crossed to his car. It was a gray Ford sedan but he didn't look at the plates so I didn't get a glimpse of a number or a letter or even if it was a California tag. His eyes were on the unlatched trunk.

He worked the trunk lid open with his foot and laid the dead woman into a nest of blankets. Little Josephina Fleet screamed. Blackout reached in to finish off the baby when a voice called out.

Blackout swung his gaze away from the woman and child and located the voice in the predawn light. Maybe fifteen feet away, just downhill from where Blackout stood at the rear of his car, was an elderly man in shorts and a tennis shirt, a phone in his hand.

"Pardon me. Do you need some help there?"

"Enter Jacob Johnston," said Cappy.

The man's expression changed from "Do you need help?" to understanding. He was witnessing a crime.

The video cut out.

My phone rang and I picked up.

Blackout's distorted video voice came over my phone.

"Sergeant? How do you like it?"

"Why did you send it *now*?"

"I wanted you to see, that's why. My best video so far, I think. My homage to Burke. But look. I've already told you to release Burke in exchange for Cindy. Don't make me say, 'Or else.' Aw shit. Or else, Sergeant. How badly do you want her?"

"Badly. Very damned badly, you fuck."

He laughed. Then, "I could send you an email with the location for the swap."

I had just started to say, "It's not up to me!" when there was a click and then, I was yelling into a dead phone.

CHAPTER 80

YUKI WAS IN court on Friday morning for Lewis Sullivan's sentencing. He had been found guilty of all charges, but the sentence for each of those charges was left to the discretion of the judge. Judge Froman, not the jury, would decide what punishment would fit the crime.

Yuki had been the first to speak that morning.

She had summarized her case to Judge Froman, saying, "Despite Lewis Sullivan's apparent clean arrest record until the horrific final battering of his wife, he had been terrorizing her for years. She called the police but was too frightened of him to press charges. He threatened her in this courtroom, Your Honor, because he didn't get his way. He has terrified his children. He wreaked bloody mayhem on his wife, crippling and blinding her for life, and was found guilty of attempted murder. We ask the court to sentence him to the maximum for all charges, and further, we recommend that he not be eligible for parole. Ever."

Mo Switzer smiled when Yuki sat down. Then, he'd made his case to the judge, the truncated version of the one he'd made to the jury. His principal points were that Lewis loved Barbara. That she had baited him until he snapped. Despite Barbara's claims, there was no proof that he had beaten her before. And he has sworn never to do it again.

Switzer said, "Lew loves his wife and children and they love him. On behalf of my client, I am asking Your Honor to please show mercy to this flawed man. Give him the opportunity to get the therapy he needs, make peace with his family, and resume life as a free man in the near future."

Judge Froman showed no expression, but she did drum her fingernails on the desk, an indication of impatience that no jury would see.

"Would Mr. Sullivan like to speak?" she asked Switzer.

"Lew?"

Sullivan stood and said, "Your Honor, I'm a broken man. I have admitted guilt. I have apologized, in writing, to my wife. I'm more remorseful than any words I can say. I understand that I must pay for what I've done, and I promise you, I will be a model prisoner. I can again be a productive member of society if given another chance."

Froman said, "Thank you, Mr. Sullivan. Ms. Castellano, does Mrs. Sullivan wish to speak?"

"She does, Your Honor."

Nick Gaines went down the aisle and navigated Barbara's wheelchair through the gallery and into the well. He asked her if she was okay, and she said that she was. He stood with her as she spoke.

"Your honor, I am nervous about public speaking, but I must say for the record that my... That Lewis hit me many times before. I was always afraid to be with him. I was afraid to leave him because of what he might do to the boys. The incident he cited, that I had purposely flirted with a neighbor, is a lie, Your Honor. Tom knew that Lew was abusing me and was trying to protect me. No one was able to do that, myself least of all.

"Your Honor, I beg you to put him away for good. He shouldn't ever be free to hurt anyone else. I would like a favor. May I go with you to your chambers? I want to show you my injuries."

Switzer stood. "Your Honor, this should have been done during the trial, if at all."

"Sit down, Mr. Switzer."

The judge came out from behind the bench and wheeled Barbara through the door to her office. The door closed. Time went by. Yuki wondered how long it would take for Barbara to disrobe. She exchanged texts with Nicky, sitting next to her, and with Len Parisi, who was out in the hallway. After fifteen minutes, Judge Froman reappeared with Barbara, who'd obviously been crying.

Gaines went to Barbara and returned her to her place in the aisle. Judge Froman, back at the bench, banged her gavel and the room became still.

The judge adjusted her glasses and read the sentences in order. One year for each count of child endangerment. Four years for aggravated assault. Life in prison for attempted murder but the judge did not say "without possibility of parole."

Yuki looked into Nick's eyes. It was clear now that while Yuki had proved Lew Sullivan's intent to kill his wife, by leaving his sentence open to parole at some distant year, the judge showed that she believed in redemption.

Lew Sullivan's face was expressionless. He was looking at lifetime incarceration in a maximum-security prison. Maybe less, if he was very, very good.

If he ever came up for parole, Yuki would be there. And she would be there with Barbara.

CHAPTER 81

YUKI WAS AT her desk, a mug of oolong tea to the right of her open laptop. It was Saturday, but her work inbox was a font of chaos: hundreds of memos, transcripts, and all manner of email that had backed up during the Sullivan trial.

She was five minutes into turning the tide when her cell phone rang. She grabbed it without looking at the screen, sure that it was Brady, hoping he would say that he had Cindy.

She said, "Brady?"

"Yuki, it's Mo Switzer."

"Hi, Mo—"

"Yuki. I'm sorry to say, she's dead."

"What? *Who?*"

"Sorry. I'm a mess. Barbara Sullivan. I dropped over to hand deliver a note from Lewis. He wanted Barbara to know that he was truly sorry. And though I cautioned him against it, he made a confession. Lew was the one who wrote 'I love you' in blood on the basement wall. The door was unlocked. I found Barbara in bed. Dead. Her throat was cut."

"She killed herself?"

"Unlikely. There were words written in blood on the bedroom wall. 'I love you,' just like in trial evidence. This time with a signature. 'Blackout.' I'm on her porch right now with Inspectors Alvarez and Conklin. I thought you'd want to know."

"Oh my God. I can't believe this."

"Poor effing Barbara," Switzer said. "May she rest in peace. By the way, Lewis Sullivan is still in lockup awaiting transfer to prison."

Yuki thanked Switzer for the call. Then, she speed-dialed Lindsay and without preamble told her, "I think Blackout killed Barbara Sullivan."

Lindsay said, "Are you serious? Says who?"

"Mo Switzer. He's at her house."

"Why does he think it was Blackout?"

Yuki said, "The wall. Bloody finger-paint writing."

There was a long silence.

"Lindsay?"

"Yuki, you okay?"

"Not at all."

"Did you tell Brady?"

"Not yet."

"Okay," Lindsay said. "I'll do it and call you back."

CHAPTER 82

BRADY STOPPED ME before I could say a word.

"Boxer. Hold up."

I said, "Barbara Sullivan was murdered."

"I know. I spoke to Hallows. I've assigned Conklin and Alvarez. You're needed here. Task force meeting down the hall."

I pictured Barbara: half blind, mostly crippled, maybe sedated, alone in a dark house. Her sons with their grandmother because Barbara was too sick to care for them. She'd never had a chance. I updated Yuki, then walked along the corridor to the war room.

Team Blackout was less than half present: Joe Molinari, Mike Wallenger, Brady, and me. The others were checking out tips, leads, and a fresh murder.

Brady said, "Cindy's been missing for seventy-two hours. We're borrowing time from a serial killer."

He locked the door and said, "Boxer. You're up."

I reported on Barbara Sullivan, waiting now for the ME report, for the forensics lab, and added her to the Blackout case files. I wrote her name at the top of a whiteboard and leaned it against the wall. Then we compared notes, triple-checked procedures for oversights, anomalies, unfounded coincidences. We watched Blackout's video reel again as well as the bookstore surveillance footage from different camera angles. I kept one eye on my inbox to see if Blackout had sent a new murder tape.

In that intense frame of mind, I silenced my phone. Brenda had called and finally knocked. Instead of screeching *What?* I got up and answered the door.

"You have a call from the tip line," she said. "I screened it. You should take it."

"Transfer the call. Thanks, Brenda."

I picked up the receiver, said my name, and the caller told me hers. Marion Witmar. She sounded youngish and rattled. I was impatient, thinking about Barbara Sullivan and at the same time urgently wanting to get back to the meeting.

Witmar said, "Sergeant Boxer. I saw that YouTube and I recognized his voice. The man who called himself Blackout? His real name is Bryan Catton."

That focused me.

I asked Witmar to spell the name and typed it into my browser while asking, "How do you know him?"

"He's my ex. We lived together for two years. It ended five or six years ago. His face looks different in the video, like maybe he's had work done. His nose is smaller. His eyes are narrower, and his hairline has receded. But that's him."

"You're sure?"

Witmar got louder.

"I'll never forget his voice. The rhythm of his speech and the volume when he's making a point. Listen, Sergeant. I'm lucky to be alive. He choked me nearly to death. That woman in the video is in serious danger."

"How can we find Catton?"

Witmar didn't know. Last time she spoke to him, Bob Brooks had hired him to work in the stockroom of Brooks's Books nights and weekends. Then he joined the Marines. Last she heard he'd been sent to Afghanistan.

"The important thing," said Witmar, "is that he had a 4.6 grade point average without trying. He's cold, brilliant, and loves an audience. I loved him. Crazy neurotic kind of love. Now he terrifies me. I despise him. If you find him, don't mention my name. I'm certain he'd kill me."

Marion Witmar doubted that she had any old contact info for Catton, his friends, family, or his photo. "I burned all of it. But a guy named Austin Reynolds was Bryan's roommate at Berkeley, and they moved back in together after Bryan and I split up. They were both drama majors and movie freaks. I heard Austin stole an idea for a play from Bryan. Austin would steal toilet paper from your bathroom. What a jerk. I haven't seen him since I last saw Bryan."

I signed off with Witmar and briefed the team. Our meeting broke into individual parts as we plugged Catton's name into databases from DMV to USMC. Twenty minutes later we had three addresses for Catton. His last-known residence was a house in the Haight-Ashbury district, currently listed as a short sale by the bank. The ad read, "Classic Victorian in the Haight. Former beauty, now a teardown or candidate for total renovation. Uninhabitable."

Downstairs at the motor pool, Joe and I signed out a patrol car. Wallenger and Brady took another squad and Reg Covington pulled up in a Bearcat fully loaded with his SWAT crew. With all lights and sirens blaring, we headed to U.S. 101 North.

We had a location, an A-plus team, and a clear shot to a teardown in the Haight. I could see Blackout/Catton stashing Cindy at this unoccupied wreck—because that made total sense. Who would look for her there?

CHAPTER 83

THE SULLIVANS' WOOD-FRAME house on a well-kept street near Alamo Square was being cordoned off by uniforms when Conklin and Alvarez finished taking Switzer's statement. They said hello to Sergeant Nardone who said, "You're not going to like what you see in there, kids."

"We've heard," Conklin said.

Officer Einhorn, Nardone's partner, approached from a house across the street. He said, "Barbara's neighbor Tom Watkins lives over there. Here's his number. Ever since the trouble started with Barbara and Lew, Watkins took to watching the Sullivan house. He says he saw a car he didn't recognize waiting two houses down from the Sullivan house before sunup. The car was there for about a half hour. He also saw the driver, a man, when he opened the door to drive away. Watkins might be able to identify him."

"Tell Watkins we'll be with him in a few," said Alvarez.

Nardone lifted the tape and Conklin and Alvarez proceeded up the walkway to the Sullivans' front door. CSU director Gene Hallows opened it, saying, "Welcome to hell. Glove up," Hallows said.

"Put on booties and mind the scene and I'll give you a peek at the victim."

The primary crime scene was a pale-green bedroom featuring a hospital bed with a raised head section, a vanity, a floral area rug, a nightstand, and a standing lamp that had fallen to the floor.

Barbara Sullivan's body was in the bed, half covered by a sheet. There was a white patch over her left eye and her mouth was open above the gaping slash across her throat. Her right leg, encased in a plaster cast from ankle to mid-thigh, stuck out over the edge of the mattress. She'd bled out, her blood soaking the bedcovers, pooling onto the floor. If she'd struggled, it hadn't been for long.

Alvarez asked Hallows, "Estimated TOD?"

Hallows said, "The ME will have a better fix, but I'd say this only happened two, three hours ago."

"And the weapon?"

"We haven't found it. Looking at the neck wound it's going to be a fixed-blade weapon."

Alvarez looked at Conklin. She didn't have to tell him what she was thinking. Evan Burke's weapon of choice was a straight-edge razor. Blackout was Evan Burke's number one fan.

Conklin asked, "Where's the mirror?"

Hallows said, "Stay out there and one at a time, peek around the door frame and take a look at the wall."

Conklin peered first. From fifteen feet away, he couldn't believe what he was reading on the pale green wall.

Alvarez spent long minutes taking in the bedroom, finally saying, "Frickin' psycho. It was dark when he did this. Looks to me like he walked behind the bed, leaned over, and made his cut."

She said to Hallows, "Looks like he wrote that message with a bare finger. You think you can pull some prints off that?"

"Don't bet on it. The moving finger smears as it writes. We'll try. Anything else?"

"Send pictures," Rich said.

Hallows nodded. Conklin and Alvarez carefully left the scene.

Nardone was waiting for them on the sidewalk with a man in his forties, wiry, wearing sweats. "This is Mr. Tom Watkins."

Conklin introduced himself and Alvarez and asked Watkins if he would come with them to the Southern Station.

"We have some photos we'd like you to look at."

"Absolutely," said Watkins. "Can we do it now?"

Conklin noted that there were tears in his eyes.

Just then, Brady's voice crackled over Conklin's radio.

"Conklin. Alvarez. Get in your car and drive."

CHAPTER 84

BRYAN CATTON'S LAST known address had been a "Painted Lady" in the Haight-Ashbury district. Online photos of the Victorian home showed that it was in serious disrepair. Paint peeled, columns tilted, and the yard was overgrown with California buckeye saplings. Vegetation pushed through the roof. The house appeared to be utterly abandoned, no signs of life whatsoever.

Still, was Blackout hiding out in this abandoned wreck with Cindy? I'd run a lot of scenarios through my mind about meeting Blackout. Right now, I was preparing for a shoot-out.

Brady called in a half dozen cars to form a perimeter around the block. When they arrived, Joe manned the rear door and Mike stayed inside what was now a command post. SWAT captain Reg Covington's team exited the Bearcat and braced their weapons on the roof and door frames. Brady and I zipped up our Kevlar vests and approached the front door. There was a flash-bang in Covington's hand and our guns were drawn.

The front porch was sagging with planks of rotted wood. Covington advanced to the front door on cat's feet, twisted the doorknob, and shook the door in its frame. The door was locked but not secure. Covington kicked it in, tossed the stun grenade into the parlor and closed the door. We covered our ears and closed our eyes as the flash-bang went off. Its blinding light and high-decibel blast shut down sight, hearing, and thoughts of anyone inside that house long enough for us to find them.

When the sound died out, Covington opened the door and the tac team ran in, guns out, three commandos clearing the ground and second floors, two taking the basement. Only three minutes had gone by and the house was pronounced safe and uninhabited from top to bottom.

Brady and I checked out the ground floor. The floor and sills were thick with dust. Two-by-fours were stacked in front of the fireplace and a couple buckets of spackle stood in a corner, but no work had been done. We ran up the stairs and found a wide landing with a number of doors including one open to a front-facing room. When we entered, I was nearly knocked over by a blast of déjà vu.

There, against a dull, white-painted wall, was the beige three-seat sofa I'd seen in Blackout's videos. The armchair where he'd been sitting, twirling his glasses, was on a diagonal to the sofa. And behind the chair were the bookshelves Alvarez had described as a screenshot of Blackout's mind.

Brady and I took our time opening books, looking for margin notes, holding them open, upside down, shaking them, hoping that something telling would fall out.

Nothing did and the bookshelf wasn't a door to a secret room. We searched all three floors and found no sign of Blackout and no sign of Cindy. Not a hair band, a broken fingernail, not a flex cuff or a bloodstain. We returned to the second floor and Brady opened a door to a bedroom across the landing from the study.

This room had only one piece of furniture, a large metal desk standing between two unbroken windows.

Joe and Mike came into the room behind us.

"Cindy was stashed in there," I said, pointing at the kneehole, a rectangular opening between the desk's two pedestals. Joe trained his Maglite on the floor under the desk while I opened the drawers.

Damn. This was the motherlode.

My hands were shaking as I picked through layers of paper. Something here was going to lead us to Cindy. I found receipts for video glasses and black jersey gloves. The Fleet family's address was written on a Post-it note. There were clippings from the *Chronicle*, obituaries of his recent victims in an envelope, and the *Chronicle*'s front page headlined with Henry Tyler's offer of a reward for information leading to the return of Cindy Thomas. And there was a picture of Cindy taken at the Poisoned Pen bookstore. She was at the podium, talking to the crowd.

I was right there.

As if my joints were locked, I stared down at the open drawer, stunned. I loved Cindy. And I'd let her down.

Brady's voice came through to me. "You okay, Boxer?"

No.

I gathered a handful of papers and spread them out on the desk. This, along with the videos Blackout had directed, shot, and produced amounted to almost too much evidence. But the only evidence that would pay off would be capturing Blackout himself.

I opened a file drawer in the lower right section of the desk. I found a yearbook from Berkeley and an envelope full of more receipts. Items paid for in cash. A stun gun. Ammo for a .22, junk food, gasoline.

Blackout had used this desk, but he didn't live here. Not anymore.

Joe was lying on his back under the desk.

"Got it," he said.

He slid out from under the desk and stood up, showing us his right thumb and forefinger pinched together.

He said, "This was caught in a sliver under the center drawer."

Joe was holding a golden strand of hair curled like the letter "C." Cindy's hair. A picture came into my mind of Cindy balled up under the desk. I imagined Blackout pulling her out, tossing her over his shoulder and into his car.

Then dumping her body into the bay.

CHAPTER 85

BRADY AND I were back in our car when the radio crack-led and Chief Clapper's voice came over.

"Brady. Need you at the Hall. Now."

"What happened?"

"Barbara Sullivan media explosion."

"I'm on the way."

It had only been a few hours since Barbara Sullivan's body had been discovered, but to the press, a scoop beat sex, food, love, and a roof in the rain.

Brady said, "Ah, sheet," and gunned the engine. We were back at the Hall in record time. It was just past two when Brady and I went through the bullpen gate. Brady took a right and headed for his office. I looked around.

Bobby said, "Sergeant, Inspectors Alvarez and Conklin are in Interview Two."

I thanked him, left the bullpen, and took a turn down the short spur of corridor leading to the interrogation rooms. The observation room shares a mirrored wall with the box. Alvarez and Conklin were interviewing a bespectacled man in his forties wearing gray sweats. He appeared agitated as he looked at a photo array on the table; men who generally resembled Blackout along with a resized picture of Blackout cut from one of his videos, printed on photo paper to match the others.

I knocked on the glass and Rich left interrogation and joined me in observation. I'd called him from the car to tell him that Cindy wasn't at the house and the question on his face now was plain. *Where is she?*

I said, "How're you holding up?"

He shrugged and looked down.

"Who's that?" I asked, indicating the man sitting across from Alvarez.

"Thomas Watkins," he said. "Lives across the street from the Sullivans."

If memory served, Watkins was the neighbor who, in helping Barbara with her groceries, had triggered Lew Sullivan's rabid, near fatal attack on her.

Rich said, "This morning, Watkins saw a gray car parked a couple of doors away from the Sullivan house. He described the car's driver as white, slim, wearing black."

"Did he pick Blackout out of the array?"

"No. No can't positively ID any of them."

"What about the car?"

"Early 2000s gray Ford four-door sedan. But don't worry about the six thousand other aging gray Ford four-doors in California. The plate number doesn't compute."

"Cop car?"

"Yep," said Rich. "Somehow the perp got his hands on a retired police car with municipal plates."

"So says Watkins. Is he a suspect?"

"He has an alibi. His wife," said Richie. "When we catch Blackout, Watkins might pick him out of a lineup."

Then, Rich looked me in the eyes and I couldn't look away.

"I need to know more about what happened at Blackout's house," he said.

"Let's talk down the hall," I said.

Alone together in the war room, I told Rich what we had found at the house in the Haight: papers showing the purchase of weapons, obituaries of his recent victims, and the front-page article in the *Chronicle* offering the reward for information on Cindy.

Rich said, "So the paper proves he was in the house recently. Did you find anything useful? Like his phone?"

"Joe found a hair that could be Cindy's caught under the desk drawer. It's at the lab. But, Rich, we knew she was wedged under a desk. Now we know where."

Richie's face just fell apart. "This is so wrong."

The brother I'd never had, my dear friend, crossed his arms on the table, put his head down and broke into sobs. I understood that this was yet one more breaking point. The chances of finding Cindy alive were minute, but finding a strand of her hair felt like proof of death.

I said, "We didn't find any other sign of her, Rich. Nothing. He probably moved her. Uniforms are sitting on that house 24-7. If he comes back...Look. That scum made us an offer—Burke for Cindy—and that offer is still standing. He's not going walk away from that."

We both knew that exchange wasn't happening, but I said it to comfort us both. Richie didn't answer me. He cried and I sat with him, rubbing his back and heaving shoulders.

About then, Brady burst through the door. "Sorry," he said, seeing Conklin's distress. "We're not done, Boxer. Come see me."

Brady left.

There wasn't a paper towel or a napkin or a dollar pack of tissues in the room. Rich wiped his face with his sleeves and said, "The contact info for Bryan Catton's school friends is old. We checked. The numbers are no good anymore. The bookstore where Catton worked on weekends is out of business."

"We have two more addresses," I said.

"Lindsay, I want in on the search for Cindy. Or I'm going to fucking quit."

CHAPTER 86

THIS WAS PURE desperation time and we knew it. Cindy had been missing for too long and we hadn't been prodded by Blackout. So, we were scraping the bottom of Marion Witmar's tip list. She had given us names that we'd connected to locations where Catton may have lived years ago—or where he might be living now. Or we'd never know.

With no sand left in the hourglass, we'd committed to checking out Witmar's leads with Blackout's given name—Bryan Catton.

Cappy and Chi had drawn the name Bennet Frank, a Catton high school friend. After running Frank's name and finding nothing criminal, they were driving to his house in the Marina District.

Conklin had pressed Brady to the wall until he relented and put Rich back in action on the search for Cindy. Brady had too many balls in the air, and now he had to neutralize the Barbara Sullivan media bomb that was radiating out to all points.

Richie and I pulled the name Austin Reynolds, an actor/ stand-up comedian who knew Bryan Catton through their drama classes at Berkeley. Reynolds's bio on social media listed his day job as a copy editor for a small publishing company.

So on that hazy Saturday afternoon, two weeks after Blackout had put a couple of rounds into Ralph Hammer's head, we were squeezing out a few unexplored leads. I knew Rich and I were both thinking of Cindy, last seen balled up under a desk and no longer there. We met Alvarez at the garage and checked out a tech-tweaked unmarked police car and headed out to Dolores Heights.

We had a dedicated radio channel connected to Brady's office, two FBI special agents in the form of my husband and his former partner for a half-dozen years. We also had the assistance of two undercovers driving an unmarked Chevy sedan following us to Austin Reynolds's address. We had no search warrant, no probable cause, and I could only hope that Reynolds knew where Bryan Catton lived. And that at the end of this blindman's bluff we'd find Cindy Thomas alive and planning her next true-crime tour de force.

Rich parked our car on 20th Street under a tree across from a clean white apartment building with balconies and city views. Joe and Mike parked a half block away and the undercovers found a spot a couple of car lengths from the entrance to Reynolds's building.

The undercovers stayed at the curb. Joe and Mike left their car and took up positions at the back of the apartment building. Rich and I zipped up our Kevlar vests, clipped our badges to our windbreakers, and got out of the car. Dodging traffic, we crossed the street and entered the building's foyer. On the wall to our right was a bank of mailboxes and intercom buttons.

Witmar had told us that Bryan Catton and Austin Reynolds had been roommates in college and again before he enlisted. The name "Reynolds" was on the mailbox for apartment 1R. That meant ground floor, rear. I took in a long breath and exhaled as Rich pressed the bell.

No answer.

We counted to ten and pressed it again.

Still no answer.

We returned to our car and I texted Joe. "He's not home. Let's wait thirty mins."

"Copy that," he replied.

But Rich couldn't wait half an hour. Ten minutes was his limit. We got out of the car, re-entered the lobby, and out of pure frustration, Conklin pushed the buzzer again, *leaned* on it.

This time a male voice spoke.

"Who is it?"

"Mr. Reynolds? This is the SFPD."

I texted Joe. "Stand by."

CHAPTER 87

THE VOICE AT the apartment end of the intercom said, "What can I do for you?"

"This is Sergeant Lindsay Boxer, SFPD. We need you to look at some pictures," I said. "Take two, three minutes."

"Can you come back later? I'm in the middle of something," Reynolds said.

I tried to listen to the rhythm and tone of his voice. There was classical music playing in the background. The voice itself was distorted through the intercom.

"Mr. Reynolds," Rich said. "We're going building to building, knocking on doors. Let's do this quick and we'll get out of your life."

The buzzer sounded. Rich pushed on the lobby door. I notified Joe that we were in, then Rich and I headed down the corridor until we stood in front of Reynolds's door.

I pressed the doorbell. I heard footfalls coming closer, then the peephole cover sliding open, the chain moving along a track and the hard click of a lock opening. At last, the door opened and I was staring at the face of a white male in his twenties, under six feet, dark haired, wearing black-rimmed glasses.

This was Blackout.

I clamped down on my startle reflex. He looked at me seemingly without recognition, then shifted his eyes to Richie and stepped aside.

"Come in, I guess," said the man with the glasses.

We stepped inside and Reynolds closed the door behind us. Bryan Catton was a strangler. I lifted my shoulders an inch or two, retracting my neck out of pure instinct as Rich and I entered his long, narrow living room.

It was a straight shot from the door, past an eat-in kitchen and a number of closed doors along the left-hand wall. The right-hand wall was all bookshelves and movie posters from *Casablanca* to *Avengers*. The room ended at a pair of sliding doors fronting a terrace.

I walked down to the sliders, opened them, and Joe and Mike vaulted over the terrace railing and walked in. They were big men, armed, wearing FBI windbreakers.

"Who are you?" Reynolds asked. "What is this?"

I made introductions and took a seat at the round dining table. We all did, including a reluctant Austin Reynolds. I looked into our subject's face and thought, *It's happened.*

We've got him. We've got Blackout.

But at the same time, I thought, *Down, girl. Play this right.* I didn't dare look at Richie.

Reynolds said, "Why do I think there's more to this than looking at pictures?"

"We're investigating a series of crimes," I said. "You may be able to help us."

Reynolds's voice sounded the same as when I spoke to him on the phone, but I couldn't be sure. I was expecting him to bolt, and at the same time, thinking he was going to say, "Nice to meet you, Sergeant Boxer," in the sassy, nasty way he'd been dealing with me since Hammer's murder tape arrived in my inbox. But Blackout was reputed to be a brainiac. If so, he would want to know what we knew. He'd play us, just like Burke.

"Reynolds" said, "What kind of crime? And why do you think I can help?"

Joe said, "Mr. Reynolds. Is anyone else here?"

"No. No one at all."

"Okay," Joe said. "We're permitted by law to do a walk-through of your rooms and the building's basement to make sure no one's in hiding."

This was true. We were not allowed to open any space too small to enclose a body, so furniture was out, but closets and rooms were fair game.

Mike said, "I'll take the basement."

He left by the apartment's front door, while Joe opened interior doors with gun drawn and checked the rooms.

He came back to the table and said, "All clear."

When Mike also rejoined us, I said to Reynolds, "Are you familiar with the name Bryan Catton?"

"Catton. Hell, yeah. What's he done?"

"How do you know him?"

"We studied drama together at Berkeley. We were also roommates for a while in this apartment, but I've lived here alone since he enlisted. I haven't seen him in over six months. Are you saying you're looking for him?"

The way "Reynolds" spoke about Bryan Catton in the third

person was raising some doubt in my mind. However, they were both actors. This evasive technique could be easy for him. Blackout had lured people to their deaths.

Rich said, "These are the photos. Can you show me if you see Catton?"

The photo array was the same deck of six photos we'd shown to Tom Watkins, five mug shots and a photo of Blackout lifted from one of his videos, reduced to the size and shape of the other five.

Rich fanned all six out on the table. Witmar had described the results of Catton's plastic surgery: his nose was smaller; his eyes were positioned differently in his face.

Reynolds hovered his right forefinger over the second photo and then the fifth, then shook his head.

"I don't recognize any of these people," he said. "I can't make a positive ID."

CHAPTER 88

AT MY REQUEST, Austin Reynolds produced his ID. He had the usual wallet-full: driver's license, insurance, and credit cards.

While I studied the picture on his license, I asked him to take off his glasses. I placed the picture of Blackout beside the one of Reynolds. Reynolds had crow's-feet at the corners of his eyes and no surgeon's scars at the temples. Reynolds's eyebrows were closer together than Catton's. His hairline was deeper, and his mouth was wider.

It had taken me fifteen minutes with Austin Reynolds to conclude that while he and Bryan Catton looked similar, they were not the same dude. Still, I hated to give up my conviction that we'd nabbed Blackout, and I needed more than a photo comparison to be absolutely sure that Reynolds was not Blackout before letting a killer walk free.

I said, "Mike, can we see that SEEK?"

Wallenger pulled the SEEK, a handheld forensic fingerprint device about the size of a small phone, from his windbreaker pocket.

"Here's what you do," said Wallenger. "You put your thumb right here and this little critter will send your print to Quantico. There it will be compared with Bryan Catton's prints in the military database."

"Oh. Oh, I see," Reynolds thumbed the reader, laughing, "Oh, this is good. You think I'm *Bryan*? Really? No, listen don't feel bad when you guys turn out to be wrong. We used to get mistaken for one another a lot back in school."

While we waited for the print to enter the government store of fingerprints, Reynolds answered Richie's questions about Bryan Catton. No, he'd never seen any signs of violence when they were in school. Catton was extremely smart and the two of them competed for the best roles in plays put on by the drama department. Later, they competed for roles in commercials. People liked Bryan, Reynolds said, but he never made real friends.

"Except you," I offered.

"Not even me," said Reynolds. "But he was a good roommate. He had a sense of humor. He picked up his clothes and ran the dishwasher and that was all I cared about."

"Got it," said Wallenger, looking at the LED on the print reader.

"You," he said, looking directly at Austin Reynolds, "are *not* Bryan Catton."

"You were the last to know," Reynolds said with a grin.

We wrapped it up quickly after that. I gave Reynolds my card, asked him to call me if Catton contacted him, but to keep walls between them.

"He's a killer," I said to Reynolds. "Don't let him in the door."

CHAPTER 89

I CHECKED IN with Brady as we set off for the Hall. Conklin was deep in his head when I broke in to say, "Listen, Rich. We know more than we knew twenty-four hours ago."

"It still adds up to zero."

I sighed. He was right.

Rich said, "But, we left a box unchecked."

"Brooks's Books?"

"We should do a ten-minute detour and take a look."

I pictured Cindy as we'd seen her last in Blackout's video, curled into a ball under a desk. The bookstore was a good bet. Better than no bet at all.

"You're on," I said.

Rich made a U-turn on Oak Street and headed us east toward Hayes Valley, an eclectic shopping and restaurant area with businesses on the ground floors of Victorians and other older buildings, apartments above. It was Saturday, nearing 6:00 p.m., and the street was quiet.

Rich was staring straight ahead and he stopped for a traffic light at the intersection of Gough and Hayes. I saw Brooks's Books up ahead, an old vacant bookstore wrapping around the corner of Hayes to Gough on our right. According to our tip-line witness Marion Witmar, Bryan Catton had once worked off-hours in the stockroom. Now there was an epitaph painted on the inside of the plate glass window: "Out of business."

Richie looked past me to the store that was already showing signs of neglect. The sidewalk was littered. Windows unwashed. It was as if the store had given up and gone into retirement.

Rich said to me, "Maybe it's a wild-ass idea, but it's the only one I've got."

"You had me at unchecked box."

I got a smile from him, then it faded again into a frown of apprehension. I radioed Brady and told him our change of plans.

The traffic light changed. Rich took a right at the corner and we drove slowly along Gough, which would take us to the bookstore's rear entrance, a small lot for employee parking, and a loading dock. Beyond the entrance to this lot was a row of attached houses with small shops on the ground floor.

We were coming up on the entrance to the bookstore's parking lot when Rich slowed way down. There was only one car in the lot, and it took a second for my brain to register what my bucking heart already knew. That the car parked to the far side of the lot was a gray Ford four-door sedan with municipal tags. It could be, had to be, the car Tom Watkins had seen across the street from Barbara Sullivan's house this morning. And maybe also the same car I'd glimpsed in Blackout's video of Catherine and Josie Fleet's murders.

"Stop here," I said to my partner. He braked hard enough to make our car shudder. An angry driver in a red Saturn behind us honked, pulled around our squad, and flipped us off. I hardly noticed. I was too busy running the gray Ford's plates through our car's mobile data computer.

The MDC came back with an answer: "Not in the system."

It was a retired cop car. A "ghost car." A junkyard retread with fraudulent municipal plates.

Rich said, "That's Blackout's car. *No doubt.*"

He put our car in reverse, wrenched the wheel, gave it some gas, and backed us into a spot at the curb with a prime view of the lot, the gray car, and the elevated loading dock at the rear of the bookstore. Rich cut the engine.

I locked my eyes on the loading dock, noted the typical aluminum roll-down door.

I said, "Rich, look at the door at right angles to that roll-down."

The much smaller second door was the kind used for workers on foot or with hand trucks. Even from where we were parked thirty yards away I could see that it was open, maybe six inches. And above that door was a glass transom window about three feet wide by one foot high.

"See the transom window?" I said.

"I do now."

It added up. The old gray former cop car, parked at the place where Catton used to work — and a transom window over a metal door that looked identical to the one I'd seen in the Blackout video. The one where he'd dragged Cindy across a warehouse floor.

Conklin said, "I can hear you thinking."

"Yeah?"

"Blackout is here and so is Cindy."

I grabbed the mic off the hook and radioed Brady to tell him that this was no longer a drive-by. It was a full stop and we needed backup, SWAT, drones, complete cover, and Blackout's reason why.

Brady asked, "Have you seen any movement?"

"No."

"Lights?"

"No."

Brady said, "Don't approach that building until I say so. Keep your eyes on that car and the open door. SWAT is still assembled. They can be there in ten. I'll get a perimeter in place and get back to you."

"Copy that, Lieutenant."

"Don't get twitchy," Brady said. "Once we've got that store locked down, we'll have all the time we need to reel him in."

Unless Catton puts a gun to Cindy's head and bargains his way out. I canceled the thought. Rich dialed down the radio volume and we sat there waiting for the troops to arrive.

I wanted to jump out of the car and run for that open doorway. I worried that if she was inside the bookstore, she was dead. I also knew that the correct and only thing to do was sit, watch, obey orders.

"I'm sure of this," Rich said.

He wasn't but he wanted to be. I felt the same way. I kept my eyes on the door and the car under the dusky sky and felt time drag slowly by. I kept my hand on the door handle and waited for Brady's order to go in.

CHAPTER 90

A DUN-COLORED ARMORED vehicle pulled into a parking spot behind us. It was an MRAP, an army surplus light tactical vehicle originally made for military use in Afghanistan; now some were used by municipal police departments who needed them. I was glad to see this one.

Brady's voice sputtered over the radio.

"Boxer, Conklin, the core perimeter is in place. The secondary perimeter is nearly set. The command post is on Ivy and Hayes. I'm there. So is Alvarez. Stand by."

I heard the squeal of a bullhorn, then Covington's voice boomed loud enough for us to hear from the storefront around the corner.

"Bryan Catton. This is your SWAT captain Reg Covington speaking. You are surrounded. Come out nice and slow with your hands up. No one needs to get hurt."

Back behind the parking lot, eight men in full tactical gear scrambled out of the MRAP and grouped around it. I knew one of them, Lieutenant Chris Martin. Black, late thirties, five ten, he's a former Ranger and experienced in dynamic entries and special equipment. He came over to my side of the car and made the universal sign to roll down the window.

He said, "Sarge, Conklin, can you come on out for a minute?"

When we were standing alongside our car, Martin opened a foam-lined transportation case and showed us a robot mounted on tanklike treads and that looked to be twenty inches wide by nearly forty long and thirty high.

"This is Mastiff," said Martin. I'd taken two classes in SWAT robotics and had worked around similar bots. I knew Mastiff weighed over a hundred pounds.

Martin said, "If you haven't seen this SuperDroid before, introducing HD2-S Mastiff, an all-terrain tactical robot, new and improved."

"Impressive," I said, impressed.

"I'm now giving you a crash course in bot reconnaissance. First, why do I need you outside at the controls? Because I need your eyes with Mastiff while we're inside a dark place we've never been, looking for a homicidal maniac, likely armed, and a hostage.

"Second, the bot is programmed and knows its job. The controls are intuitive, less complicated than your phone.

"Third, if you need to get out of here, you're inside a vehicle. If you need to talk to your commander, you have the radio."

Martin continued the lesson, opening a large Pelican case. "Here is the Operator Control Unit, easy as one, two, three."

I tried to take in what Martin was telling me, but the one message that was as easy as one, two, three was that Martin was putting me in charge of Mastiff. I knew the tactical breach and clear drill. Flash-bangs went in first to stun any living thing. Next, the robots went into the room and scoped out the place, sending visual to the tac team outside. If necessary the robots knocked down doors. Before the tactical team went in, we would have received full images of the interior. If a subject was found, he'd be down and out for a few minutes, enough time to find him, disarm him, cuff him, extract him. If no one was home, the same procedure would be repeated in the next room.

Mastiff's control board and view screen looked like a laptop computer game. The joystick was at the top of the screen surrounded by marked buttons for override manual control. But I knew this bot could go full auto if needed.

Martin said, "She's called Mastiff after the Alpine dogs by that name. These treads allow her to travel over sand, gravel, water, riprap. She can climb stairs and can bust down a door. She's a two-way radio programmed to do a grid search in any kind or size of room."

Lieutenant Martin was describing the six-axis extending arms with grippers this beast could use to deliver a meal or a bomb or a phone. Mastiff operated off a base that could rotate 400 degrees to capture floor-to-ceiling images with its pan-tilt 20× optical zoom camera.

"Take the stick, Boxer. Give it a shot."

I pulled back on the joystick and the camera turret rose a few inches on the robot's neck. I swiveled the stick and the camera behaved accordingly. I pressed the button at the top of the stick and the camera snapped a picture.

"Very good," said Lieutenant Martin. "Hold down the button and you're shooting a video. If you see something, say something. We'll hear you and you'll hear me. The bot knows the way."

I told Lieutenant Martin, "Copy all of that," and my partner and I got back into the car. Rich was at the wheel and I had robot controls on my lap.

I was sweating. My blood was hot. Feeling that Blackout and Cindy could be yards away inside the bookstore was making me hyper. What Rich was feeling must be incalculable. But Martin was right not to take us into the bookstore. We weren't SWAT trained, not geared up for an out-of-control firefight.

Martin handed me a small construction-grade flip phone.

"If you need to tell me something in private, press Call. I'll answer."

I pressed the Call button. Martin grinned, picked up, and put his phone to his ear.

I said, "Lieutenant. Get Cindy Thomas the hell outta there. Do it now."

"We will damned well do our best," he said. "And that's a promise."

CHAPTER 91

THE SUN WAS just an orange streak on the horizon as I gripped the protective case with the bot control panel inside. Lieutenant Martin deployed Mastiff across the asphalt lot, with his team in a line behind him. They passed the gray car and jogged up the stairs to the elevated loading dock. A tac team officer lobbed a stun grenade overhand through the open door that appeared to lead into the warehouse.

He closed the door.

A second later, I saw the blinding flash through the transom window. The bang was muffled, but my car's window frame vibrated. As I watched, Lieutenant Martin opened the door so that Mastiff could move onto the warehouse floor. It was black inside, black on my screen, then the robot's LED lights came on.

Martin's voice came through my speaker. "We're a go. Copy?"

I said "Copy. I hear you loud and clear."

As I watched, Mastiff's four lights cut a swath about sixty degrees to each side of center. The laptop screen broke into a quadrant of four views. I saw familiar objects: cartons and odd bits of furniture. I heard muffled sounds of footfalls, and someone calling out that, as expected, there was no electric power in the store.

In the upper right quad I recognized the section of floor where Blackout had dragged Cindy by the wrists, yanked the tape from her mouth, and told her to stop screaming. Or else. Richie seemed paralyzed as he stared at the images, looking for a mad dog killer and his girl. We saw SWAT legs, boots, and camo, but I didn't see Blackout. And I didn't see Cindy. I'd begun to doubt that they were there when the bot's lights focused on a closed wooden door.

Martin called out, "Mr. Catton! Come to the door with your hands up. At the count of ten, we're coming in. Need I say, we're armed? To the teeth?"

Sitting in the car with Rich beside me, only yards away from the action, I counted to ten while staring at the image of a standard hollow-core wooden door. I touched the stick and rolled Mastiff up to the door. A member of the tac team was ready with a flash-bang when a voice, not Martin's, came over the audio on the laptop.

"Hate to tell you but she's not *here*," the voice said.

It was Blackout's voice. Even in one short sentence, I recognized the cadence, the emphasis on the last syllable.

I pressed the call button on the phone. Martin said, "Yes?"

"That's Catton. Out."

Martin shouted at the door, "I'd like to take your word for it, Mr. Catton, but that's not how we do things."

It was eerie to hear Blackout's loud, steady voice coming from the controls in my lap. He shouted, "I said, she's not here! She's. Not. Here."

Martin's voice: "Seven, six, five, four. Last chance to open the door."

A tac team commando stepped in front of the robot, kicked in the door and chucked in another flash-bang. Mastiff rolled into what had to be the bookstore's main room, the storefront rounding Hayes and Gough. The commando closed the door behind the bang and the bot. I braced for an explosion of sound and light. But nothing happened. I heard a man's voice curse the dud.

A second stun grenade was lobbed into the main room. My screen bleached to white from the blast, and when it cleared, "I" was with the robot as it searched the room, north to south, east to west, around the bookshelves and sparse furnishings in the main room. I was mesmerized until Conklin broke the spell.

"Lindsay. *Look*. Over *there*."

He was pointing, not at the screen, but to the parking lot fronting the loading dock. A man was crossing the asphalt toward the gray sedan. He was wearing black everything and barely visible against the setting sun and pale moon rising in the sky. But I recognized him. He looked to be just under six feet and was keeping his head down as he walked.

I phoned Lieutenant Martin, told him that the suspect was on foot in the parking lot and we needed backup.

Rich switched on the engine and swerved away from the curb, then wrenched the wheel hard right, and drove straight into the parking lot I knew by heart. He braked between the man we knew as Blackout and his gray sedan. Blackout had been nonchalant, certain he'd make his escape. He didn't know what was coming.

"Lights," I said.

Rich turned on the high beams and blinded by the light, Catton shielded his eyes with the crook of his elbow. Rich set the parking brake and we bolted from the car, weapons drawn.

I yelled, "SFPD! On your knees. Hands on your head. Do it, now."

CHAPTER 92

SIRENS SCREAMED. GRILL and roof lights flashed red and blue from blocks away as squad cars broke from the perimeter and converged on our location. The man in black recovered from his momentary high beam blindness and continued trying to evade us and get to his ride.

My Glock was in both hands. I shouted again, "Get down on your knees! Hands on your head. Do it. Now."

But Blackout turned on his heel and ran toward Linden Street. We were in close pursuit and then he tripped. My partner, faster than me, was on him. Grabbed his collar with his left hand, pressed his gun to the side of Blackout's face, and jerked him to his knees.

I came in close and stared at the subject of night terrors. Yes. It was Blackout. The man I'd seen on too many murder videos. Real name Bryan Catton.

I yanked his arms behind his back as he resisted. I had cuffed his left wrist and was working on the right. Rich kept his gun on Catton and began to pat him down. But the bastard was strong, and he pulled out of my grasp and backed away toward the loading dock.

He pulled a gun from somewhere and aimed it at me. Conklin was behind me. Julie's face came into my mind. And Joe's. The blood left my head and pooled in my knees.

Catton shouted, "Freeze!"

I stiffened my legs. That was all I could do.

And the man who'd told us to freeze at the point of his gun, shouted with military authority. "Lie facedown, both of you! My gun is mad. I can fire or I can bolt. Choose option two. When I'm outta here, we all live."

I knew "we all live" was a ruse and that someone would die in the next few seconds. I was rigid. It was a lose-lose situation. We could die here. Or, if we killed Catton, we might never find Cindy.

I said, "All right, all right. There's my gun."

I dropped my weapon and began to kneel. I was buying only seconds to give Rich a better shot.

He fired. Twice.

We are trained to fire two shots to center mass but Catton was an athletic genius. He'd turned sideways, avoiding probable kill shots, taking a .9 mm round in his right forearm. He grabbed his shattered arm and as blood streamed down, he screamed, and his weapon clattered to the ground.

As Rich bent to pick up the gun, Catton took the opportunity to knee him in the face. Rich's head snapped back from the blow, but he wasn't out. He balled up his fist and delivered a bone-breaking punch to Catton's nose.

Catton screamed again. Blood flew from his face. My cuffs were dangling from his left wrist. Richie's cheek radiated red even in dim light, but he was otherwise unharmed. Catton was wailing, Rich rolled him onto his belly and I finished cuffing the monster.

When Catton was immobilized, I leaned over and grabbed a

handful of his hair. I lifted his head from the ground and looked into the bloody face of the man who'd murdered so many innocent people, who'd taunted us, who'd abducted our close and beloved friend.

I said, "Where's Cindy? Tell me where she is and I'll help you. This offer expires in ten seconds."

This man had talked before, sent video evidence of his murders with cinematic flourishes. Now he said, "I don't know who you're talking about."

Stepping back, I said to my partner, "He's all yours."

Rich Conklin and a uniformed officer hauled Catton to his feet. I fished my phone out of my vest, set the camera to video, aimed it at the bloody tableau in front of me, and pressed "record."

Inspector Richard Conklin said, "Bryan Catton, you're under arrest for murder. You have the right to remain silent. Anything you say can and will be used against you..."

Brady pulled up in his SUV, Alvarez in the passenger seat. Our Godlike lieutenant got out first.

He called out, "Is it him?"

"Yes, sir."

Brady went over to Catton, asked him questions starting with "What is your name?"

Our prisoner had taken the right to remain silent to heart. He said, "Lawyer," and then he didn't say another word.

CHAPTER 93

BROOKS'S BOOKS WAS an active crime scene inside and out.

Spectators gathered across Gough Street asking questions, taking photos, getting in the way. A satellite truck arrived from one of the big three networks. Damn it. Local press showed up, too.

Inspectors Michaels and Wang drove Catton back to the Hall to be booked. At the same time, Catton's gray sedan was on a flatbed truck speeding out to the crime lab. A CSI mobile edged through the crowd and set up on Gough. They snaked electric cords from the van to the store and set up klieg lights in both the main room and warehouse. Until San Francisco PG&E turned on the power, CSI would have no shortage of light.

The store was filled with police and crime scene techs who couldn't work until other law enforcement cleared out. We couldn't leave yet. I was overwhelmed by my own near-death experience and still focused on Cindy. I desperately wanted to find her alive.

Brady was senior officer and with his okay, Alvarez, Conklin, and I began pulling bookshelves away from the walls in a frantic hunt for an access point to the building next door or hidey hole where Catton could have stashed Cindy.

Lieutenant Chris Martin stood near me in the wreck of the former bookstore and spoke into his vest mic saying, "The hostage has not been located. We need Holmes and Crispo."

Who?

A white van pulled up in front of the plate glass window at the front of the store. Martin opened the doors and we heard excited barking as two canines and their handler exited the van. Holmes and Crispo, both German Shepherds, were trained search and rescue dogs. They ran into the store, eyes bright, muzzles lowered, pulling along Sergeant Betsy Park. The handler for SWAT's K-9 division was a white-haired woman in her sixties, wiry, strong. She gave sharp one-word commands and unclipped their leads. The K-9s immediately went to work sniffing out corners, cabinets, and cartons, before going into the warehouse.

Cappy arrived. He found Conklin and as requested, handed Rich a sky-blue cardigan that Cindy had left in his car. Rich handed it off to the canine handler, who called the dogs and gave them a good sniff of the sweater.

While the search and rescue dogs looked for a living, breathing person, I took a seat at the long service desk at the rear of the main floor and began to snoop.

If Catton had been bunking here or even just dropping by, he might well have left some artifacts for us. I opened the center drawer and aside from some pushpins and Post-it notes, it was empty. Next, I went to the left-hand pedestal of the old desk. There were two drawers of empty file folders and three-ring binders filled with book invoices. I opened the file drawer in the right-hand pedestal and found sandwich bags of men's toiletries.

I opened the last drawer in the desk with low expectations, but there was one intriguing item in that last drawer. It was a leather-bound journal, a diary. The title was "Blackout. Last Night in Helmand Province," by Bryan Catton.

I nervously flipped through pages of heavy-grade paper that had a handmade feel, scanning for names that I may have known. Finding none, I flipped the book open toward the end. If Catton had kept this journal up-to-date, there was a chance that he'd recorded what he'd done with Cindy.

But the journal didn't end with Cindy. She wasn't even mentioned. The date on the last entry was three years prior to Blackout's appearance in our lives. A huge disappointment, yet, when I started to read the final pages of the journal, I couldn't stop.

CHAPTER **94**

IN THE DIARY, Catton wrote that he was in country, a door gunner inside a helicopter on an enemy suppression mission in Helmand Province.

The sky was hidden by dense cloud cover, what he thought of as a blackout. He was wearing a headset and night goggles, listening to the pilot when he saw muzzle flare coming from the ground below them. The situation went ballistic, he wrote.

I had to stop reading.

There was a loud commotion from Holmes and Crispo. I didn't know which was which, but the one with the black muzzle and matching saddle was barking at me from my left side. The other was yelping at my feet, digging at the wooden floorboards under the chair behind the desk.

I stashed the journal in the drawer.

My mind was half in a helicopter in Afghanistan, half shrinking from two large K-9s who saw me as an obstacle. I like dogs, love them, but my supply of adrenaline was depleted and I didn't know what to do.

I looked up when Betsy Park, the dog handler for SWAT's K-9 division, called my name. She stood with me and two powerful sets of jaws.

"Sergeant Boxer. They're harmless," she said. "Stand up slowly and step away from the desk. And don't bark at them."

I laughed nervously and did as I was told. I met Conklin's eyes, and when I was away from the desk, he grabbed my arm and pulled me to him. "You okay?"

"What just happened?"

"The sniffer dogs got a hit. You were sitting on it."

I stood with him against empty bookshelves as uniformed officers moved the chair and then the desk, which wasn't as heavy as it looked. There were wheels under the pedestals and Lieutenant Martin directed that the desk be pivoted on the left rear corner. Once the desk was moved, I saw something odd where the chair had been. It was a yard square of crosscut boards, a pair of inverted hinges, and a cut-out handhold opposite those hinges.

It was a trapdoor.

Conklin stepped forward and opened the hatch. We surrounded the opening and looked down a flight of stairs into a basement. Martin directed Mastiff down on the steps, the LED lights came on, and the robot bumped down, step-by-step into the hole.

The pack of us, Conklin, Alvarez, Martin, Brady, Park, Holmes, and Crispo, followed Mastiff down the stairs. I brought up the rear and, honest to God, I had a bad feeling.

CHAPTER 95

THE BASEMENT WAS a quarter the size of the store. It had a sloped ceiling that followed the lay of the land above. Wires and pipes ran across the length and width of the ceiling, and the robot provided enough light to see the furnace and other mechanicals.

Lieutenant Martin's gun was in hand. Brady and Conklin turned on their flashlights. Sergeant Park gave the dogs another deep sniff of Cindy's cardigan and the canines were off, vacuuming up skin particles from the air. Rich frantically called out to Cindy, tripping over various old tools and odd parts, cursing loudly. He was understandably crazed. Cindy could be here—or nowhere.

There were too many people in that basement room, so I climbed a short flight of stairs in the farthest corner to get out of the way. I sat on the top step, hugged my knees, and watched everything.

There was an oil tank next to me and that made sense. The oil company would pull into the lot, plug in the hose outside, and fill 'er up.

I reached overhead. The roof above me sloped toward the parking area. It was halved in the center and hinged at opposite ends. This was a bulkhead. It opened for use by electricians or any workmen to do repairs without tracking dirt through the store.

I called out to Brady. "This hatch opens out."

He was with me in two steps. He tested the bulkhead doors.

"It's not locked," he said.

He pressed his hand against the doors, and they opened with a terrible whine. Fresh air poured in over my head. Park leashed the dogs and we all headed outside. One thing was clear: this was how Catton had made his earlier near-escape. He'd gotten out of the store through this bulkhead, without us seeing him do it.

A new moon gave off a pale, haloed illumination as we stared around the parking lot. Martin and Brady scrutinized the loading dock. Betsy Park, Conklin, Alvarez, and I walked every inch of the asphalt with Crispo and Holmes.

There was nothing to see. Until the dogs pulled their handler and alerted at a dumpster up against the house and flower shop next door to the former bookstore.

Dogs barked. Rich ran to the dumpster, leaned over the edge of it calling, "Cindy! Cindy, answer me!"

I heard a faint cry. *Please, God let it be Cindy, not a bag of kittens.* Rich vaulted over the side of the dumpster and started throwing things out. Cartons, paint cans, rags, drop cloths and other trash.

He called again, "Cindy! It's me."

I joined him at the dumpster. "Rich, do you have her?"

I heard the sound of a zipper opening and Rich yelling, "Call a bus! Hurry!"

I called for an ambulance as Rich stood up, holding a very limp Cindy Thomas, our girl reporter, in his strong arms. But he was standing on shifting piles of trash and couldn't keep his balance.

"Boxer," he said, "Give me a hand."

I stretched out my arms and he lowered his and transferred Cindy's body to me.

Cindy was almost weightless. Her skin was pale, bloodless and her lips were cracked. She looked close to death but moaned softly.

"Cindy, Cindy. We've got you. We're here. You're going to be fine," I told her. I was overwhelmed with relief that she was breathing. I set her down gently on a stinking drop cloth, moved her hair away from her face, put two fingers on her wrist. Her pulse was thready, but she had one.

I ignored everything but Cindy and Richie as I listened for the ambulance.

"He put her in a garment bag," Rich said.

"Blackout? Plastic? With a zipper?"

"Yes. He knew he was asphyxiating her or maybe he thought she was dead."

Rich asked Cindy to open her eyes, but she didn't do it. He told her his name and that he was there for her and that help was on the way.

I shouted out over the now crowded lot, "Where's the ambo?"

It had been only minutes since I'd called them but Cindy's breathing was irregular, her pulse feeble.

Rich said again, "Cindy, open your eyes. It's Richie. I'm here."

She cracked open her eyes, looked at Richie, and closed them again. Cindy wasn't speaking. She took in air through her mouth and sometimes she didn't seem to breathe at all.

The small parking lot was filled with squad cars when finally, the ambo's siren reached us. I don't know from which direction it had come, but the EMTs were here. Doors opened and running footsteps came toward me. I heard the wheels of a gurney rattling over asphalt and when I looked up, I saw white uniforms. I was asked to step aside, and I scrambled up.

Two EMTs lifted Cindy onto the gurney and wheeled her to the rear of the ambulance. Rich climbed in after it and seconds later he called out to me, "We'll be at Metro."

Doors slammed and the ambulance went Code 3, its sirens screaming, lights blazing as the bus edged out of the lot and into the dark street.

Brady came up to me.

"Report from the EMTs?"

They weren't saying if Cindy was a DOA or if a twenty-four-hour saline drip would bring her back to life.

I said, "She's still breathing. Just. I saw bruises around her neck and eyes and that's all I could see of her body. Brady, he left her in a plastic shroud inside a dumpster. God, I hate him so much."

"Are you hurt, Lindsay?"

"You mean physically?"

He nodded.

I looked down. My hands were sticky with Catton's blood. His blood was on my shoes, and there was a good chance I'd smeared some across my face.

"It's his. Catton's. From the gunshot. Is Richie going to be okay for shooting that scum?"

"You would have been dead if he hadn't. Conklin'll be behind a desk for a week or two, but that's what he needs."

"That, Brady, is the truth."

I felt tears I'd been holding back for hours and days welling up. I turned away from my friend. Took some breaths. Then said, "I'm glad Rich didn't kill Catton. That would be too easy an out for that psycho. And too much added stress on Rich." I turned back and looked into Brady's face.

I swear he'd aged years since this morning.

I asked him, "How are you?"

"Better now. We got the bad guy. Cindy's in good hands and I say she's going to make it. There were a hell of a lot of pieces to this case, but I'm proud of how well alla y'all worked together. Will you burst into tears if I tell you that you did a *fan*-tastic job?"

I nodded yes, and he put his arms around me and patted my back and let me cry against his coat. I tried to apologize but he wouldn't hear of it. I was cooked, done, ready to call home, where Joe was watching Julie.

While Team Blackout was searching the basement, I had phone calls to make. Richie at the hospital first and then about ten other people who'd been going through hell out of fear for Cindy.

I was about to tell Brady I'd see him in the morning when he said, "Before you leave, we found something you'll want to see. Take a minute."

"What kind of something?"

"You're going to want to see it," he said again.

"Then show me. Show me now."

CHAPTER 96

I FOLLOWED BRADY through the bulkhead and down the stairs to the cellar. Under CSU's klieg lights, the dark and gloomy room was now bright and gloomy in shades of gray and brown. The floor and a worktable were littered with pipes, partial rolls of wire, and broken parts that were of no use to Bob Brooks when he'd abandoned his business.

Alvarez was taking pictures of the basement for our files.

Brady said, "Sonia found Blackout's lair."

"It was a team effort," she said.

"Sonia found it," Brady repeated. "Say the magic words and show Boxer."

Alvarez laughed and walked to the base of the long flight of stairs that ran from the trapdoor in the main room down to the basement floor. She edged in between the staircase and the furnace, then, using a spackle knife, she pried a wide, vertically placed board from the side of the stairs.

She shot a grin at Brady and said, "Open Sesame." Then she propped the board against the wall, leaving a void where the piece of three-quarter-inch ply had been. The narrow opening was a doorway. Reaching inside, Alvarez flipped a switch that turned on an overhead light and an exhaust fan.

What the hell?

"Our guy has been using the neighbor's juice. Come on in," said Alvarez. Brady and I ducked and entered a small subterranean flat underneath the staircase that extended into a carved-out section between the bookstore basement and the building next door.

I took in the compact three hundred square feet of hidden real estate, every inch of it in use. The walls were white. To our right was a bunk bed with a toilet below it. Across from the bed and WC was a kitchenette. I mentally catalogued the microwave, small sink, and a dorm-sized fridge. Above the kitchen counter were cabinets for dishware and packaged foods.

Looking ahead to the far end of the room was an office consisting of a long narrow ledge for a desk, a wheeled chair, a high-end laptop, centered on the desk with the lid open. A thirty-two-inch screen was affixed to the wall above the computer.

To the right of the laptop were a printer and a framed photo of a Venom helicopter with Marines posing in front of it. I couldn't be sure, but the young man in uniform, standing a foot or two apart from the rest, could be Blackout.

To the left of the laptop was a fireproof box, a cube about twenty inches on each side.

"Locked," said Alvarez. "And look here."

A pair of black-rimmed glasses was clipped to a charging station. Blackout had left his video glasses behind, surely with the expectation that he would be back.

Brady lifted his chin, indicating the computer screen mounted on the wall.

"Boxer. This was on when we got here. It's in plain sight, so no problem. As for the fireproof box, it's closed and locked."

What was inside that fireproof box? It was important enough to Blackout that he'd kept it locked even inside his cave. The press clippings we found at the old Victorian were meant to distract us. Here was where Blackout kept his treasures. I was pulled from my thoughts when Alvarez called my attention back to the computer screen on the wall.

She said, "This is going to shock you, Lindsay, but it's a good thing disguised as a bad thing."

Before I could say "I don't get it," Brady stretched out a gloved finger and touched the laptop's "on" button and the screen on the wall lit up, displaying a grid of edge-to-edge photos, each about two inches square. It looked like a double-page spread in a school yearbook and was too much detail to take in all at once.

Alvarez explained that the photos were interactive. Tapping an image played embedded audio features. Voices. Music.

I stepped closer and saw that each photo showed a subject of Blackout's past murders, taken with his video glasses, cut from the videos to still shots.

I said, "It's a hit list."

"Hammer, meet nail," said Brady.

CHAPTER 97

I STARED AT the screen. The top row of photos documented Blackout's murders of Catherine and Josie Fleet and his disposal of her baby and body. My eyes scanned downward to shots of the rest of his known kills and crime scenes.

Toward the bottom of the grid, the photos came closer to home: Claire at Baker Beach; Brady and Yuki holding hands as they left the Hall; Brady addressing the press; Yuki in court facing Barbara Sullivan in her wheelchair; Barbara Sullivan at home in bed, her mouth stretched wide in a scream as a blade slit her throat. It was a horrible portrait, so graphic that even in miniature I could feel her terror and pain.

There were a dozen pictures of Cindy, each one ratcheting up my overpowering fury at Blackout; Cindy with Rich at the book signing; Cindy approaching the brightly lit windows of Susie's; hugging Claire outside the Hall; and individual shots from Blackout's videos of Cindy, tied and gagged. Helpless. Terrified. He'd displayed that vignette in various angles; gag removed, screaming, curled under the desk.

My eyes skipped to the last line of photos on the screen. I felt Alvarez standing beside me on my left, Brady on my right.

I had chosen to look at the images in order. But now I was up against the wall. There was a shot of me in front of our apartment holding Julie, handing her to Joe, me waving goodbye as Joe's big black car drove up Lake Street. Mrs. Rose taking Martha's leash while I dashed across Lake Street.

Blackout had been watching us all.

Beside me, Alvarez said, "It's history, Lindsay. The bastard is in the hospital under heavy guard. His right arm will never hold a gun or a comb or a spoon. He's out of business. There is enough evidence in this room and in the videos he sent you to convict him a hundred times."

"I know, I know, I know. It's too much, Sonia. Too close. I'm processing that every one of my friends were his targets. He tried to kill Cindy because she refused his demand to talk about Burke. He sent *me* the videos because killing me was supposed to be his finale."

Brady said, "Let's get out of here before I lose my breakfast."

When we were outside, my mind was still whirling with everything I knew about Blackout. I flashed on his diary. I could see it, still in the desk upstairs in the store. I had to get that, voucher it, and most important, read every word.

If there was an answer to the black hole that was Bryan Catton, I wanted to know what it was. Why had he gone from a would-be actor with a wide-ranging and high IQ to a serial killer?

I hugged Alvarez, told her I'd see her in the morning, then took the long staircase up to the chaotic scene on the main floor. I hoped Blackout's war journal would still be in the desk drawer.

CHAPTER 98

WHILE BRADY ASSIGNED uniforms to protect the former bookstore against looters, press, curiosity seekers of all kinds, I searched Blackout's desk. I located the journal, took it out to Brady's SUV and began to read. The journal's title, "Blackout. Last Night in Helmand Province," had been written in longhand with a fine-point Sharpie.

A quick flip through the pages had told me that this journal was about a night mission that took place during Catton's yearlong tour in Afghanistan. He had been a helicopter door gunner in a reconnaissance chopper.

He described his mission as one of resistance suppression— clearing the field of enemy fire in advance of a squadron of heavy-lift choppers in their wake, ferrying in fresh troops to the battlefield.

Catton wrote:

"Once the troop transport following us to the Landing Zone put down, our job was to orbit the field, keeping track of and quashing additional resistance.

"Our pilot, Jamie Jackson, was nearing the end of his third tour and he was in charge. Smart guy. Well trained. Great instincts. From liftoff to our return to base, his job was twofold. Pilot the chopper and look for the enemy.

"Our gunship holds twelve people: pilot, copilot, crew chief; eight combat-ready Marines; one gunner who stands in the doorway with a large M240 machine gun and takes out the enemy. I'm the door gunner.

"That night our pilot was talkative.

"'Hey, gunner, they're down there, left side beneath those trees and they're live. Keep an eye out and if you see them, do what you do.'"

"We were flying over a wide-open terrain, very few trees, and this couldn't be missed. It was a unit of about a dozen or so to my left and then, when we were in range, a tight burst of muzzle flare erupted below.

"I opened up on the enemy, firing, firing, holding the trigger down."

*   *   *

I stopped reading Blackout's journal to take a breath and look around the parking lot behind the store. There were cop cars everywhere, but no muzzle flare. Law enforcement and CSU were going in and out of the abandoned bookstore.

I looked down at the open book on my lap and sent my mind back to the firefight.

*   *   *

Blackout wrote, "We were flying low under total cloud cover, but below the chopper's belly was a different kind of night sky, one pocked not with stars but gunfire. It's common to be crapping yourself in situations like this, but I wasn't afraid. I felt high.

"I had a heavy-duty gun and more ammo than I'd ever thought I'd need. I fixed on the location of enemy fire, aimed, pulled the trigger, and held it down again.

"The belts fed the ammo smoothly through the chamber and as the rounds discharged, the links came undone and a pile of metal parts and casings mounted around my feet. The ground below me was dark.

"Jamie's voice in my ear was like that of a supreme being. 'Catton. Thirty degrees left of center. Do you see it?'

"'Got it, bro.'

"There was a new field of enemy fire as we were tracked. I responded in kind, knowing full well that all there was between the chopper crew and the incoming rounds was a quarter-inch of aluminum—which doesn't stop bullets.

"Again, I fired, sending as many of those dirtbags to hell as I could.

"Jamie's voice: 'Okay, Bry, check fire. Do you hear me? Check fire! Stop now.' But I couldn't stop even with Jamie's voice crackling repeatedly in my headset: 'Check fire, check fire, check fire.'

"I ignored him. I wasn't ready to stop. We'd counterpunched the enemy with deadly precision but more, I knew, would be waiting. And there it was.

"A bus had just sped through the broken wall of a compound up ahead. I dropped a payload on the vehicle, lighting it up. Beyond the explosion, people ran, spreading out as they hit open terrain. I sprayed them with gunfire, ahead of them and to both sides.

"Again, I heard Jamie Jackson's voice—now urgently screaming at me 'Check fire. Check fire.' Too bad for the enemy. I'd stopped listening."

CHAPTER 99

BRADY KNOCKED ON the driver's-side window and got into the vehicle. He shoved the key into the ignition, slapped his vest pockets, said, "Shit. I'll be right back. Left my phone."

He got out of the SUV and headed toward the bulkhead, where a uniform opened the winglike doors.

I went back to Blackout's diary.

After a blank page, he had written an epilogue entitled "After the Fall." His story continued in lines of black inked letters marching across rough, handmade paper.

*   *   *

He wrote: "After that night's mission, a year after signing up, I was drummed out of the Corps and sent home.

"Captain James 'Jamie' Jackson had told me that for many reasons, atmospheric conditions, comms confusion, my age and time in grade, he'd worked at and succeeded in getting my insubordination buried.

He said I would be discharged honorably but there would be no more USMC for me. There would be no medals, no promotions, and I was told to consider myself lucky. And I did.

"Three years after that night in Helmand Province, having made many one-on-one kills near home and small but perfect videos recording my work, every minute of my tour is all still with me. The skills, the pride, anger, and self-knowledge are priceless. I am not ashamed. I enjoyed it. No, I loved it. I was being myself but battle-tested and although unacknowledged, in my mind my chest is covered with stars.

"These days I have a friend who is like me, but older and more experienced. He has been a great supporter. One day I hope to make him proud by beating his body count. But for now, since I cannot hunt with Evan Burke, I make my way surefooted and alone."

*   *   *

I closed the diary and leaned back against the headrest. I heard Brady get into the car.

He said, "Why don't I drive you home, Lindsay? Tomorrow is Sunday, your day off. I'll have someone bring your car back to you in the morning."

"Thanks," I said. "And this is for you. Catton's war journal."

Brady reached into the glove box for an evidence bag and carefully stored the book. Then he unhooked the mic on the car radio and spoke with the dispatch supervisor, telling her who was still at the scene, who was off duty, asking her to pass it on to Clapper.

I called Joe.

I gave my off-duty FBI liaison and on-duty husband all of the bottom lines. Cindy had been found alive and was at the hospital. Rich had saved my life by shooting Bryan Catton, who was injured and in custody. That I was beyond exhausted and Brady was driving me home.

"Good," he said, "Julie's waiting up for you."

CHAPTER 100

DINNER WAS ON the table when I came through the door. I ate something for show, then, moved to my recliner in the living room and pulled Julie into my lap. She had a lot of questions I couldn't answer so I asked her to tell me a story and she did. It was her version of an old favorite of mine that my mom had read to me when I was Julie's age. The story was about the unstoppable little engine that could. In Julie's version, the train could not only climb mountains but it could sing and fly to the Planet Moon Pie. This little girl of ours made me laugh.

I woke up sometime later in bed with Joe, having no memory of getting there. I touched his shoulder, and he pulled me into his arms. I held onto him and said, "Lucky me."

My eyes opened again as light came through the blinds. Joe felt me stir and turned toward me. He looked into my face.

"How do you feel?"

"Ten years older than this time yesterday."

I didn't say that my waking thought was, *What if Catton had put a couple of rounds through my head?* That could've been well within the realm of possibility. What would happen to my family?

I sat up in bed, saying, "What day is it?"

"Sunday."

"I have today off," I told my husband. It was just after eight. I grabbed my phone from the nightstand and speed-dialed an important number and left a message.

"Hi, it's Lindsay Boxer. I know it's short notice, Dr. Greene, but if you have time for me, I can be at your office any time tomorrow."

I called Richie and left him another message. Between last night and this morning, it was my fifth or sixth. Worried, I said, "If you don't call me back, I'm sending the police." I clicked off.

Joe said, "Talk to me."

I got back under the warm bedclothes and my husband's arm.

I said, "I don't know where to start."

"Try."

I told him everything, or tried. About Catton aiming at me, telling me to drop my gun and that I'd done it putting well-placed faith in God and Richie. "Richie shot him in the arm."

"Bad aim?"

"Catton swerved, but Rich's shot was good enough to put him out of action."

I fell asleep in the middle of a sentence. Woke up. Apologized to Joe. I said, "Where was I?"

"The basement room and the pictures of Blackout's hit list."

It was right there before my eyes, but I couldn't bear to describe it. I woke up again when my phone rang. Dr. Greene. We confirmed an appointment for tomorrow at four.

The smell of brewing coffee and cinnamon buns brought me to my feet. I got out of bed and stumbled into the living room, which shares a large, open loft space with the kitchen and dining room. I was safe at home. We were all safe.

Joe was dressed, pouring coffee.

He said, "I can't stop worrying about you, Blondie."

"I know. I'm sorry, Joe. Dr. Greene will weigh in. Where's Julie?"

Joe said, "With Mrs. Rose next door. Eggs with everything?"

"For sure. Did I eat last night?"

"Sort of. You shower, I'll cook."

The phone rang again only inches from my hand. Richie.

"Cindy's responding very well," he told me. "She's out of the ER and in observation, as of just now."

"Thank God."

"She's weak but she knows what happened to her."

I signed off with Rich and sat at the kitchen table, let my husband take care of me. He set down a plate of scrambled eggs with cheese and mushrooms and a cup of coffee, heavily sugared. A cinnamon bun on a little plate. And he propped a drawing of Julie's against the coffeepot; a crayon drawing of me, Julie, Daddy, Mrs. Rose, and Martha. I had to frame this precious drawing of everyone I loved. And they loved me, too.

I wondered. Could I retire? Stay home and take Julie to the school bus...?

"Eat," Joe said.

"Cindy's in observation," I said, again.

"Wonderful news. Eat."

I dug in.

"There's something I need to discuss with you," Joe said when my mouth was full.

"Good or bad?"

"You'll tell me," he said.

CHAPTER 101

BRADY CALLED BEFORE I'd finished my coffee.

"What news?" I asked.

"We've got Bryan Catton's fireproof box in the war room. If you want to see the contents, come now. I can hold it until about 10:30."

My day off faded out to nothing.

Joe was loading the dishwasher. "Joe? Can you drive me to work?"

He looked at me, resigned, and said, "No problem."

"It's just a meeting."

"Uh-huh."

I found clean jeans in the dryer, a pressed pink shirt in the closet, and after a search, I found both of my shoes. Twenty-five minutes later, I was in the war room, feeling edgy and curious to know what Blackout thought important enough to keep locked in a safe, inside a secret room, inside an abandoned store.

Brady stood up, dragged a chair over to the table, and sat down. Alvarez grinned at me and said, "Starting to feel a lot like Christmas."

I held up crossed fingers, wheeled my chair close to the table.

Cappy came in and sat in Richie's empty seat. He asked me if there was any news of Cindy.

"She's out of the ER," I said.

"Aw-right. That's tremendous."

Hal Williams from maintenance knocked on the doorjamb, holding a crowbar. Brady asked him to come in and as four pairs of eyes fixed on Williams and his crowbar, he popped the lock on the fireproof box.

He asked the group of us around the table, "Anything else?"

Brady thanked him and when Williams had gone, Brady lifted the lid. I stood up to see. The box was filled with about a dozen eight-by-eleven-inch brown envelopes.

Brady gloved up, took one out of the box, and peeled up the flap. He reached inside the envelope and pulled out a paper-clipped packet of papers. He reviewed the packet and we waited for him to say something.

"These appear to be photocopies of letters 'B.C., Esq.' wrote to Evan Burke, care of San Quentin State Prison."

I was the one who said loudly, "He was writing to Burke?"

Brady said, "Catton was posing as Burke's attorney. He visited Burke in disguise, and they exchanged unmonitored letters under Burke's constitutional right to counsel."

He spread the papers out on the table. Cappy called out for Brady to read a letter or two.

Brady picked one up.

"This is from Catton, dated about three months ago.

'Hey there, Evan, I want you to know that I enjoyed our meeting yesterday. I like your idea very much and will be scouting for appropriate candidates. Meanwhile, I've contacted your publisher asking for an advance copy of *You Never Knew Me*.

'Let me know if you need anything. I'll be in touch.

Best regards,
B.C., Esq.'

Brady said, "Gloves, please."

He handed out the brown envelopes saying, "So. We'll read the letters while in this room. Make note of anything we should all know and return them to me in ten minutes. I'll get them to the DA. By the way, Catton is being arraigned tomorrow."

I opened the large brown envelope in front of me.

It held eight photocopied letters from Catton to Burke, and a newspaper article I knew by heart. The article was on the front page of the *San Francisco Chronicle* posting a reward for information leading to the return of Cindy Thomas.

I said, "This is different."

There was a note scribbled on the back of an A2 envelope in small, neat handwriting, and it was paper-clipped to the article.

I read it out loud. "Good job, my friend. I look forward to hearing more. To you from the hole at the Q., E.B."

Up until the last few days, Burke was coaching Blackout, mentoring him. They were some kind of team. At least, that's how it sounded to me.

CHAPTER 102

IT HAD ONLY been two weeks since I'd last seen Dr. Greene but it seemed like a year.

I was ten minutes early to our Monday appointment, so I used that time to make myself presentable. I tipped the rearview mirror toward my face and took note. My hair looked like a tumbleweed that had blown in from Texas. I finger combed the hay-colored mess as best I could, found a band in the console, and pulled my hair into a pony. I pulled a few strands of hair forward to soften the stress lines in my forehead. Next, I slicked on "burnished bronze" lipstick, pinched my cheeks, smoothed my brows.

I got out of my Explorer and stood for sixty seconds in the fair spring afternoon. I went to my happy place: a field of daisies and bluebonnets. My family was there along with my dog and a tennis ball. I locked up the car, crossed the street, and rang the bell next to Dr. Greene's nameplate.

The buzzer sounded, unlocking the door.

I walked up two flights to Dr. Greene's office, opened the outer door to his waiting room, and sank into a seat by the window. I stared at a piece of artwork that looked like a portrait of a woman who'd been through a car wash. What else could it be?

The door to Dr. Greene's office opened and he stuck his head out and said, "Hi, Lindsay, come in."

I returned the greeting and followed him into his cozy, pale-carpeted office and took a seat opposite his recliner.

He tucked a folded newspaper into a magazine stand and said, "How are you doing?"

"How do I look?"

"Like you're trying hard to seem okay. What's happening?"

"Start at the beginning, right?"

"Any place you like," said my paid-for-by-the-city shrink, whom I actually liked quite a bit.

I said, "Ah, you usually ask, 'How was your week?'"

"Fair enough. How was it?"

"I'm looking for a way to tell you about it, Doctor. I may need more than one session."

"Of course, but see what you can do with this one. I'm a good listener."

I exhaled loudly and leaned back in the chair. "Where did we leave off?"

He said, "You were telling me about the stress of your work, wondering if you should still be a homicide investigator and I asked you if you might be happier in a staff job. And I suggested that we should spend time talking about that. We can talk about anything that's on your mind."

"Well, Dr. Greene. In the two weeks since I last sat here, we—me, my partner, and the team—bagged a serial killer and rescued our friend Cindy Thomas, who'd been kidnapped and nearly murdered."

"Oh, good God."

I outlined last night's ride with Rich to the last resort abandoned bookstore, working with SWAT, manually manning a robot, tearing the store up. I was seeing it as I was saying it. The descent to the basement, the big reveal that the killer we were chasing lived there, a place where he had worked before he enlisted, now his home base.

I said, "This psycho, Bryan Catton, had a hit list."

"An actual list?"

"You betcha," I said. "He displayed his victims on a grid projected on a backlit screen in full color. It looked like an ad for something. 'Come to San Francisco and have a good time.' If you pressed the picture, the audio would come on. Voices. Music."

I stopped talking, panting a little as I visualized that large screen.

"Keep going," Dr. Greene said. "I'm with you, Lindsay."

I looked at him. "There were a lot of people on this—computer screen. Blackout had killed half of them. And the rest were on his to-do list. All the ones left on the list were friends of mine."

I detailed the Women's Murder Club, our partners and spouses including my husband and daughter and Mrs. Rose.

"I was on his list, too."

"Did you listen to the audio?"

I shook my head no. I'd lost my nerve and I couldn't talk anymore. Blackout's hit parade was really getting to me. My snarky pen pal had been teeing me up, waiting to kill me.

"Take your time," said my therapist. "When you're ready to speak, tell me the story however you wish, whatever occurs to you."

When my hands unclenched and I was breathing normally, I told Dr. Greene about Catton's sneaky escape past all the cops in the world. I described the showdown in the parking lot. Blackout aiming his gun at my head, telling me to put down my weapon. Which I'd done. His gun was still pointed at my head when Rich fired a couple of good shots, hitting Catton in his gun arm, ending a standoff that could have meant my life and probably Rich and Cindy's, too.

I told him about our desperation, Cindy still missing until finally the search and rescue dogs sniffed her location.

"He'd stuffed her in a garment bag, Dr. Greene, thrown her into a garbage dumpster. If not for those good dogs, a carting service would have mangled her in the back of their truck when it got light in the morning."

I told Dr. Greene that Cindy was at the hospital and that we had enough evidence on Catton to put him in prison for life. I gulped. I tried to swallow.

"I'm here," the doctor said.

I leaned my head into my hands and let it out. I was sobbing from too much trauma, in too little time. I cried until I became self-conscious, grabbed some tissues and mopped up.

I said, "I've been terrified. And now relieved. And I'm wondering if I can trust relief to last. It's not over yet. The trial and sentencing are going to take months and I'm going to be thinking and dreaming about Blackout for years. Maybe forever. What do you think?"

"I'm sorry. Sorry you went through this—what else can you call it?—real-life nightmare. But you got him, Lindsay. Take that in. It's the end of his story, but not yours. The more we talk about him, the more the terror will fade."

"Promise?"

"It won't be a straight line up, but I think more up than down.

Some pitfalls. Some great revelations. You were heroic, Lindsay. I say that without prejudice."

Dr. Greene reached over to the magazine rack, found the paper, and opened it up. He showed me the front page of today's edition of the *Chronicle*. The headline was in huge type. "SFPD CAPTURES SERIAL KILLER. CINDY THOMAS IS SAFE."

Dr. Greene said, "Lieutenant Brady lauded you and Rich to the press. I hope you can give that to yourself."

I shrugged. "Did I mention that Richie saved my life?"

"Yes. Tell me again."

I did.

Dr. Greene said, "He's another of a rare breed. It's called self-sacrificing."

We all did that every day. It was never just a job.

"Where are you, Lindsay?"

"I'm very tired, Doctor. But as I've said before, I work with great people. I work hard to get bad people off the streets. Murder is always on the table. Today, despite everything that happened, I'm feeling pretty good about cuffing that son of a bitch. That's the truth."

Dr. Greene smiled at me.

He said, "How would you feel about taking some time off?"

"That sounds like a good idea. One snag."

"Which would be?"

"Joe has a job offer from the FBI. Full time. Right away."

I told Dr. Greene that Joe hadn't accepted the offer yet. He was still caring for Julie from after school until whenever I got home. We still had to discuss how to fill the "daddy gap" for Julie. I knew we wouldn't be the only working parents with a nearly five-year-old, but I didn't have a nine-to-five job and if Joe went back to the

FBI, his day would have elastic hours, too. Even with Mrs. Rose as backstop, I didn't know how we would manage it.

The last time I'd seen Dr. Greene, I'd asked if I was done with therapy when I could decipher the modern art paintings on his walls. It had been a joke, but I'd been itching to get out of this enforced psychotherapy. Now, I was glad for the therapy, but needed to go home. I looked at the set of three paintings and the white walls. They were all composed of lines and swirls and colors without names.

I said, "I can interpret the paintings all right, but I'll save that for another time. Our hour is up, Doc. See you next week?"

"Yes, of course. And call anytime if you need to talk."

He offered me the *Chronicle* and I was glad to have it. I thanked the doctor and headed home.

CHAPTER 103

THE WEEK AFTER Cindy was released from the hospital, twenty-three days after her launch event at Book Passage, Claire, Yuki, and I had a conference call with Rich from Yuki's office.

Yuki asked, "Okay for us to come over?"

Rich said, "She's still, you know, fragile. She would like to see you guys, but no dancing."

Claire said, "If no dancing, what then?"

"You know. Girl talk. Say she's looking good. And no spicy food, either."

I said, "Flowers okay?"

"Pastel colors should be okay."

I laughed at his joke and said, "We'll be careful."

We'd stopped at Lucky to buy flowers, soup, and ice cream, piled into Claire's Escalade, and drove to Kirkham Street. During the drive, we all got quiet. I was thinking about Richie's dumpster dive and Cindy's survival about a minute short of death.

Claire said, "I know we're scared, but she made it, girlfriends. Our mission is to get her to smile."

Rich and Cindy live in this small three-room apartment, a cute place that's, as the saying goes, as snug as a bug in a rug.

Claire parked her boat. Yuki rang the bell, jogging in place as we waited at the doorstep. Claire and I laughed at her, but we were as eager to see Cindy as she was. Rich opened the door and the three of us greeted him with hugs.

"Come on in, Murder Club ladies. What can I get you?"

Yuki, Claire, and I edged past Richie and found our dear friend in PJs, lying on the sofa under a pale blue blanket. Yuki called over her shoulder, "We're good, Richie. Oh. Could you put this in the freezer and this in a pot. And these in a vase."

Richie took our shopping bags, and we each leaned in and gave Cindy gentle hugs. Then Rich was back. He moved over a couple of chairs as we told our friend how good it was to see her.

Cindy beamed and waggled her fingers at me which I translated as a request for another hug. I got down on my knees so she didn't have to move or strain vocal cords injured by Blackout's hands. She whispered in my ear, "Tell me everything."

"We will."

Yuki went into the kitchen, heated up the chicken soup, and poured out five mugs. Rich sat down at the table with his mug o' magic healing soup, our bright red roses, and a big bowl of corn chips that he passed around.

"Music?" he asked.

"Got something reggae?"

He shook his head as if we were all crazy, but he dialed up Spotify on Cindy's laptop and—suddenly we were at our booth at Susie's. No beer, no margaritas, no pulled pork, but we were together and that was a blessing.

Claire fluffed up Cindy's pillow and Yuki leaned in to say,

"Here's the scoop. Blackout aka Bryan Catton was arraigned on Monday, charged with seven murders and the abduction of you, Girl Reporter, attempted murder on you and Lindsay, plus a charge of aggravated assault for good measure."

Cindy whispered, "When's his trial?"

Yuki said, "It's in the works. Len will want to be lead prosecutor. I'll be second chair."

Cindy smiled and made a V for victory sign with her fingers. Then she asked, "Catton on suicide watch?"

Richie said, "You bet."

Cindy reached for a pad and pen on the coffee table, wrote in big letters: HEADLINE NEWS. ME = STAR WITNESS.

"For sure," said Yuki, fist-bumping her.

I dished up the ice cream, everyone's individual favorite flavor, and when the music came to an end, we unanimously agreed that for now, it was time to hug Cindy goodbye. As we were leaving, Cindy waved me over again.

I bent to hear her.

"You and Richie saved my life."

"He saved mine, too."

"Will you be my maid of honor?"

"Aww Cindy. You know I will."

"Shhhh," she said. "He doesn't know."

I buttoned down a smile and said, "I promise. It's off the record." I hugged her again, kissed her cheek, and as we'd come in, we swept out of the apartment, got into the big black Escalade SUV. Claire let me drive. Yuki stretched out in the back seat and we headed back to the Hall.

Speaking for myself, I was elated.

CHAPTER 104

ALVAREZ, CONKLIN, AND I were at our desks that morning talking over coffee about last night's spring training game. We were in agreement that the Giants had been cheated of a win by a bad call that video replay should have overturned. Rich was vehement.

He was saying, "It was clear from that second angle that the kid leaned over and prevented Wade from making the catch. Bang. Fan interference. You saw it, right, Alvarez? Pure and simple, we was robbed."

Alvarez said, "So kick it to Robbery."

I laughed. We didn't have a Robbery division anymore. But Central Station had one.

I said, "Central would love complaints from sixty thousand PO'd fans."

Rich said, "It would please me, no end."

We were all emotionally tapped out and had been hoping for a win. Blackout was in jail awaiting trial and forcibly retired from the snuff video business, but he'd left dread behind. I couldn't open an email without fear that a murder-in-progress as seen through the sick eyes of the killer could jump out of the screen.

I cut the thought off at the knees and replaced it with the advice from Dr. Greene. *Take some time off.* I planned to put it to Brady this afternoon.

And then, there he was, coming down the aisle toward us. He stopped just short of our pod and I shrank back a little bit. It was involuntary. I just didn't want another case. Not yet.

Brady looked at me and said, "Sergeant, got a moment for me?"

I sighed. "Sure, Lieu."

"In my office," he said.

Reluctantly, I got out of my chair and followed him back down the aisle. He held his door for me and I took a seat, put my feet up on the side of his desk.

He settled into his chair and fixed me with his sharp blue eyes. "Got any big plans?" he asked.

"No, and I'm liking that."

"We need to go out to San Quentin."

"Why, Brady? What for?"

"Trust me now," he said. "Thank me later."

As my more spiritual sister, Cat, likes to say, "Let it go." So I tried that and found my morning thoughts were still circling. Things to do, things not to do, and a premonition of something behind the curtain about to jump out and yell, "Gotcha."

I went back to the pod, shut down my computer, told my partners to hold the fort.

"Wassup, Lindsay?"

I shrugged, grabbed my phone, and took the fire stairs with

Brady down to Bryant Street, where his favorite SUV was waiting. He signed the log and we both got into the vehicle. I buckled up. Brady started the engine, then, turned to me and said, "You're going to be glad you did this, Boxer. For years."

Prove it.

CHAPTER **105**

BRADY AND I were escorted by guards to a big concrete room with a cage at the center and a man in the cage. There were two doors, each one twenty feet away from the cage, one to the left, one to the right. The room was not the attorney-client one Burke had earned by his six murder confessions and cold-case assistance but served as a pass-through. As we sat in folding chairs looking at the killer inside the cage, a number of guards came through one door and left by the other.

Brady had spoken with Warden Hauser early this morning and told me the plan during our drive. I knew what to do, what to say, but I didn't know what to expect. Now, looking at Evan Burke, his face four feet away from mine, he raised hackles I didn't know that I had.

Burke's shaved head had grown in since I'd seen him last week. His face was stubbly and his fingernails were rough. But he was jocular in that know-it-all way he has, even with a stack of life sentences against him and no possibility of parole.

Today he wore an orange jumpsuit and shiny metal accessories:

cuffs, chains, and shackles. We'd exchanged greetings and now that we'd had a chance to sniff each other out, Burke said, "How's Cindy? I hear some criminal roughed her up?"

"She's doing fine," said Brady. "The criminal's name is Bryan Catton."

"Oh?"

Brady said, "He claims to know you."

"Me? How?" said Burke.

"You don't know his name?"

"How'm I supposed to know him? You know more about me than just about anyone. I don't have friends. I moved around a lot… Now I'm in solitary."

Brady said, "Boxer?"

I said, "Okay, Evan. Catton came to visit you every few months, posing as your attorney. He wore minimal disguise, signed the log Brian Catalina—an alias varying his first name plus your 'Ghost of Catalina' nickname. Here's a copy of the sign-in sheet."

Brady produced pages folded lengthwise from his briefcase and passed them to me. I flattened them and held them up one at a time against the wire cage.

Burke said, "You're saying he came here? I don't see a Bryan Catton. Len Woods, an ad man. Wyatt West. Some kind of a producer. Oh. Okay, that one is Brian Catalina. Oh. I think he was interested in the book I did with Cindy than anything to do with my appeal." Burke was getting impatient. "What the hell is this about? I hate cops. If you're still here in three minutes, I'm calling the guards."

I said, "Three minutes is all it's going to take, Evan."

"Call me Mr. Burke."

"Okay, Mr. Burke. Bryan Catton came to see you multiple times. But you know that, right?"

"So the fuck what? Guy comes here, spends five minutes with me, makes his pitch that I'm not even listening to, and then he's escorted out."

I said, "We have a few other papers to show you."

Brady reached into his briefcase again and brought out a manuscript box and a brown eight by eleven envelope.

Brady asked Burke, "Interested? Or should we call the guard?"

"You son-of-a-bitch."

I glowered at Burke as I'd been told to do.

"What's with you, Lindsay?" Burke said.

"You give me the creeps. That's all."

"So who invited you?" Burke said.

I said, "I'll tell you what's in the box. It's a first draft of a manuscript called "The Last Face You'll See: The Life of Evan Burke."

"Let me see that," Burke said.

"The writers are you and Bryan Catton," I said. "But wait, the best is yet to come."

Brady opened the brown envelope, took out the papers and handed them to me, saying, "Sergeant, why don't you read this one?"

"Your handwriting," I said to Burke. "See?" I flashed it so he could see the letter and then I read:

"'Hey, Bryan, my daughter-in-law was about twenty, and my granddaughter was a toddler. One was a brunette and the other a strawberry blonde. I think females like that would be suitable targets. Get me?'"

Burke became livid. His face turned red and his eyes bulged and he tried to stand, but with the handcuffs, the chain between them to the shackles around his feet, he only managed a crouch.

"What do you think you're doing, Brady? You trying to accuse me of something? I've been tried, convicted, sentenced, and locked in this cinder block hole. You're accusing me of murder?"

Brady said, "This is one of many documents like this one," he said, patting the large envelope. "They're proof of conspiracy to commit murder."

I said, "Here's the note Catton wrote back to you, saying 'Yeah, those seem like appropriate targets,' and then a dark-haired woman and her redheaded baby washed up on Baker Beach.

"Look familiar?" I said.

I held up a photo of Catherine Fleet, lying on a gurney with the baby on her chest, water dripping from her coat and the ME's van as a backdrop. Then I whipped the photo away so that there wouldn't be enough time for Burke to get much pleasure from it.

"And here's the letter you wrote to Catton saying, 'If we want a big boffo ending to the script, you need to take out the nutty blond reporter and the big pushy female homicide cop.'"

I put the letter down on my lap and said to Burke, "That would be Cindy Thomas and me."

Burke said nothing but looked at me with his mouth hanging half open. We'd blindsided him, but the meeting wasn't over yet.

I said, "You put hits out on me and my friends and I have to tell you, Bryan followed your directives and he had plans of his own. He's been hospitalized and, I heard, is in excruciating pain. And he's been indicted on seven charges of murder one and attempted murder on me and on Cindy."

Burke shouted, "Are you threatening me, Sergeant? Because I'm fine. 'When you got nothin', you got nothin' to lose.'"

I kept going. "Mr. Catton's video glasses were working perfectly and he filmed his kills. He's already talking, Mr. Burke, and as for me, I'm waiting to see if the death penalty can be revived especially for the both of you."

"Good luck with that. I wouldn't bet against me, Sergeant." He tapped the side of his head. "It's all in here. Things you couldn't possibly imagine."

I snorted, "You're pathetic," and having had the last word, I stood up. Brady called the guards and they were showing us out when Burke called out, "Leave that manuscript."

Brady shouted back, "Sorry, Evan. It's evidence."

Four guards walked past Burke's cage holding overflowing cardboard cartons.

Burke yelled, "Hey! Where you going with my stuff?"

A feather mattress topper was bursting out of one box. Another held a terry cloth robe, a TV, and a radio. I knew but Burke did not. All of the comfort items he'd negotiated for in exchange for his confession to innumerable murders and input on unsolved cases were now being removed. I heard Burke screaming "Nooooooo," as we passed from the private room through the metal door and out to the public area and exit from the prison.

Back in the car again, I buzzed down my window so I could feel the breeze blowing in from the bay.

Brady said, "Well?"

I turned to look at him. He smiled and I smiled back.

"Thanks, Brady. That was a peak experience."

He said, "For me, too. Talk to Joe and plan your vacation."

I said, "Will do. How long can you get along without me?"

Seabirds circled. A ferry blew its horn. Sunlight capped the waves.

Brady said, "Take the time you need."

I hugged him, and as he started the engine, I lowered the seat back and closed my eyes. Something Richie and I had said to each other many times came to me now unprompted.

I turned my head and said it to Brady.

"This is a good day to be a cop."

ACKNOWLEDGMENTS

Our thanks to the exceptional people who shared their time and expertise with us during the creation of this book: the real Rich Conklin, Assistant Chief, Bureau of Criminal Investigations, Stamford, Connecticut Police Department; Michael A. Cizmar, Special Agent FBI, retired, and former private military contractor in Afghanistan; Donald Blaufuss, former door gunner in Vietnam, 1966; Ann Payne and the pros at Superdroid, Inc.; and our first-class legal advisor, Steve Rabinowitz, Attorney-at-law, LLP, in New York.

As always, we're grateful to our talented researcher, Ingrid Taylar, in San Francisco, and Mary Jordan, who keeps track of the parts and pieces and keeps the whole shebang together. And, many thanks to the talented Team Patterson at Little Brown.

JAMES PATTERSON
THE WORLD'S #1 BESTSELLING WRITER

ABOUT THE AUTHORS

James Patterson is the most popular storyteller of our time. He is the creator of unforgettable characters and series, including Alex Cross, the Women's Murder Club, Jane Effing Smith, and Maximum Ride, and of breathtaking true stories about the Kennedys, John Lennon, and Princess Diana, as well as our military heroes, police officers, and ER nurses. He has coauthored #1 bestselling novels with Bill Clinton and Dolly Parton, told the story of his own life in *James Patterson by James Patterson*, and received an Edgar Award, nine Emmy Awards, the Literarian Award from the National Book Foundation, and the National Humanities Medal.

Maxine Paetro is a novelist who has collaborated with James Patterson on the bestselling Women's Murder Club, Private, and Confessions series; *Woman of God;* and other stand-alone novels. She lives with her husband, John, in New York.

JAMES
PATTERSON
RECOMMENDS

JAMES PATTERSON
AND
BILL CLINTON

THE
PRESIDENT'S
DAUGHTER

"PROPULSIVE, EXHILARATING, AND
UNNERVINGLY BELIEVABLE." —KARIN SLAUGHTER

THE PRESIDENT'S DAUGHTER

I can't think of a more terrifying prospect than your child being abducted. And it is exactly that situation that I've thrown at former US president Matthew Keating. He has always defended his family as staunchly as he has his country. Now those defenses are under attack. A madman abducts his teenage daughter, turning every parent's deepest fear into a matter of national security. As the world watches in real time, Keating—a retired Navy SEAL—embarks on a one-man special-ops mission that tests his strengths: as a leader, a warrior, and a father.

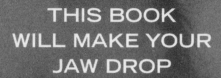

THIS BOOK
WILL MAKE YOUR
JAW DROP

INVISIBLE

THE WORLD'S #1 BESTSELLING WRITER

JAMES PATTERSON
& DAVID ELLIS

INVISIBLE

Have you ever known something and no one believes you? It's the most frustrating thing and—in this book—deadly. Everyone thinks FBI researcher Emmy Dockery is crazy. Obsessed with finding the link between hundreds of unsolved cases, she has newspaper clippings that wallpaper her bedroom, and has recurring nightmares of an all-consuming fire. Not even her ex-boyfriend, field agent Harrison "Books" Bookman, will believe her. Until Emmy finds a piece of evidence he can't afford to ignore.

JAMES PATTERSON

JUROR #3

AND NANCY ALLEN

JUROR #3

As a thriller writer, I'm always creating powder-keg situations that push my characters to their limits. That goes for the citizens of Rosedale, Mississippi. Ruby Bozarth is a newcomer, both to this town in the Deep South and to the bar. Now she's tapped as a defense counsel in a racially charged felony. The murder of a woman from an old family has the upper crust howling for blood, and the prosecutor is counting on Ruby's inexperience to help him deliver a swift conviction. Then her case is rattled as news of a second murder breaks. As intertwining investigations unfold, no one can be trusted, especially the twelve men and women on the jury. They may be hiding the most incendiary secret of all.

JAMES PATTERSON

THE MIDWIFE MURDERS

AND RICHARD DiLALLO

THE MIDWIFE MURDERS

Imagine the outrage when new moms become the victims of two kidnappings and a vicious stabbing. To senior midwife Lucy Ryuan, nothing could be more heinous. Something has to be done, and she's fearless enough to try. Rumors begin to swirl, blaming everyone from the Russian Mafia to an underground adoption network. Lucy teams up with a skeptical NYPD detective to solve the case, but the truth is far more twisted than a feisty single mom could ever have imagined.

From the Creator of the #1 Bestselling Women's Murder Club

JAMES PATTERSON

2 SISTERS DETECTIVE AGENCY

FIRST TIME IN PRINT

& CANDICE FOX

2 SISTERS DETECTIVE AGENCY

Discovering secrets about your own family has a way of changing your life...for better or for worse. For attorney Rhonda Bird, she learns that her estranged father had stopped being an accountant and opened up a private detective agency—and that she has a teenage half sister named Baby.

When Baby brings in a client to the detective agency, the two sisters become entangled in a dangerous case involving a group of young adults who break laws for fun, their psychopath ring-leader, and an ex-assassin who decides to hunt them down for revenge.

JAMES PATTERSON
J.D. BARKER

ONE KISS
AND YOU'RE DEAD

DEATH OF THE
BLACK WIDOW

DEATH OF THE BLACK WIDOW

A twenty-year-old woman murders her kidnapper with a competence so impeccable that Detroit PD officer Walter O'Brien is taken aback. It's pretty rare for my detectives to be this shocked. But what Officer O'Brien doesn't know is that this young woman has a knack for ending the lives of her lovers—and getting away with it.

Time after time, she navigates her way out of police custody. Soon, Walter becomes fixated on uncovering the truth. And when he discovers that he's not alone in his search, one thing is certain. This deadly string of secrets didn't begin in his home city...but he's going to make sure it ends there.

For a complete list of books by

JAMES PATTERSON

VISIT
JamesPatterson.com

Follow James Patterson on Facebook
@JamesPatterson

Follow James Patterson on X
𝕏 **@JP_Books**

Follow James Patterson on Instagram
@jamespattersonbooks